Children of Tarnuz

Book One in the

Clara Overton series

By

Dan Scarro

Children of Tarnuz

About the Author

Dan Scarro is a music teacher based in Kent, UK. He is married with one daughter and a cat. He wrote 2 Young Adult fantasy books during the COVID pandemic and released these under the name Dan Saunders. This is Dan's first adult steampunk novel.

You can follow Dan on instagram @scarro_saunders_stories

Acknowledgements

I would like to thank my lovely wife and beautiful daughter for listening to my endless story ideas, formatting this book and for their love and support. I would also like to thank my wonderful Beta readers Wayne and Janelle and my bookstagram community. You know who you are! Thanks to my family and friends for your ongoing support.

Children of Tarnuz

Contents

Chapter One: Next Stop, Oblivion! 7

Chapter Two: The Rose of Death 21

Chapter Three: Crime Scene Revisited..........46

Chapter Four: Lipstick and Guns 54

Chapter Five: An uncomfortable meeting.....87

Chapter Six: Following a lead 117

Chapter Seven: Unseen Dangers.................139

Chapter Eight: Civil Unrest 159

Chapter Nine: Not All the Lost Are Saved 182

Chapter Ten: Confessions 193

Chapter Eleven: A Bad Choice of Friends....................237

Chapter Twelve: A Common Cause.............245

Chapter Thirteen: Upcycled 264

Chapter Fourteen: A Very Suspect Circus 269

Chapter Fifteen: Shattered Flint 305

Chapter Sixteen: Where Are The Wolves?..................320

Chapter Seventeen: Painful Memories 390

Chapter Eighteen: Revelations....................422

Chapter Nineteen: Evil Tightens Its Grip.....................444

Chapter Twenty: Pick a Side........................485

Children of Tarnuz

Chapter One: Next Stop, Oblivion!

Steam was progress. Progress to some, but to others, it was destruction, upheaval, and sometimes death. Some twenty years ago, people were displaced from their homes to make way for a high-speed train network. A few folks had done well out of it, receiving quaint farmer's cottages and a handful of livestock. Others were forced from their homes with nowhere to go. There were stubborn people too, who refused to give up their land, making the train company take legal action. While some embraced the change, others opposed it. Opposition was the reason Clara was boarding the train today.

An hour earlier, Chancellor Patrick Theodore Spencer had snipped the golden ribbon and declared the rail link open, accompanied by excited cheers and whistles from the enthusiastic crowd. Young women twirled parasols and held eye contact with their men as they wittered on about locomotives and the steam revolution. Angry protesters from The Workers

Liberation Front (TWLF) chanted "Fair pay, for fair jobs" and waved placards.

Children licked large round lollipops decorated with red and white swirls, which reminded Clara of Catherine Wheels, spitting flames and Clara bit her lip. Grey clouds obscured the sun, followed by a clap of thunder. The crowd grumbled as they put up their umbrellas.

A security team buzzed around the chancellor like flies and one of his team leaned forward and whispered something in Patrick Spencer's ear. When the man had finished speaking, Spencer dipped his chin ruefully.

"The storm is already here, Winston," Spencer said, pointing at TWLF.

Spencer had receding swept back curly silver hair and thoughtful brown eyes. His hands were holding the lapels of his black suit jacket, and he had a red cravat fastened at his neck.

"Sadly, I will not be travelling on this magnificent locomotive today," Spencer said, his deep voice booming out across the crowd. "Something of uttermost importance has come to my attention, and I must deal with it. I wish you all a pleasant trip and I look forward to joining you on future journeys. Good day to you all."

And then he was escorted away by his beefy bodyguards.

I wonder if the good chancellor was privy to the same information as me. Clara thought.

Clara had been tipped-off about a terrorist planning to detonate a bomb on this train. Note after note had been slipped under her door recently, asking her to reprimand a suspect. The first note asked her to investigate a local cat burglar who was planning to steal a precious royal diamond. Royalty no longer existed in Tarnuz, but the treasures still remained. A relic of a bygone era. It turned out the thief was a child. She caught the tyke and marched him off to the authorities. Fortunately for the child, the judge had compassion on him and awarded him a scholarship. Clara was a young detective who had shown promise on a child kidnapping case, and somebody had noticed. After the crime was solved, the notes started appearing under her door. Today's note was her third. Each letter was eloquently written in neat cursive, but the latest one had the seal of the vampire council. Glancing around the carriage to make sure no one was looking; she reached into the back pocket of her black leather trousers and pulled out the note. Before opening the message, she traced her finger over the black wax symbol. It looked like a throwing star with a rose in the centre.

She opened the letter and perused its contents:

Dear Miss Overton,

We have been observing you for some time, and we are most impressed with your meticulous investigations and would like to meet you. After you have dealt with the troublesome Artimus Vengeford, we would like to discuss something that has come to our attention. Best of luck stopping

Vengeford from destroying the 2.10 pm to the capital.

Yours sincerely,

Vampire Council.

This is considerably more serious than the last crimes, so I guess it makes sense that they would contact me now, she pondered.

She reached into her satchel and checked her clockwork laser pistol.

A blue Number 10 was displayed on the screen.

I have to work fast. There are only 10 minutes left on the charge.

The ticket officer entered the carriage. Clara put her gun away before he got to her.

"Tickets, please," the inspector said, as he weaved his way around the carriage as it swayed and clattered along the tracks.

The ticket collector had a salt and pepper curly moustache and lamb chop sideburns.

He wore a black wool coat with gold buttons, a black waistcoat and black cotton trousers. A gold name badge was fastened above his left breast. "Brian" it read. Finally, he reached Clara. A blue, telescopic eye clicked and whirred in his eye socket.

"Tickets please, miss," the ticket inspector said, breaking her train of thought. His clockwork eye turned red. Offering him her sweetest smile, Clara gave him her ticket. His eye extended, producing a red line that scanned the ticket from top to bottom. When it had finished, the light turned green, and the inspector smiled and gave back her ticket.

There's a story behind that eye. I wonder if he lost it in the Birikian war.

"I beg your pardon sir, could I inquire about your eye," Clara said, leaning forward in her chair.

"I don't mind telling ya at all, miss. I lost it in the war, see," Brian said, chuckling at his own joke. "The train company thought I was ready for the knackers' yard, but I told em that I'm too young for that."

"So somebody threw you a lifeline, gave you a helping hand?"

The ticket collector rubbed his chin. "Yeah, a strange, tall pale fella with eyes as red as blood, approaches me and gives me his card. I think I still have it about me self. Let me take a gander," he said, patting his waistcoat. Using his fingers like a pair of pincers, he fumbled in his waistcoat pocket and pulled out a business card and handed it to her.

It was a white card with the silhouette of a pterodactyl on it.

Clara turned the card over, but there wasn't anything written on the back.

"There doesn't appear to be a telephone number, or business address on here. How do you contact them?" Clara said, frowning at the card.

Brian grinned broadly. "He gives me these weird goggles and it reveals the address on the back. I went to the address and they fitted me with this telescope," he tapped the side of his mechanical eye.

"It must have cost you an enormous amount of money."

"On the contrary, miss, it was completely free."

Clara parted her lips and touched them with her leather glove. "How wonderful. It's rare to see such random acts of kindness these days."

Brian nodded. "I owe them me life miss, gave me my job back."

Clara handed the card back to him, but he waved it away, saying, "No, no miss, you keep it."

"Well, thank you, if you're sure?"

"It's yours. I have another."

Clara pocketed it. "Thank you, Brian."

"You're welcome," Brian said, smiling.

"You mentioned the man had pale skin and red eyes. Was he a vampire, by any chance?"

"Yes, he told me so," he said, puffing out his chest.

Interesting. I'll have to ask the Vampire Council about this.

Brian continued. "The Birikrians are filthy war mongers and I am proud that the Tarnuzian army beat 'em," he poked his finger at his chest. "But I'm forever grateful they let vampires land on that boat two and half centuries ago, that's for sure. Now if you'll excuse me miss, I've been flapping me gums too long. Good day to ya." he said, doffing his black inspector's cap with a red band around it.

"Thank you. I will."

He left and carried on inspecting tickets.

One thing the cruel Birikrians brought to Tarnuz was a refugee exchange. Elves, dwarves, werewolves, vampires, dragons, and various other races and species, were all given asylum on Tarnuz, opening up trade, and after five years, citizenship. Once you became a Tarnuzian, you could register your child for a royal scholarship. Dragons had no use for the scholarship, but were always available to impart advice and wisdom. If the child was successful, their training would be funded by the state.

Clara welcomed the diversity of her country, and it provided stability and valuable allies. She believed these allies helped them defeat the Birikrians but she sincerely hoped the current peace treaty was secure.

Whilst I respect the cause of TWLf, fair pay and decent working conditions, I don't have to agree with their draconian methods. They have the ability to cause a civil war, Clara thought, shivering.

Before she could go over the plan in her head once more, she heard the sound of a commotion.

"How rude. You don't just barge people like that young man, especially a lady," an older woman's voice said, followed by a loud whacking sound, probably a parasol hitting an arm.

"Ow, that hurt." The victim said.

"Serves you right, you bad-mannered little upstart."

Clara leaned forward and peered down the carriage. She saw the old lady, clad in a white bustle dress, tap a weasel-faced man on the arm. The man's eyes darted around the carriage as if he was watching for the police. Nervously, he fiddled with the straps of his rucksack, then pulled at his grubby mocha-coloured cravat. He reached into his trench coat pocket and pulled out a fob watch. Popping open the device, he looked at the time. After that, he apologised profusely to the old lady and hastily walked down the carriage. As the train clattered along the tracks, the man swayed on the unsteady surface and disappeared through the carriage door.

He fits the description; the rucksack and his behaviour are very suspicious.

Clara got up and followed the man. At one point, he looked in her direction, but she turned and opened the window, pretending to smoke. At that moment, the train's whistle sounded, and Clara continued her pursuit. A carriage door opened, and Clara heard the sound of rushing wind. Leaning out of the window, Clara saw the man gingerly walk along the narrow runners of the carriage. And then he disappeared. Opening the door, Clara followed him. When she found him, he'd planted a magnetic bomb just above the carriage coupling. A ticking sound signalled that the explosive was primed.

"Artimus Vengeford, you're under…"

Artimus punched her in the jaw, and she reached back and grabbed the gold handrail on the door. With a grunt, she heard him pulling himself up onto the top of the next carriage. Dazed and with a throbbing jaw, the wind whipping at her hair and clothes, she pulled the bomb from the carriage and put it in her satchel. She climbed onto the top of the train, and Artimus swung his fist again. Clara sidestepped and Artimus rushed into the empty gap.

"Grr-ra," the weasel yelled, kicking Clara in the stomach.

Winded, she fell on her back; the movement of the train made her head wobble. Tick, tick, tick went the bomb. Artimus grabbed her throat and began squeezing her windpipe. Clara curled back her palm and drove the heel of it into his nose. As it made contact, there was a soft squelching sound. Blood poured from Artimus' nostrils as he screamed and fell backwards, dropping the satchel. Picking up the rucksack, she threw it at Artimus, who caught it and fell on his back.

"Artimus, I think this is your stop," she said, pulling him to his feet and throwing him over the side of the moving locomotive.

He screamed as he plummeted to his death. The steam engine was travelling over the Great Tarnuz Viaduct. But Artimus exploded before he hit the ocean, cutting off his agonised screams. With a screech of brakes, the train started to slow down and eventually stopped.

Clara went inside the train to check that everyone was okay. An old lady lay on the floor in a white bustle dress. A walrus of a man, in a white suit and red tie, who smelt of cigars, was waving a bottle of smelling salts under her nose.

"Excuse me, sorry, ma'am, please let me through," Brian the ticket collector said, as he made his way through the panicked crowd. His face was red, and he was out of breath.

"Where's the weasel?" he said, breathing heavily.

"He went pop," Clara said.

Chapter Two: The Rose of Death

After the eventful train journey, Clara swung back the squeaky black wrought iron gate of her house. She opened the front door, shrugged off her cloak, and handed it to Dalton Paget, her butler, who was a tall, thin man with round spectacles, a few strands of grey hair combed neatly on his head.

"Have you eaten Miss Overton? Would you like the chef to prepare you something?"

"No, that won't be necessary, Dalton. I had something at the police headquarters."

She had stayed late to write up the Artimus Vengeford case. She tried to leave work at work, but sometimes the lines got blurred.

"Very good. Would you like me to pour you a rum in your study?"

"No, I will make one myself. You may sign off for the day, Dalton. That will be all."

"Very good, ma'am. I'll see you in the morning."

"Have a splendid evening. I'll see you tomorrow."

Dalton opened the dark wood door of his room and disappeared. The grandfather clock at the bottom of the stairs chimed 8 p.m. Wearily, Clara trudged up the red-carpeted stairs and opened the first door on her right. After she had poured herself a rum, she sat down in her green studded leather armchair. She switched on her green reporter's lamp. Electricity was a new and expensive invention, but her father's inheritance was more than enough to cover the bills. Her father was a renowned psychiatrist. In truth, she didn't need to work, but being a providentia, like her father before her, or the more commonly known term, Empath, meant she could use her skills for police work. Young women often whispered when she entered a room, tittering amongst themselves. Eventually, they cleared their throats and hid their smirks behind their fans. But the eyes were the window to the soul, and Clara knew deceit when she saw it. Once, someone had thrown a stone through her window, with a note attached to it. "Witch," it read. After she read the note, she felt like she was being watched. She peered through her broken window and stared straight into the eyes of a woman twirling a grey parasol. For a moment, she glared back at Clara, then she stuck her chin out, tilted her head and then walked away.

"Whatever floats your boat, love. You better hope I don't shake your ungloved hand, ha!" Clara said to herself.

When Clara was young, she was well-liked, but on her sixth birthday, she discovered something strange. After she had opened one of her presents, a mounted beefeater on a white horse, she went into a trance. There was a flash, and she saw Abigail, the child who gave her the present, push a boy down a well and steal the toy. After Clara dropped the toy, the connection was broken, and Clara opened her eyes. Breathing heavily, she made her excuses and ran to the bathroom, where she promptly threw up.

A few days later, Clara dressed in a yellow pleated frock and Abigail was dressed in a black pleated frock, and they were walking in the woods. Relentless June sunshine had persuaded them that a walk in the Overton estate forest was what they needed. Sighing deeply, Clara turned to Abigail and said, "I love the present you bought me. The beefeater is so handsome, and the horse is divine."

Abigail smiled sweetly. "I'm glad you liked it."

Clara wrung her hands and chewed her bottom lip. "Where did you get it?"

Abigail's smile faded, and she looked at the ground.

"Oh, I don't know. Papa takes me to toy shops all the time. I saw it in the window and I know how much you love horses, so I asked him to buy it."

Clara looked at her, smiling weakly. Then, she turned away, her hands making nervous gestures. "It's just… when I unwrapped it… I saw...had a vision."

Abigail touched her lightly on the shoulder. "What did you see, Clara?" Abigail said, an accusing edge to her voice.

"I…err.. I saw you push a boy down a well and steal the soldier."

Abigail squeezed her lips together. "Clara, turn around."

Clara did as her friend asked, and as she did so, Abigail's fist crashed into her eye. Abigail's face was red with rage, her eyes blazing with hatred.

"Take that, you evil witch. How dare you say such a wicked thing," she said, picking up a sharp stone and scratching above her own eyebrow, drawing blood.

After that, she burst into tears and ran screaming back to the Overton house. Rumours spread by Abigail circulated after that, and from that day forward, Clara was alone. No child wanted to play with her; no one wanted to be her friend. When her father had talked to her, he listened to her side of the story. For a moment, he said nothing, then he picked up his phone and called his best friend, police Captain Peter Harris, and told him what Clara had seen. Later that day, the police pulled the broken body of little Oliver Smeardon out of the family well at the back of the property. He had been missing for a week before they found him. Abigail had gone over to play with him the day he went missing. When she was questioned, Abigail's mother lied on her behalf, and the case was closed.

Things improved when Clara got older. Not only did she have more control over her powers, but she could use them to her advantage. Poker became especially easy. All she needed to do was flash a warm smile, touch her opponent's hand, and she could see their cards. Gambling became very lucrative for Clara until Oswald Overton, her father, found out and pointed her in Captain Harris' direction. Police training was only two short years, but she had become a detective when she solved the kidnapping of somebody called David Chambers. Although she was driven, she didn't have the desire to progress further in the force.

After letting out a sigh, she put her legs on her desk and crossed them, her black leather trousers creaking as she did so. A stray lock of her brown hair dangled down the side of her face, so she unfastened her French twist, letting her hair fall down. The ice clinked in her glass as it began to melt, and she felt the day ebb away. A tap on the window made her jump, and she saw Dimitri floating there, his long brown hair framing his angular face. Before she could respond, there was a sound like steam being released from a pipe, and then black smoke seeped under the study door. A young woman materialised before her, also with long dark hair, a heart-shaped face, and innocent looking eyes. Red eyes.

"Do you two always have to make a vampire entrance, or do you occasionally use the door like humans?"

"Sorry, Clara," the woman said, her doe like eyes pleading with her.

"Don't do that, Velorina."

"Don't do what?" Velorina said.

Dimitri glided down and stood next to her, the tails of his navy jacket curling as he did so. He adjusted his white cravat and brushed imaginary dust from the gold leaf pattern on his lapels.

I didn't know vampires were vain. Maybe it's just the males. I hope he doesn't fancy me. Still, I need to test my stake gun on someone. I hope he can't read minds. I bet he can. Maybe my powers stop him from reading mine. I'll find out soon, I'm sure.

Clara turned her thoughts back to Velorina. "That thing with your eyes. You know the don't-be-cross-with-me, look." Clara said, folding her arms.

"I can't help the way I look."

Dimitri made a stop sign with his hand. "The vampire council needs your unique skill set."

"Is it a crime, Dimitri?"

"Yes, it is."

"Well, go down to the station and report it. I'm off duty."

Velorina moved closer, but Clara averted her gaze.

"Dmitri, will you tell your sister to back off? I will not be manipulated by you two blood suckers, especially her," she snarled, standing and planting her legs wide.

"Clara, calm down. Something untoward is happening, and it could threaten the very existence of Tarnuz, maybe the whole planet of Remina."

Clara drained her glass. "Well, seeing as you put it like that."

Dimitri took her left arm, and Velorina grabbed her right, and then they gracefully lifted in the air.

"Hang on. I didn't agree with the pair of you manhandling me like this."

Dimitri flicked up his fingers and the window slid open.

"Trust me, Clara. This is the quickest way to get there."

They flew through the windows, the mid-September wind blowing through their hair. They soared above the slate roofed houses and smoking chimney pots. A steam train blew its whistle as it sped across a viaduct. Revellers spilt onto the street from a rowdy tavern, singing songs with slurred voices. Steam curled from the smokestack of a coal fired taxi, dropping its occupants at the theatre.

When they had passed the city, they flew to the coast and landed at the mouth of a storm drain. Blood stained the floor, and it smelt of rotting flesh. A body lay motionless on the ground. Water trickled down the walls. They ventured further into the tunnel, and Clara pumped the button on her clockwork torch. Once it was lit, she handed it to Dimitri.

"Keep the light trained on the body, please."

"Sure, Clara, no problem."

The body belonged to a young woman, no older than sixteen. And then Clara spotted something.

"Dimitri, shine the light on her chest cavity."

Dimitri moved the beam over the area. There was a hole in the soft, tender flesh.

"The killer ripped her heart out," Clara exclaimed.

Dimitri turned the torch on his face and grimaced. "Why rip out the heart?"

"It could be a love crime," stated Velorina.

Clara took the flashlight from Dimitri and shone it around the crime scene. "There doesn't appear to be any signs of a struggle, and the body is facing us, so that rules out someone sneaking up and whacking her from behind."

"Well, the killer didn't eat the heart; I just found it." Velorina said.

"Thanks for that," Clara said, training the lamp on another part of the drain, illuminating a rose.

Clara picked up the rose, her eyes turning white. She saw the dead girl laughing. Someone had told her a joke. Still smiling, the girl sniffed the rose. She laughed again and then punched the joker on the arm, a male arm with a pterodactyl tattoo on it. That's the second time today I have seen that flying dinosaur. I wonder if there's a connection. And then her face went serious, the back of a male head appeared. The male sank his teeth into the girl's neck. At that moment, Clara dropped the rose, her eyes rolled back to their natural colour, emerald green and she fell backwards, gasping for air.

Velorina rushed to her side.

"Clara, are you okay?" Velorina said, looking concerned.

"I'll be okay, nothing a drink can't fix."

"Father wants to see you," Dimitri said, solemnly.

"What does Raqaknoff want with me?" Clara frowned.

"He wants to be kept informed of everything. He's very concerned," Velorina said, her voice was dreamlike and reminded Clara of mournful violins.

"Fine, a flight by vampire will help me process this God awful murder." Clara's voice was harsh like a firestarter striking flint.

"Okay are you ready?" Dimitri said, holding out his hand, eyebrows raised.

Clara nodded. "Try and make the flight pleasant, will you. The more scenic, the better."

"I promise you won't be disappointed," Velorina said, smiling.

Just stop. You can't have empathy, you're a vampire.

Lifting Clara gently off the ground, they flew back to the city. Their flight took them past dreamy church spires and away from the mustard yellow factory smog.

"Do you fancy seeing something neat?" Dimitri said, looking mischievous.

"Sure," Clara replied, chewing her lip.

Both siblings rose altitude and when the cloud cleared, a Dirigible appeared like a ghost ship through the fog. A majestic but disturbing sight.

"Here watch this," Dimitri said, steering them towards the observation deck of the balloon.

The vampire siblings switched from horizontal flight to vertical and floated in front of the windows of the huge craft. People pointed at the strange sight, some taking out spy glasses for a closer look. Others waved or cheered, some clapped. For a moment, they floated on the breeze, then they opened their mouths, revealing their large fangs. Women fainted, men shook their fists, some of them drew pistols. Feeling pleased with himself, Dimitri gave them a small wave, a smug grin splitting his face. After that, they turned and sped towards the ground like a bullet, making Clara retch.

"Can you set me down? I think I'm going to be sick."

The vampires glided down into a deserted park, and Clara stepped onto the path that circulated the recreation ground. An owl hooted just as Clara vomited into a rubbish bin, masking the sound.

"Here, breathe into this," Velorina said, handing Clara a brown paper bag.

"Thank you," Clara said. She breathed in and out for a while until she felt better. And then she said, "How did you know about the murder tonight?"

"One of our jobs as part of the vampire council is to patrol the whole of Tarnuz," Dimitri said. "I smelt the blood and I summoned Velorina telepathically and we investigated."

"You expect me to believe you're both some kind of night watchmen or something? Who's to say you weren't looking for someone to feast on?" Clara narrowed her eyes and jammed her hands into her pockets.

Dimitri turned his back to her, placed his hands on his hips and shook his head.

Velorina looked hurt, or Clara thought she looked hurt, but the moonlight made it difficult to tell.

"I don't know what we need to do to make you trust us, Clara," Dimitri tutted, staring at the ground.

"We only drink animal blood. You have probably eaten some of our meat. Moonlight Meals is our butcher and delicatessen chain, the finest quality cuts in the whole of Tarnuz," Velorina said, with a trembling voice.

I don't understand these creatures. I thought they were blood sucking leeches, lurking in the shadows, draining the life out of people. It seems they are sensitive and have feelings.

"Yes I have eaten Moonlight Meal products. They were delicious, I'll give you that. Look, I'm sorry," she said, looking at each sibling in turn. "You'd better take me to your father now. He must be wondering where we are."

"Apology accepted," Dimitri said, offering his hand to Clara, which she took and the three of them flew to the vampire council palace.

The palace was a Gothic church once, a sanctuary, a place of salvation, holy ground. Stained glass windows changed the sun's rays to red, green, blue and yellow, showing off creation in all its glory. But at night, ghastly gargoyles glared at you from lofty perches. Darkness and light, night and day. Two sides of the same coin, both demanded a blood sacrifice, both promising eternal life.

Clara felt a sense of foreboding. Something terrible happened here a long time ago, she could sense it.

I'm not touching anything in there. I don't need a sensory overload. I have only seen a padded cell once and that was enough. I am so grateful for Emmeline and her exquisite gloves. I won't be removing them here.

She paused before she went in.

Dimitri and Velorina stood at the top of the stairs holding the huge dark oak doors open.

Dimitri beckoned to her.

"Clara, are you coming? We don't bite," he and Velorina both sniggered.

"Not funny. Actually you do," Clara said, glaring at the sinister siblings.

A chill breeze blew, shielding the moon with a cloud, darkening the sky.

Now the cathedral spires looked like black bony fingers scratching at the ebony sky. Shuddering, she took a deep breath for composure and climbed the steps.

Clara's boots echoed on the white and black tiles as she walked. All the pews had been replaced with three thrones, each one had a white kid goat standing on it. Raqaknoff sat in the centre throne stroking his goat with long slender fingers. The animal bleated softly, nuzzling his round chin. Raqaknoff fixed his luminescent blue eyes on Clara and smiled a chilling smile. A knot formed in

Clara's stomach, as those eyes bored into her soul. Swallowing hard, and licking her lips, Clara tried to focus. Dimitri picked up the goat on the left and sat down. Velorina sat on the right. Both of them stroked their goats.

One half of Raqaknoff's face was shadowed, the other was lit by the moon. His hair was longer on the top, slicked back from the forehead. Nothing he could say or do would put Clara at ease, she was sure of that.

Raqaknoff stopped stroking the kid and frowned. "Clara, you're trembling."

"I..I feel… uncomfortable. I have never been so close to so many vampires," she said, looking nervously at the goats.

"Well, I don't know if this will help, but your providentia abilities prohibit vampire telepathy. You can trust us, there's no need to be afraid. On the contrary, we..." he gestured to his offspring, "...should be afraid of you."

Clara's whole body slumped, then she grunted. "You do know a cathedral is shaped like a cross, right?"

Raqaknoff handed his goat to Velorina, lent forward and clutched the arms of the throne tightly. "Is that some kind of veiled threat, Miss Overton?"

Hair bristled on Clara's arms and at the back of her neck.

"No, no, I didn't mean to offend," she said, her voice shrill, her leg muscles tightening.

It's not too late to run, Clara.

The master vampire held out his hand and Velorina gave him his goat. "Good. I am glad we have come to a mutual agreement."

Clara sighed. "Is that true, you really can't read my mind?"

Dimitri and Velorina nodded.

Raqaknoff said, "We have no reason to deceive you. I would, however, like you to tell us what you saw at the crime scene."

Clara breathed in and out and paced the floor.

"When I was in the trance state, I saw a young man talking to the victim. I think she knew him well. Perhaps he was her brother."

Dimitri stopped stroking his animal and lent forward this time. "Did you see his face?"

"No, I only saw the back of his head."

"What colour hair did he have?" Velorina inquired.

"Platinum blonde, or white."

"This is very good. Clara. Please continue," Raqaknoff said, trying to sound encouraging.

"Thank you. I saw a tattoo of a bird. No, wait... a dinosaur," she revealed, closing her eyes and massaging her temples. "A pterodactyl. It was a pterodactyl."

The three vampires looked at each other, then Raqaknoff spoke, "What do you think the significance of this prehistoric monster is?"

"The murderer could be a member of a cult," Velorina said, and the three vampires nodded.

Are you sure about this mind reading thing? I am yet to be convinced.

Clara and Velorina glanced at each other; Velorina's face was impassive.

"Yes, cult or organisation. I was handed this today," Clara said, passing the card to Raqaknoff, who inspected it before passing it on to his two children.

Raqaknoff steepled his fingers under his chin. "Which one do you think it is, Clara? A cult or an organisation?"

"There's another option we need to consider too: a gang," pondered Clara.

"Criminal gangs often brand new members as a rite of passage. It's normally awarded after some task is completed. Usually something dangerous or with a high risk value."

"So, do you think he's killed before?" Dimitri inquired.

"Possibly. It depends what the gang wants. His first task might have been stealing something of value from a museum or to inflict a severe beating. Difficult to tell without knowing what is required of new recruits." Clara said.

"Well, this is highly irregular behaviour and something that we have not sanctioned. Someone or something is causing suspicions to be cast at the vampire council and we want it stopped," Raqaknoff roared, slamming his fist on the arm of his throne, making Clara gasp and step backwards.

"Please try to remain calm, father. Clara has shown tremendous bravery coming here today. I apologise for my father's outburst, we have worked very hard on building trust with humans. It's still terribly fragile, even after two hundred and fifty years," Velorina said, her voice soft and reassuring, those innocent eyes pleading with her.

Clara looked away.

"Restraint is something we have striven to maintain for decades now and this incident, this murder," Dimitri said, waving his fist in the air, spittle dripping from his snarling lips, "has threatened our very existence, our way of life, how we conduct ourselves."

He slumped back in his chair, and Velorina patted his hand like a mother reassuring an angry child.

"We are exercising self-control at this very moment. Myself and my children haven't fed in hours," Raqaknoff revealed.

"The nature of the attack was one of desperation, without self-discipline. I want to reiterate what Velorina told you earlier this evening. We don't feed on humans anymore," Dimitri said, having regained his composure.

"Are you saying there's a different breed of vampire out there, a vigilante?" Clara asked.

Velorina nodded. "This doesn't have anything to do with us. Normally, a fledgling has a mentor to show them how to feed, and how to conduct themselves. This was a crime where that poor girl was drained dry. It's barbaric."

Clara pondered this for a moment. "Do you think someone created this creature, this fiend, you know, in a lab or something?"

Raqaknoff smiled. "Glad to see you're thinking like a detective again, Miss Overton. Yes I think that is definitely a possibility. There's a lot at stake here. Gone are the days of vampire slayers and angry mobs with pitchforks. But it doesn't take much for folks to slip into old habits. People are always looking to pin something on us. We don't need another war, we lost too much in the dragon battle. Please let us know what your investigations reveal."

"Thank you for enlightening me, Raqaknoff. I had no idea how serious this was. I'll be sure to let you know," Clara said, sounding relieved.

"Now if you don't mind we'd like to feed," Dimitri said.

"Okay, I'll see myself out," Clara said, leaving.

As the large oak doors closed behind her, she heard three goats screaming.

Chapter Three: Crime Scene Revisited

An unseasonal frost welcomed Clara and Detective James Bronze as they arrived at the crime scene. Fog crept along the ground choking out the sun, hiding the evidence like an evil accomplice. An unpleasant stench of death tormented Clara's nose. She took out her perfume and instead of dabbing it behind her ears, she smeared it under her nostrils. The scene was already a hive of activity. Officers scribbled things in note pads, some shook their heads in disgust. One muttered something about his daughter being a similar age to the victim. The forensics team meticulously placed items in evidence bags: a watch, bracelet and a necklace. A meagre collection of a person cut down in the prime of their life. Everything would be catalogued and archived, waiting for grieving relatives to collect them. Nothing would replace the warm smiles, the heartfelt hugs, the love. The family would be faced with probing questions from stony faced police officers, presenting cold hard facts and distressing evidence. A crime photographer took pictures of the area. Clara clutched the rose again, but the vision was the same as the night before.

James stood next to her. "They found boot prints. Identical to the ones you normally wear, but not today," he began, staring at her footwear with raised eyebrows. "They also found bite marks on the neck.

"So are you accusing me of murder, Bronze, or what?" Clara spat.

"You tell me. It's either you or your merry band of vampires."

Clara took him to one side, away from earshot. "So you're following me now are you?"

James gazed at his boots.

Clara grabbed him by the lapels, forcing down a trance before it took hold. "Answer the bloody question, you piece of shit," she hissed.

James rolled his eyes. "Once or twice."

She swore again. "I knew it," she said, turning her back, then she turned round again. "The vampire council are as concerned about this as we are," she said, jabbing her finger as she spoke.

James grunted. "Do you expect me to believe that? I knew you would defend those blood sucking bastards. A freak like you. I have seen your eyes roll back in their sockets like a Great White Shark."

"So the police still employ bigots. What happened to diversity? Did it pass you by, James, or were you just too lazy to embrace it?"

James said nothing.

"Is this the you-made-detective-before-me thing again?"

James shrugged his shoulders. "You did leapfrog me."

"Rib-it," she said.

"That's not funny," he huffed.

"Come on, Bronze. It was one year, that's all. Twelve short months. If I were you, I'd be thanking me right now."

James smirked. "Clara the narcissist, who'd have thought it."

"That's not what I meant. When you saw me advancing my career, you got the bit between your teeth. It galvanised you, gave you a purpose, a goal, something to work towards. You're a damn fine detective."

James smiled coyly. "Do you mean that?"

"Of course I do. I have confidence that we will solve this case, because we are both as determined as each other."

"That sounds like a winning hand doesn't it?" he said, smiling.

"It most certainly does," she replied, returning the smile.

James puckered his lips. "I still don't trust you, Clara. And what's with the bodice, and leather trousers."

"Ha! Like that is it?" Clara said, putting her hands on her hips, chest puffed out, jerking her head upwards. "A bodice can take a bullet you know."

"Is that so? Just one bullet?"

"Yes, as far as I know."

"I'll have to test it before my transfer comes through." James said, straightening his topper, the googles staring blankly at her. Judging her, mocking her.

"Transfers can take at least six months. Can you put up with me for that long?" Clara said, raising one eyebrow.

James grunted. "It's a dangerous job being a law enforcement officer. You might die in the line of duty. If that happened, I could stay put." He stroked the vulture on top of his cane, his eyes blazing.

Clara stared at him for a long time.

Damn this man! We are already a fabulous crime busting duo. If only he would lower his defences and let me in. I find him infuriating and handsome all at once!

I'd better bury the handsome part, I don't want him thinking I am going soft or something.

"Are you done?"

"Yes, Clara. I think I've made my point," he said, with a cruel smile.

After they hailed a Hackney carriage, neither of them spoke. The silence was broken by the sound of the horse's hooves on the cobblestones, the occasional snorts from the animals and the sharp crack from the driver's whip. A whistle blew and a policeman shouted "Stop, thief!", as he chased a street urchin clutching a large white loaf. The air was filled with the stench of horse manure, fish, baking bread and frying sausages. Market traders tried to entice customers like entertainers at a freak show.

"We're here," the driver said, bringing the carriage to a halt.

They stepped onto the cobblestones and James paid the driver, tipping him generously.

The driver's face lit up. "Gawd bless ya, mate. If there's anyfink I can do, just let me know."

"I'll be sure to call upon your services again my good man," James said, doffing his top hat.

"Feeling flush today are we, Detective Bronze."

"No need to scoff, Detective Overton. You're not the only one who comes from an affluent family."

"Really? I heard you grew up in the workhouse," Clara remarked.

"I am sorry, Miss Posh Knickers. We don't all have a world renowned therapist as a father."

Clara rolled her eyes. "And what's wrong with trying to fix people, Detective Bronze?"

"Not everyone needs fixing."

A small smile flicked across her lips and she stared at him flatly. "Everyone needs fixing, even a child with a grazed knee."

James's face reddened and he clutched his fists by his sides. "That was a low point in my family's life. We rose from the depths and I'm here now." He said, breathing heavily.

"Impressive, a real rags to riches success story. Let's go, Horace is expecting us."

It was a nice thing to do, tip that driver like that. No doubt business is flat with TWLF forcing strikes on workers again. Bully boy tactics never achieved anything. I've seen the bloody noses and the black eyes on strike breakers faces. Tarnuz is a bubbling cauldron, threatening to spill over at any moment, Clara thought.

Chapter Four: Lipstick and Guns

When they stood in front of the armoury, loud hammering could be heard coming from Horace's workshop. James rapped the handle of his cane on the door.

"What the hell is that supposed to be?" Clara said, pointing at the stick.

James threw the stick up and then caught it just below the handle. "This is a vulture handle."

"Looks expensive."

"It is. It's bespoke, I have the only one. It has rubies for eyes."

Clara snorted. "I wouldn't leave that lying around in the wrong neighbourhood. Those rocks would be on the black market before you could shout, "Stop, thief!""

"They've got to take it from me first," James said, pulling a blade from the walking stick.

"You're just trying to impress me with the size of your sword. A bit thin, though, isn't it?"

But before he could reply, the door opened. An old man's face appeared, half-moon glasses perched on his nose. A frown creased his brow, then he smiled, recognising the detectives.

"Come in, come in," Horace said, stepping aside to let them pass.

No one would know he was an armourer, he wore a navy blue tailcoat, with gold buttons and a plum waistcoat. A gold fob watch chain poked out of his waistcoat pocket.

The room smelt of grease, oil and fried fish. In the centre of the room was a bench with an ornate sub-machine gun clamped to it. Next to the rifle, a goggle- wearing tiny tree elf studied the blueprints of a Dirigible. Machines were everywhere. Devices for wood and metalwork, as well as soldering. On one wall there was a weapon rack. Next to that was a bookshelf. Opposite that was a leather chair and a Chesterfield. There was a large arched window, a double bed, a child's bed, an en-suite, behind that a kitchen diner.

"Coffee, tea?" Horace offered in a sing-song voice.

"Coffee, white no sugar," Clara and James said together

A few minutes later Horace reappeared and gave them their drinks. Clara sipped hers. It had a rich aroma and a velvety taste.

"Has Adamar introduced himself to you?" Horace said, gesturing to the elf.

"Oh, sorry. Please forgive me," Adamar said, sliding his goggles onto the top of his head. "I'm Adamar, a former tree elf. My tree house caught on fire and Horace was walking in the woods and rescued me. Being of my short stature, the rest of the elves ostracised me. They said I was cursed, so I had lived on my own for decades. I am eternally grateful to Horace for taking me in."

"And what an asset you are too," Horace said, smiling at the elf. Adamar returned the smile. "Have you taken your elixir today, Adamar?" Horace said, peering over his glasses at the small elf.

Adamar pointed his forefinger at the ceiling. "Ah, thank you for reminding me, Horace. I'll do that right away."

He disappeared into the kitchen diner. A scraping sound followed by a creaky cupboard door could be heard from the room.

"I'm genuinely sorry to hear about your younger days, Adamar," Clara offered, putting her coffee mug on the workbench. "I thought elves were respectful to their own kind."

"Dark elves don't work that way I'm afraid," Adamar revealed, scratching his brown goatee beard.

Clara reflected as she took the elf in. I do feel sorry for him. I know what it's like to be alone. I never knew my mother and now my father is dead, I don't have anyone. I suppose I have Dalton. He's the closest I have to family I suppose.

"Anyway, enough about me. Horace has some new toys he wants to show you."

"Thank you, Adamar, I do indeed. I heard that you lost your firearm in that unpleasant business with Artimus Vengeford. I understand their plight, but I feel the methods of The Workers Liberation Front are a trifle on the zealous side. Anyway, Clara, this is for you," Horace said, unclamping the gun from the bench and passing it to Clara.

She tested the weight and the sight, aiming at the Chesterfield. It was a brass gun with a drum magazine and a few holes in the muzzle to let out high pressure gas.

"It's very nice, but it would be even better if it had a lipstick compartment."

Horace smiled. "I thought you'd say that," he said, leaning over and pressing a button just above the magazine. A panel slid open revealing two lipstick tubes and Clara smiled.

"Adamar, can you help James with his weapon please?"

"Sure," Adamar said, showing James the wall-mounted weapons.

Horace moved with Clara to the kitchen. "Use your ability to see what each lipstick can do. This is a top secret prototype."

For a brief moment, Clara stood there, and then she massaged the lipstick in her hands. When the trance was over she rejoined the others.

"So, why did you want the lipstick?" James asked.

"Because if I'm going to have a kiss of death, I want to leave a good looking corpse."

Horace laughed. "I thought you wanted to kiss Detective Bronze."

Clara grimaced. "The trouble with frogs is they don't all turn into princes."

Horace and Adamar laughed, James scowled, crossed his arms and widened his stance.

Horace's smile faded. "Now, pay attention, Clara, James. Could one of you give me your gun please?"

James sighed and passed the weapon to Horace, handle first, muzzle down. "Thank you, Detective Bronze. As you can see, this machine gun is fitted with four different barrels. A quick press of this button," Horace said, pressing at a red button just above the trigger. The barrel rotated and another one slotted into place. "This barrel fires grenades or tear gas, depending on the user's loadout preferences. The other settings are regular machine gun ammunition, grappling hook and electric shock charges."

"The regular ammo makes sense, but how does it charge the electricity?" James said, verbalising Clara's thoughts.

Horace smiled. "It's clockwork. You pump the switch on the side, and it gives you a charge for one shot," Horace revealed, demonstrating the action. The machine made whirring noises as it powered up.

James curled his lip as he pointed it at Clara, Horace stepped in front of him, gripping the muzzle with both hands. "If you have to try it on someone, I'd rather it was me."

"Really? Are you serious?"

"Yes I am," Horace grimaced, standing back, puffing out his chest.

"Okay old man, brace yourself," James said, assuming an aiming stance.

James pulled the trigger and a two pronged dart embedded itself in Horace's chest buzzing with electricity. The inventor convulsed like a fish caught in a net. When the charge was spent, Horace bent over, breathing heavily, his clothes smoking.

"I thought it would have knocked you out cold," James said, inspecting the weapon.

"I asked you to shock me so I could test another prototype, wearable body armour. It appears to be working just fine," Horace said, smiling at Adamar, who smiled back, and then shook Horace's hand vigorously.

A confused look swept across James's face and he scratched his head. "I don't get it. I shocked you with several thousand volts and you are still standing upright. You should be flat on your back!"

"My waistcoat is made of leather, an excellent defence against electronic discharge."

"Does this armour come free with the gun?" Clara asked, raising her left eyebrow.

"Adamar and I need to run more tests, but when it's ready, we'll get you both in for a fitting. Have I answered all of your queries satisfactorily?"

"I don't have any further questions. Do you, Overton?" James asked.

"No, I don't, Bronze," Clara replied, scowling at him.

"Well, if you don't mind, Adamar and I have very important research to conduct. If there are any further developments with my inventions, I will contact you forthwith. It's been a most pleasant experience, and I look forward to seeing you again soon." Horace said and shook hands with them both.

They thanked him and left.

***

Later that evening, Clara climbed down from her cab outside the Arch Tavern. A thick fog clung to the harbour like a blanket. Bells on fishing boats dinged softly as the vessels lightly bumped each other, buffeted by ripples from the sea. Moist air smelling of algae assaulted Clara's nostrils, and the fog smothered the gas lamps like a killer suffocating his victim. Teenage boys in peak caps and dirty cravats sat on wooden beer barrels in front of the pub and leered at Clara as she walked towards the tavern.

"'Ere, darling. I can give ya a real good time. Better than anyone in that bloody place," one boy said, hooking his thumb over his shoulder.

The rest of the gang sniggered and said, "Go on Chris, show her a good time."

"How 'bout you plant one on my kisser?" Chris smirked, puckering his lips, leaning forward.

"You want me to kiss you?" Clara said, raising her eyebrows and putting her hands on her hips.

"Yeah, if you're game," Chris replied.

"Very well. Let me put my lipstick on first," she said, taking a gold cylinder from her pocket. After she had applied the make-up, she said, "Come and get me lover boy,"

"Go on Chris, you're in there!" a gang member jeered.

Chris took off his cap and kissed Clara. After she had kissed him she stepped back. For a moment, Chris smiled savouring the exchange. And then his face turned red and his eyes bulged. He clutched his throat and tried to tear the cravat from his neck.

"I…can't breathe…," Chris wheezed, sliding to the floor and falling backwards.

Children of Tarnuz

"What have you done to him? You fucking crazy bitch!"

"Nothing. I just kissed him. He must have had an allergic reaction to my lipstick."

"He's convulsing, I don't know what to fucking do," a young gangster said, fear in his eyes.

"Give him mouth-to-mouth," Clara said.

"What? Ah, yeah, good Idea. We'll take it in turns," the scared youth said, leaning down and putting his mouth on Chris's lips.

One by one the youths placed their mouths on Chris's lips.

"Good job, guys. Before you know it, he'll be as right as rain." Clara said, with a cruel smile, stepping into the tavern.

When Clara opened the door, thick tobacco smoke wafted towards her. The air was filled with the stench of cigarettes, cigars, beer and seafood. Sawdust swished under her boots as she walked. Men stared at her, some undressed her with their eyes.

"I thought pork was off the menu, but I see a pig has just walked in. Don't you coppers have ya own bar or somefin'?" A yellow toothed man said, pointing at Clara. His friends guffawed loudly, slapping him on the back, spilling his beer.

"You sound like you have something to hide. Is there something you need to tell me? You could accompany me to the station and we could discuss it."

Yellow teeth licked his lips and swallowed hard. "N…no, officer. That ain't necessary. Let me buy ya a drink, my way of sayin' sorry."

Clara narrowed her eyes. "Are you trying to bribe an officer of the law?"

"No, mam, I wouldn't dream of it."

"Well, I suggest you carry on drinking and leave me be."

"Right-ho, Miss," Yellow Teeth, said, looking sheepish, sipping his beer and turning back to his subdued mates.

A self-playing piano played singalong songs, accompanied by drunken singers who slopped ale onto the floor. Billiard balls could be heard clacking together. Clara perched herself on a bar stool. The barman had his back to her, he was sharing a joke with a regular. He turned to face her. He had curly ram horns and a black fleece instead of hair. His smile faded when he saw Clara, his brown eyes blazing, his ebony mouth tightening.

"What can I get you, Officer Overton," the puck bartender said.

"Some of your unwatered down beer if you don't mind, William," Clara said, flashing her sweetest smile and sliding a dark brown penny across the counter.

William shook his head, took a tin tankard down from a hook above the bar and pulled the bar pump. When the flagon was full, he slammed the drink down in front of her, spilling the golden liquid on the bar.

After he pocketed Clara's coin in his waiter wallet, he said, "You've got a nerve showing up here again," William hissed.

"Why shouldn't I? This tavern was owned by my great, great, great…"

"You've already told me about your grandmother.."

Clara held up her index finger for silence.

"I haven't finished. Great Grandmother."

William dipped his chin, "I get it she was great, truly marvellous."

Clara drank some of her beer, wiped her frothy lips and placed her drink on the bar.

"I am merely trying to point out how great she really was and how far from greatness you have fallen."

"Well, your unique gift keeps me honest these days."

"I only touched that ugly diamond skull knuckle duster of yours, that's all," Clara said.

William stared at her for a while, then grabbed a tumbler and poured a glass of whisky.

He sighed. "I guess I should thank you for stopping me from ripping off the punters."

Clara threw up her arms and smiled. "Just doing my job, serve and protect. Anyway, what have you got for me, my good man?"

William leaned closer, glanced around the pub to make sure no-one was listening and said, "There's something strange going on at the metal foundry. You should go and check it out."

Clara snorted into her beer. "I can't go poking my nose into everything that's a little out of the ordinary. If I looked into everything that was unusual, I'd never go home. This is Tarnuz, unusual is what we do."

William lowered his whisky, took out a handkerchief from his white shirt breast pocket and wiped his black handlebar moustache. "What if I told you, Detective Overton, that people were going in and not coming out. Disappearing into thin air. Poof!" he said, with a flourish of his hands, his voice gradually getting softer.

Clara stared at him without emotion and sighed. "If a missing person's report comes across my desk I'll look into it," she said flatly.

William scrutinised her. "You know what you remind me of, Clara?" he said, sifting his weight, his hooves clacking on the wooden floor.

"Please tell me," she said, not looking up from the menu she was studying.

"A thistle. Prickly and difficult to handle," he chuckled.

Clara lowered her menu, narrowed her eyes and tightened her sultry lips. "What's good on the menu barkeep?" She hissed.

"The oysters,"

"Really? Okay, I'll have those then," she said with a grin like the sun appearing from behind a dark cloud.

"You can't, they're off," he said, laughing again.

Clara fixed flinty eyes on him and his smile disappeared. She lunged across the counter trying to grab his ring, but William pulled away before she touched him.

"You're lucky you have quick reflexes, puck. I bet there are a ton of dirty little secrets hiding behind that easy going facade of yours," she shouted, raising her chin and slamming her fist on the bar.

William backed away, fear in his eyes. "The honey glazed garlic pork chops are delicious. Chef's dish of the day with fried rice."

Clara smiled smugly. "There, that wasn't so hard, was it? I'll have that," she said, tossing the menu across the bar like a discarded playing card.

William licked his lips. "Coming r…r…right up, d…d…detective," he said, scribbling down her order with shaking hands.

"And another beer, please," she said, placing a coin on the counter like she was flicking a tiddlywink.

After he had handed the chit to a server through the service hatch, he took her money and poured her another beer.

"Thanks," she said, slurping noisily.

People talked amongst themselves like children sharing Chinese whispers and she could feel eyes boring into the back of her skull.

Sometime later, she tucked into her meal. A man cleared his throat and stood next to Clara.

"Excuse me, miss."

Clara turned and saw a tall man with a brown beard.

"I think you should eat your food and leave," he said. "Apart from being rude to William, you are a woman on her own and the law…"

Clara huffed, made a show of getting her police badge out and flashed it at the man, a smug grin plastered on her face. "I am the law, bud," she said, finishing her food and paying her tab, leaving a generous tip.

Brown beard stood there with his mouth open as she left.

A crowd had gathered outside the tavern and the police were trying to hold them back.

"Ladies and gentlemen, this is a crime scene. Please stand clear and let us do our job," one uniformed officer said, trying to pull away from a woman grabbing at the silver buttons on his blue coat.

James Bronze spotted her and barged his way through the unruly crowd.

"Just as I thought all coppers are pigs," a woman shouted after James as he ploughed through the crowd. The crowd cheered the woman and showered her with praise.

Bronze grabbed Clara by the arm and pulled her across the cobblestones as bewildered market traders stared in disbelief.

"Let go of me, Bronze, or I promise you'll regret it," Clara demanded, wrenching her arm away from him.

James bared his teeth. "There are six dead young men over there," Bronze said, jerking his head in the direction of the corpses. "It seems wherever you go there's at least one body.

Clara raised her hands, palms up. "Well, those boys over there must have had the oysters. William told me they were off."

"I find your cavalier attitude insulting."

"Well, you won't have to put up with me much longer. You put in a transfer, remember?" Clara said, blowing him a kiss and walking away.

James took his topper off and gripped its brown rim so tightly, his knuckles whitened.

He huffed like a bull, his nostrils flaring, as Clara sauntered away from him.

Rowdy dandies sped round the corner in a black carriage. Some were hanging from the roof, one slopped red wine from his bottle onto the cobblestones. Another cracked his whip at the black horse and the animal neighed, showing the whites of its eyes, a terrified look on its face. The carriage swayed left and right as it narrowly missed shoppers and pedestrians. Clara tutted and shook her head.

A whistle sounded followed by shouting policemen sprinting after the runaway carriage, waving their batons in the air.

"Bring them in, boys," Clara said softly to herself.

The faint aroma of newly cooked bread wafted up Clara's nostrils as she strolled past a bakery. Walking further, she passed 'Cotton and Couture', a high end boutique, where she saw women in expensive silk bustle dresses examining fabrics whilst flustered seamstresses' pulled cloth from overhead shelves.

She smiled as she approached 'The Spine Mine' book shop. Its gold paint never dulled or peeled and the books in the front window glowed softly from the lantern light that illuminated them.

As Clara entered the store, a heady scent, a mixture of old paper and leather comforted her.

A man cleared his throat. "Are you with us, Miss Overton, or have you slipped into one of your trances?"

Clara opened her eyes with a smile and turned in the direction of the voice.

Edwin Buckle was a tall man in his forties. He had a square jaw and brown hair, parted on the right

"Edwin, so great to see you! How the devil are you? My fine fellow."

Edwin returned the smile and they hugged, his maroon silk cravat rustling as they embraced.

Children of Tarnuz

"Clara, you look tired. Are you getting enough rest, my dear?"

Clara rolled her eyes. "I have a tough job, it keeps me awake at night," she said, blinking hard and rubbing her temples.

Edwin walked behind the counter. He took a bottle of brandy and two glasses down from the shelf. He poured two fingers in each tumbler and handed a glass to Clara. She took it and thanked him. She sipped her drink.

He stood up, his black tailcoat fluttering lightly. He took out his gold fob watch from his grey waistcoat pocket.

"Are you expecting company, Edwin? A young lady perhaps?" Clara said, arching one brow.

Edwin cleared his throat. "Huh, ah, no. Not really. I have only just got this watch. It's still somewhat of a novelty to me. I lost the last one whilst swimming."

Clara smiled and tapped her lips with her index finger. "Were you inebriated when you decided to take a little paddle?"

Edwin's cheeks coloured and he looked at his black shoes.

"I was merry, but I wouldn't say I was inebriated. I think that is far too strong a word to use," he said, taking a gulp from his brandy glass. "Anyway, you happened to mention you were having sleepless nights. I have always found reading before bedtime incredibly therapeutic," he said, holding his arms out, palms up, and rotating on his feet.

"You are a bookseller, you're obliged to say that," she said, pointing her glass at him.

Edwin snorted. "I wouldn't want people to spread wild accusations about me. My reputation would be in tatters," he laughed nervously.

"Okay, what would you say if I said I was in the market for a book. What would Edwin Buckle recommend?"

Edwin tilted his head to the left, then he placed his drink on the counter. A slight smile twitched at his lips as he walked over to a shelf, took down a maroon coloured, medium sized book and handed it to Clara.

Gold writing was written on the spine: "Orphan to Opulence" it read.

"I don't think this story would be very good for my mental health," Clara said, sliding the book across the table counter and stepping away from it as if it was a burning coal.

"To experience vulnerability is to know the true power of strength," Edwin said.

Clara flashed a fake smile at him. "My vulnerability could put me in the hospital. I can't afford such luxuries."

"I can assure you there is nothing luxurious about a mental institution," Edwin shuddered.

Several years before, Edwin had a bad bout of depression and was committed. Clara and Eme battled the authorities for eighteen months. Edwin battled for a further two years before Clara and Eme secured his release. Edwin coughed. "Besides, I thought Eme had crafted you some rather fine reading gloves."

Clara snorted. He's got me there. Bang to rights.

Edwin stared at her, his eyes pleaded with her, like a child trying to get his own way.

Clara narrowed her eyes, extended her index finger, and hooked the book towards her. "Is it a true story?" she said, frowning at the book.

Edwin cleared his throat "It's based on true events, I believe."

Clara lowered the book. "How much do you want for it?"

"Six shillings" he said, beaming a large smile.

"Six shillings?" Clara screeched. "It better be a bloody good read, Buckle," she said, shaking her head, fishing around in her purse for the coins.

Edwin slid the coins into his hand and rang up the price on the cash register.

"There, that wasn't as painful as all that, was it?" he said, a smug smile on his face.

Clara sneered at him. "Good job I love you, Edwin, isn't it?

"I love you too," he said, clasping her hands. "I don't know where I'd be without you and Eme."

"You'd still be in that God forsaken place, wearing a skull cape receiving shock treatment."

Edwin unclasped Clara's hands, sighed deeply and put his hand on his brow.

"I think you'd better leave. I feel a headache coming on. It's time for me to close for the night anyway."

Clara froze, stretched out her trembling hand, then she turned, looked over her shoulder, lip quivering and left. She stood with her back to the book shop and with leadened steps, made her way to Emmeline Miller's glove making shop.

"Fit Sew Good" was painted in red calligraphy on the shop front. Clara smiled at the wordplay, as she always did. Before Clara could knock on the shop door, Emmeline flung open the door and pulled her friend inside.

Emmeline promptly kissed the air near Clara's right cheek, then her left.

Strewn about the place were reams of cotton, silk, lace and leather. It smelt of clean linen, cow hide and of a burning jasmine joss stick.

Clara smiled. Eme, you're such a creature of habit.

Hand mannequins reached out as if they were asking for help, making Clara shudder. If this place was properly illuminated, I wouldn't feel terrified every time I stepped in the shop.

"Clara darling, how are you?"

Clara sighed and puffed out her cheeks. "Got another violent murder and I think I have upset Edwin again."

"Ah, for fuck sake Clara. You have to tread with exceptional care around Edwin. He's still frightfully fragile. Come here you silly goose," Emmeline said, opening her arms and the two women hugged.

Suddenly, Emmeline started kissing Clara. Clara pulled away and pushed the other woman, who fell against a hand mannequin, knocking it to the floor.

"Enough, Eme," Clara yelled, eyes blazing, her nostrils flaring.

"You didn't say that the other night," Eme said, picking up the fallen mannequin.

"It was a drunken exchange, nothing more."

"My, you really know how to make a girl feel special, don't you?" Eme retorted, her eyes wide and brows furrowed.

"I've just got a lot to contend with right now. My life is… complicated."

"It's the life you chose, sweetheart."

"You could choose this life too. The force would definitely benefit from another providentia."

"I'm still considering my options," Eme said, rearranging the glove on the mannequin.

"You wouldn't need to be a police officer for very long. I know business has been slow lately. You could run the glove shop as a side-line."

Eme stared at her, took down a bottle of red wine from a shelf, poured herself a glass, swallowed the contents in one gulp, then poured another glass. She wiped her lips on her brown leather glove, then she pushed her fedora up, the googles around the rim glinting in the lantern light. Eme glared at Clara before taking down another wine glass and poured a drink for her friend. They clinked glasses and drank.

"But you're my best customer," Eme said, making a toasting gesture at Clara.

Clara flashed a half smile. "You can't support yourself on my business alone."

"You go through gloves like there's no tomorrow," Eme said, smiling.

"I cannot deny that. Are they ready?"

"Reading gloves, right?"

"Right."

"I have them right here," Eme said, turning to two hand mannequins, each one wearing a black lace glove. "These have other uses too, you know," she added, pouting her lips and giving Clara a sultry look.

Clara shook her head, replying, "Don't push your luck. Anyway, I thought you and Edwin were very intimate with each other, now."

"Yes, but I'm after a little fun, a light, feminine touch," Eme said, stroking a feather seductively.

Clara rolled her eyes. She's certainly persistent, I'll give her that.

"Suit yourself," Eme said, dumping Clara's gloves on the counter.

"How much do they cost?"

"82 shillings," Eme said, biting her lip

Clara spat out her wine, "82 Shillings? I expect the gloves to be made of the finest elven lace for that price."

Eme's eyes darted about nervously, she fumbled in her leather waistcoat pocket, then smoothed her sweaty hands on her black and white leggings.

Eme cleared her throat and tugged at the collar of her white blouse.

"Err, it is Elven lace, actually."

Clara tutted and shook her head. "You need to find more well-heeled customers. I can't keep propping up your business like this," she said, fumbling in her purse for the money. "Also, don't hurt Edwin. He's in love with you and you know how fragile he is." Clara slid the money across the counter and Eme snatched it up like a bad mannered child.

Eme stared at Clara with a pained look in her eyes, then she looked away.

"I can't help the way I feel about you, Clara."

Clara reached out and touched Eme's hand, Eme grasped it tightly.

"Do you love Edwin?"

Eme nodded rapidly.

"Good. Then you need to devote all of your time and attention to him. I don't love you in the way you love me. You're like a sister to me. We're peas in the same pod. Providentias in arms, you might say."

Eme snorted and half smiled. "Look at us, Clara. Reminding each other how delicate Edwin is."

Clara took both of Eme's hands in hers. "That's because we both care very deeply about our friend and we both want what's best for him."

"He is rather dishy I have to admit," Eme said, giggling and twirling mousey hair around her forefinger.

"I knew it! Your attraction to him is undeniable, you should see yourself in the mirror. You're blushing," Clara laughed.

Eme peeled off her left brown leather glove and dropped it on the counter, then she pressed the back of her palm against her cheek.

"Stop it, you rascal," Eme said, picking up her glove and playfully swatting Clara on the arm with it. Both women laughed.

Clara yawned and stretched her arms above her head.

"I am absolutely beat. Let's agree that we will do everything we can to make Edwin happy and help him get back on his feet. Agreed?" Clara said, holding out her hand for Eme to shake.

"Agreed," Eme said, shaking Clara's hand and smiling.

Eme yawned this time. "Now you've got me yawning."

"I'll see you soon Eme." Clara said, rotating her wrist, fingers pointing to the ceiling.

Eme returned the gesture and then Clara left.

Children of Tarnuz

Chapter Five: An uncomfortable meeting.

Dew glistened on the forest floor, and the trees creaked in the wind. The horses snorted and shook their heads as Clara and police Commissioner Peter Harris pushed their animals harder. A scampering sound could be heard to Clara's left. She turned her head and saw the handsome face of an elf attached to a spider's body. The elf's eyes turned from beautiful emerald orbs, to horizontal red slits. Large fangs replaced the elf's canines and it used its black spindly legs to climb a tree, where it sat staring at her through the foliage, gnashing its teeth together. Clara shivered, as if an icy finger had traced the length of her spine, or maybe a dark spider's leg. A short time later, Clara and the Commissioner reached a clearing with two archery targets in the centre. Both riders pulled their steeds to a stop and dismounted.

Clara loaded her bow, aimed and fired, hitting the bull on one of the targets.

"Did you see that Elf Spider back there, Commissioner?" Clara said, waiting for her friend to load his bow.

Peter Harris strung his bow, aimed, fired and hit the inner gold. "Yes I did. They are more scared of you than you are of them."

"Do you think? I was scared shitless!"

Peter snorted. "We were lucky to see one. They are pretty rare these days."

He mounted his horse, lifting his bottom to free his light brown trench coat before he sat. Clara mounted her horse, her black leather jodhpurs squeaking as she did so, and they rode to the next target.

"What can you tell me about the fanged fiends?" Clara said, cocking her head.

Peter pulled his horse parallel to hers. "Some say dark elves bred with Midnight Spiders, but I think that is unlikely."

Clara dismounted and said, "Do you have a different theory?

Peter nodded. "Yes I do."

"Well, don't keep me in suspense, pray tell."

Peter sighed. "I think because the dark elves fell out with the elven council and were forced to leave, I think they made their homes near a Midnight Spider colony and the arachnids turned them into what you saw."

"I think you might be onto something. I haven't seen a Midnight Spider in years."

"It gets worse Clara. The Elf Spiders hunted The Midnight Spiders until they were extinct. Dark Elves fought the Elf Spiders until they too were on the brink of extinction. It was a short but brutal battle and the Dark Elves were forced to flee."

"What a terribly sad story."

Peter produced an ornate silver cigarette case from inside his coat pocket and took a cigarette from it. He lit his smoke with an elaborate lighter. He sighed, massaged his forehead with his ebony hand, then he sat on a tree stump and crossed his long legs at the ankles.

Clara squeezed his shoulder. "You are reliving a painful memory, aren't you, Peter?"

Peter sighed and stared into the forest, then he nodded.

"You are not obliged to tell me anything, but I am prepared to listen if you do," Clara said, lightly touching Peter's leg. Peter squeezed her hand gently, turned his head and looked at her with moist eyes.

"I really appreciate it. I was about your age, Clara. Had been in the force for about 18 months or so. The dark elf and spider war had ended, but there were still rebel fractions, still fighting, each side refusing to surrender to the other. Looting and pillaging was still taking place, and we were assigned to keep the peace. As myself and my fellow officers approached a war torn village, broken and smouldering, a woman with pointed ears, dark hair and eyes ran towards me. Her face was streaked with tears and dried blood. Her dark maid's dress was torn and her bare feet were black and sore. Next thing I knew, she tripped and fell forward. I lunged and caught her. When she woke up, she looked startled and talked rapidly. I asked her to calm down and I reassured her she was safe," Peter said, taking another drag on his cigarette.

"Had you taken her to an inn or something?"

Peter nodded. "The inns and taverns had become makeshift hospitals and shelters for the wounded and the dying. Most landlords put aside their prejudice and helped the elves. Others refused to cooperate, even after we threatened to arrest them." He sighed again.

Clara shook her head. "War can do one of two things: bring out the best in people or the worst."

Peter flashed a half smile and nodded. "I saw both," he said, looking at the leaves on the woodland floor.

Clara wrung her hands. "What did the maid tell you?"

Peter took a deep breath. "The maid said she had been separated from her son in the fighting and begged me to go and look for him. I said I would do my best to find him."

"Did you go and look for him?"

"Yes, you know I am a man of my word. I always have been and always will be."

"Yes, that's always been true. That's why my father trusted you."

Peter smoothed the front of his white shirt, a distant unfocused smile on his lips. He dropped his chin and then he said, "When I got to the heart of the village, the scars of war were everywhere. Buildings were shells of their former selves. Large oak beams charred by fire looked like black fingers extended in prayer towards the heavens. Bodies littered the streets and the air was perforated with sobs, moaning and the smells of smoke and rotting flesh. If prayers were uttered that day, I don't think they were answered."

Clara squeezed her eyes shut and felt a chill run down her arm. She rubbed the top of her forearm. "Do you think it was magic that obliterated the village, Peter?"

"Yes I am certain of it. There were no explosives found after forensics had combed the area."

"Did you find the boy and reunite him with his mother?"

Peter swallowed hard and pressed his left fist to his lips, he still held his cigarette in his right hand.

"I carefully picked my way through the village calling the boy's name: Luvon. I called. I tried to block out the horrific scenes around me and concentrate on the task at hand. You know how this job works, don't you?"

Clara nodded. "Oh, yes. All too well," Clara said, a grim smile on her lips.

"I saw an elf with an elf spider on his chest, colour draining from his face, his glass eyes staring into space, his hands still clutching a sword that was protruding from the spider's abdomen. Black blood oozed from the arachnids fatal wound. A one-legged spider limped around helplessly, hissing and baring its teeth before one of my colleagues shot it. Eventually, I could hear muffled cries from a pile of rubble and I called over some of my co-workers and we carefully removed the bricks. We pulled Luvon from the debris amongst joyous cheers, whistles and applause."

"So, this dreadful story did have a happy ending after all," Clara said, squeezing Peter's shoulder again.

"I haven't revealed everything that happened that day." Peter finished his cigarette. "There were things I chose to leave out of my story. Some of the things I saw that day were completely barbaric and they still plague me from time to time."

"We all have that one case that lingers like a rotting corpse," Clara said.

Peter snorted, "You only have one?" He said, wrinkling his brow.

Clara held up her hands in mock surrender. "I have narrowed it down to one."

"That reminds me, how is the murder case going?"

"I have managed to piece together a profile of a male face."

"Ah, yes. The police sketch artist has released the picture to the press."

I haven't seen the Tarnuz Standard today. Clara thought.

"Has it developed any leads, Commissioner?" she asked.

"Not sure. You know what it's like when an award is attached. It always attracts the crazies and the opportunists."

"How much is the reward this time?"

"£200"

"Golly, that is frightfully generous. Who put that up?" Clara said, her black gloved hand flying to her chest.

"Jedidiah Lewis."

Clara's eyes widened and she stepped backwards. "The wealthy industrialist?"

"The very same."

"He must have a vested interest, or maybe he has some kind of connection to the girl. Has anyone formally identified her yet?"

"Yes. Violet Taylor. The victim's brother, Andrew Taylor, is missing. Didn't you say in your report, Clara, that you were certain Violet knew her murderer well?"

"I did say that, yes."

"I think Mr. Taylor is probably our man."

"Possibly, but I'm not entirely convinced he is still a man."

"Are you referring to Violet's body being completely drained of blood?"

"I am indeed."

"You found two puncture wounds on the neck, didn't you?"

"Yes I did."

"The pathologist confirmed that. Do you think it was a vampire attack?"

"The vampire council seems to think so."

"You went to see them?"

"I had the pleasure of their company, on their terms of course."

"Ah, for fucks sake, Clara! You stay away from them, you hear?" Peter bellowed, wagging his finger at her.

Clara backed away from him, covered her mouth with one hand, the other clutched the ruffle on her white blouse.

"I…I…I don't have a choice. They just turn up. They can be very persuasive."

"Everyone has a choice, and, of course, they can be persuasive - they're fucking vampires."

"It seems they are interested in me."

Peter stood up and turned Clara to face him. "I bet they are. They'd love to sink their fangs into your beautiful young neck."

"I don't think it's like that. I think they are curious."

"They are curious?" Peter shouted, his voice climbing the octaves.

"Yes, they said that they can't read my mind."

Peter's shoulders slumped a bit and he rubbed his hand over his grey beard.

"They can't read your mind, you say?"

"That's what they told me."

"Hmm, that is interesting. Very interesting indeed."

"Look, I didn't ask to be in league with the vampires, but these notes started appearing under my door after the Toby Fuller case."

"That case did raise your public profile a lot, I'll admit that."

"I didn't expect my name and face to be splashed all over the tabloids, heaven forbid, but it happened, and there's nothing I can do about it."

"Yes, you were also in the papers almost on a daily basis after your father died. God rest his soul," Peter said, crossing himself.

"I miss him too, and I was starting to adjust to a life without him, before that case."

"Sometimes, we have to live our lives in the limelight and other times we live them in the shadows. It's the nature of the job. You'll get used to it over time."

"Have you ever gotten used to it?"

"I did in the end. Besides, press conferences are very tedious."

"They are very much part of the daily grind for you, aren't they?"

Peter barked a laugh.

"Very much so. Anyway, what would you like me to ask Patrick Theodore Spencer, Jedidiah Lewis and Zintius anyway?"

"You're meeting with the bigwigs. When is that?"

"Tonight."

"I'd like the law changed on women having to be accompanied by men to enter pubs if you don't mind."

"I can't promise anything, but I'll bring it up. I can certainly see how this hurdle would scupper your investigations."

"Thank you, Peter. I would truly appreciate that. Obviously, I know who Spencer and Lewis are, but who's this Zintius?"

Peter looked away from her and cleared his throat.

"He's a vampire."

***

The steps to the Chancellor's house were very busy that night.

Dignitaries from all over Tarnuz began arriving at 7PM. The din in the main assembly hall was deafening. Servants handed goggles to everyone when they reached the top of the stairs. Peter Harris turned them over in his hands, a deep frown creasing his forehead.

"They are for the voting process later this evening," said the male servant that gave Peter his goggles, as if reading his thoughts.

"Thank you, but what happened to the old polling booth and the pencil tied to a piece of string?" Peter said, leaning forward.

The servant swallowed hard, licked his lips and backed away, with a wild look in his eyes.

"T…T…these are modern times, sir, err, Commissioner. It's a new and progressive way of voting, but these goggles are so much more than an elaborate toy, or a tacky gimmick. There will be a public demonstration tomorrow in the marketplace at 2PM. It would be delightful if you could attend."

"I wouldn't want to miss it for the world," Peter said, doffing his front pinched hat and walking away.

Chancellor Patrick Spencer approached Peter, his hand extended and Peter shook it. The industrialist Jedidiah Lewis stood with Lewis and the vampire Zintius. Lewis gestured to a servant to clear away some men standing in front of large dark oak doors.

"So good of you all to join us this evening. Please take a seat at the table," Patrick Spencer said, gesturing at the table. The men walked across a large maroon carpet and took their seats.

A server appeared and poured them red wine and gave Zintius a goblet that Peter suspected contained blood, and he clenched his fist and then released it again.

"Our friend, Zintius, is Managing Director of a new company, Agreeable Solutions, and has success in Birik controlling gang crime."

Zintius gave a curt nod, his long white hair brushing his alabaster cheeks as he did so. He smiled a cruel smile and his red eyes flashed like blood stone diamonds. He wore a black trench coat, a white shirt and red cravat at his throat, fastened with a ruby.

A boisterous wind battered at the windows briefly, then everything went still again.

Peter felt a chill run down his spine. I don't know how he did that, but I think it was for dramatic effect.

"We are all very aware of the gang problem on Tarnuzian soil," Spencer continued, shifting in his seat, stroking his left grey side burn. He ran his fingers through his thinning hair and pulled on the lapels of his plum coloured jacket.

"I am intrigued," Peter frowned, leaning forward. "How did you manage to get the gangs to work with you, Zintius?"

Zintius smiled and stroked the metal goblet with his long elegant fingers.

"We mix human genes with those of vampires, werewolves or other creatures, producing a calming effect on the subject," Zintius replied smoothly.

"But those are naturally predatory beings." Peter said, with wide eyes.

Jedidiah moved his red and yellow striped tie, opened his fawn suit jacket and took out what looked like a fob watch and lit his pipe with it. When he dragged on the pipe, his bearded cheeks looked like two bellows inflating and deflating. He took his pipe out of his mouth and pointed the stem at Peter.

That's a neat lighter. I wonder where I can get one?

"There's no need to get all bent out of shape, Commissioner," Jedidiah said. "Tarnuz is well accustomed to different races and species. We have been living in harmony for over 250 years."

"The first few years weren't particularly harmonious. The vampire and dragon wars were especially bloody and very brutal. They threatened our very existence. No offence Zintius."

"None taken, Commissioner. I do want to address your concerns. We take the best attributes from a creature, say the strength of the werewolf or the speed and agility of a vampire and give them to humans."

"Bigger, better, faster, stronger. These people are very attractive employees," Jedidiah said, in between puffs.

"I think we can all agree that the ganglands are a no go area, and if we can find a solution to this, then everyone is happy," Lewis chimed in.

"This sounds like a massive gamble to me. Turning people into super humans. These are real people with real lives and families."

"I applaud your compassion, Commissioner. I would have thought you'd have referred to them as criminal scum or a blight on society."

"With all due respect, Chancellor, that is the type of language a politician would say."

"You doubt my integrity, Commissioner?" Lewis spat, shaking his fist at Peter, his face red.

"No, I am merely pointing out that MPs are known for making broad, sweeping statements without having a clue about what the common man really needs."

"You make me sound like a pompous old fool who is out of touch with his subjects," Spencer pointed his finger at Peter. "I can

Children of Tarnuz

have you replaced, Harris. I will not tolerate this insubordination."

Peter made the calm down gesture with his hands and said, "I wasn't pointing the finger at you, Chancellor Spencer, I have found your leadership to be just and fair. I am just saying that politicians have a bad rep, that's all."

Spencer's' body relaxed a bit and he sat back in his chair.

"Well, I am glad you feel that way, Peter. The preliminary tests have been most impressive so far. In fact we are voting on a national roll out tonight. That's why we have called the delegates here this evening."

Peter did a double take, and bared his teeth. "Why wasn't I kept in the loop about this?"

"Need to know basis, old chap," Jedidiah said, fumbling in his suit jacket pocket for his lighter. Eventually, he found it and re-lit his pipe.

"Well, I'm not entirely happy with it," Peter said, sitting back in his chair and folding his arms.

"Perhaps this will convince you, Commissioner," Zintius said, reaching into his inside jacket pocket, pulling out a black six inch rectangular hinged box with a crank handle on the side. Zintius placed the box on the table and opened the lid. Inside the lid was a four inch pane of glass. Zintius cranked the handle several times, making the dynamo whirr. The black glass displayed black and white moving images of people rioting. A young man stepped from the crowd and threw a Molotov cocktail at the police. The scene changed and the youth received a shot in his arm, and a nurse fastened a cotton pad on the jab and secured it with a piece of surgical tape. After this scene, it cut to another showing the boy coming first in a 100 metre sprint, his chest bursting through the ribbon at the end of the track.

The next frame showed him talking to some of the young men from the rioting clip. He looked like he was trying to convince his friends to receive the injection.

Abruptly, the film ceased, the picture shrunk to a tiny white dot on the screen, then went blank.

Zintius closed the box and returned it to his pocket.

"That's an impressive piece of film, but I need more proof than this. Perhaps meet the young man myself," Peter said, glancing at the others.

"We thought you'd need a little gentle persuasion. You can meet Tim Mockett this very night if you wish," Jedidiah said, puffing on his pipe, a glint in his eye.

"You mentioned that these weremen or vamp humans will make, and I quote, 'very attractive employees' Jedidiah. What's your involvement in this?"

"Mr. Lewis is a very generous supporter of our cause, having seen the results for himself in Birik," Zintius said, before Jedidiah had a chance to speak.

"So you're the money then, Lewis? I thought as much. I doubt very much that you're doing this out of the kindness of your heart. What's in it for you, huh?" Peter said, raising his eyebrows.

Jedidiah toked on his pipe then he said, "We all know the slums are a difficult area. A no go zone you might say. I believe with a calmer and less...how shall I put this...feral community, everyone would benefit. The poor and the outcast on the fringes of society would have well paid jobs, respect, a future and, above all, food in their bellies."

"That's all well and good, but I know you have been after that land for years, and I know the planning office rejected your application again last week. What's that for the third year in a row now?" Peter said, cursing under his breath.

Jedidiah clenched his fists, then released them. "I think that will change now. Once the planning office has received a copy of Zintius' film, and once we roll out the injections in the slums, they will be completely convinced."

Peter held up his hands in mock surrender. "Okay, okay, you have talked this up enough. Let me meet Mr. Mockett."

Lewis and Jedidiah smiled and Zintius dipped his chin.

"Before we go, was there anything you wanted to bring to our attention, Commissioner?" Spencer said.

"I would like a slight change in the law, if that's possible. I would like women to be allowed into the pubs without being accompanied by a man."

Spencer and Jedidiah shifted in their seats.

Spencer steepled his fingers. "If you vote in favour of the vaccine roll out, then I am sure we can all agree to that."

"Vaccine? I wasn't aware that slum dwellers were sick." Peter said, his jaw dropping.

"Many of them are malnourished, living on a diet of beer and bread. The vaccine contains essential vitamins and minerals." Jedidiah said, tapping the contents of his pipe into an ashtray on the table.

"Government aid workers will hand out food packages to all of those who would receive the jab," Spencer added.

"I will have a team of medical professionals on hand to give out health checks and hand out supplements if they are needed," Zintius said.

"So, what happens to those that don't want to go along with this?"

"They will be given a food parcel for one day and then we will leave them alone," Lewis said, staring determinedly at Peter.

"They sound like they are damned if they do and damned if they don't." Peter said, shaking his head. "Right, I'm ready to meet this Tim Mockett now."

They all stood and walked into the ballroom where men stood around chatting, smoking, laughing and drinking beer and wine. Cigar smoke hung in the air like a thick fog. Patrick Spencer introduced Peter Harris to Tim Mockett, a tall, slim man with red hair. Mockett wore a dark blue tail coat, a white shirt, a black string bow tie, grey and black pinstripe trousers and in his right hand he held a cane with a pterodactyl handle. Mockett gestured to a dark door on the right before opening it. The door opened into a smoking room with a bar at the back. A barman polished glasses and smiled when they approached the bar. The barman was the only other person in the room.

"What'll it be, gents?" he asked, smiling, making his curly brown moustache twitch as he did so. His brown eyes sparkled in his red, round, jolly face.

"Two brandies and two cigars please, Frank," Mockett said, before Peter had a chance to speak.

"Coming right up, Tim," Frank prepared the drinks and placed them on the bar next to two diademas cigars.

"Thank you, Frank," Mockett said and paid the man. Mockett pointed at a two seater table by the far wall.

"Thanks for the drink and the cigar, Mr. Mockett, I truly appreciate it," Peter smiled.

"Tim, please call me Tim."

"Okay, Tim it is. So how do you feel about being the poster boy for Agreeable Solutions?"

Tim reached inside his left breast pocket and pulled out a silver fob watch lighter identical to Jedidiah's and sparked a flame, offering to light Peter's cigar. After the cigar was lit, Tim lit his own.

Tim's eyes bounced around the room and when he was certain no one had entered, he leaned forward and Peter did the same.

"Agreeable Solutions have changed my life for the better, I can't deny that," he said, softly. "Without them, I would be either dead or in prison."

"That's great, so why are you whispering?"

Tim licked his lips, then took a swig from his glass. "It turns out, I had a little bit of werewolf DNA in me. Some great, great, great, grandmother or whatever the fuck. I was fine with the injections and the heightened senses and all of that shit. It helped Zintius seal the deal with the Birikian government. Others weren't so fortunate."

"How come?"

"At first, things went according to plan. Subjects were calmer and started to build a better life for themselves. That all changed when the full moon came. People changed into wolves and began attacking people and livestock."

Peter sighed, shook his head and stared at the table. "We have strict laws about this sort of thing in Tarnuz. The werewolves, vampires, shapeshifters or whatever are allowed to live and move freely amongst us ordinary folk as long as they don't harm or kill anyone. Every community is responsible for ensuring their members are properly trained and kept in check by a mentor. If a sheep is found with its throat ripped out, 9 times out of 10 it's a dog attack, not a werewolf."

"Agreeable Solutions don't care about that. A mentor system costs money and eats into their profits. Besides, I think there's something else going on."

"Such as?"

"I think Zintius is building a supernatural army, but I don't have enough proof. Hopefully, you and your police force can find any evidence of foul play. I'm hoping you can control this before it gets out of hand."

"What do you propose I do?"

"Give them what they want, vote yes to their vaccine programme. Let them think they can trust you. It's a way to keep your friends close and enemies even closer. Look, Commissioner, I have probably said too much, and I have put my life at risk telling you all this, but Zintius needs to be stopped, he and Agreeable Solutions are dangerous." He pushed his chair away with the backs of his legs and stood up.

"Wait, how am I supposed to fight this thing?"

"Equip all of your officers with silver bullets. Good luck, Commissioner. Hopefully I'll see you after all of this is over," he said, and left.

Peter sat there drawing on his cigar, and swirling his brandy around in its glass, trying to comprehend what Mockett had just told him.

Frank came over to Peter's table.

"Commissioner, I suggest you take your place in the ballroom. The voting will take place in five minutes."

"Thank you, Frank."

"You're welcome. I hope to see you again soon."

"I'm sure you will."

Peter picked up the goggles and fondled them as he joined the other men.

Patrick Spencer stepped onto the stage and spoke into the microphone. "Good evening gentlemen. If I could have your attention please. Upon your arrival, you were given goggles. In just a few short moments, we will be voting on the slum vaccination program. I'm sure I can count on a 'yes' vote tonight."

The crowd murmured in agreement.

"That's settled then. Right, if you could all put your goggles on. You will see a screen, and it will have a message saying vote now. Peter put on his goggles and saw a screen with the words on it.

Lewis continued, "On the count of three, blink once for 'yes' to the vaccination program or twice for 'no'. Three, two, one...VOTE!"

Police Commissioner Peter Harris blinked once.

Chapter Six: Following a lead

An icy wind blew between the maze of cobbled streets, rundown houses and ram shackled huts with corrugated tin roofs. Unpleasant odours of urine and faeces assaulted Clara's nostrils, and she reached into her police issue trench coat for her jar of menthol rub. After she had undone the lid, she smeared some of the clear waxy substance under her nostrils, then passed the jar to James Bronze. He thanked her and applied some under his nose too.

They were following a white carriage with Agreeable Solutions written on the side and the trademark black pterodactyl logo above the lettering. Clara felt her stomach tighten as the carriage stopped. A tall, dark haired, slim man and a short, slim, blonde woman in white lab coats with stethoscopes around their necks stepped to the ground and lightly rapped on the door of the first house. A plump red, female face, with dishevelled brown hair appeared at a crack in the open doorway.

"Yeah, what's yers want?" the woman said, with a voice as rough as sandpaper.

"Pardon me, madam," the man said. "We are offering vaccines against Typhoid for your children, and in return, we will give you a month's worth of food."

The woman smiled, revealing crooked brown teeth. "Before I's hand me tikes over, let me sees the grub first."

"Of course," answered the man "Dorothy, would you be so kind as to fetch one of the hampers from the carriage please?"

"Certainly, Arnold," Dorothy said, smiling.

She stepped into the back of the carriage and promptly returned with a wicker basket. She opened the lid and the lady peered in. Nestling on a bed of hay, were various hams, a whole chicken, vegetables and an array of pickles and preserves.

The woman's eyes bulged like two saucers in her head.

"Give us a sec," she said and closed the door. A few minutes passed, then the door opened, and two children, a boy and girl, with dirty clothes and faces, were pushed into the street. The boy couldn't have been more than eight and the girl must have been no more than six. Although their blonde hair was greasy and unkempt, they had striking handsome features and innocent blue eyes.

Dorothy bent down to their level and said softly, "Would you like to be safe from typhoid? I hear it is very bad in these parts."

They both nodded and said in tandem, "Yes, miss,"

Dorothy smiled sweetly and said, "Very good, if you would like to step into the carriage, and roll up your sleeves, I'll give you the injection, and you'll be as right as rain."

"Miss," the boy said, raising his tiny hand, "Will it hurt?"

"No, my dear, it will feel like a small pin prick, nothing more. Now, if you'd just step up into the carriage I'll give you the jab. Right this way, if you please," Dorothy chirped, gesturing to the back of the carriage that was lit by a dull lantern suspended from the ceiling.

"Yes, miss," they both said in unison.

After a few minutes, the children re-joined their mother, who was clutching her hamper, grinning from ear to ear.

"Before we leave, all children that present this document..." Arnold said, producing two postcard sized pieces of paper from the inside of his lab coat and handing them to the woman, who snatched them from him "...will be guaranteed a job at the Jedidiah Lewis cotton factory behind us."

With that, he hooked his thumb over his shoulder at the enormous building behind them, its three white chimneys billowing smoke into the grey, dreary sky.

"Fanks so much, kind sir and miss. When does me little uns start?"

Arnold looked at Dorothy and she looked at him, then they turned to the lady and Arnold said, "How about tomorrow morning, say, six o'clock?"

"Yes, that'd be fine," the woman said.

"Splendid. Mr. Lewis will be very pleased to see you tomorrow. Good day to you," Arnold said, doffing his bowler hat and asking the carriage driver to roll forward to the next house.

Clara stepped around the carriage, quickening her pace.

"We have to work fast! Once this carriage has done the rounds, people won't be opening their doors again," she said, in a steady low pitched voice.

James nodded. "I think it's a stroke of genius on the Commissioner's part to shadow these coaches. Normally, we'd be lynched within seconds and our remains would be left out for the birds."

"Hmm, but I wouldn't want to be forced to vote for something I didn't agree with, though."

James snorted. "Clara, you don't even have the vote!"

Clara tightened her fist, then released it again.

He's trying to bait you, don't let him rile you.

"That may be true, but he did manage to get the law changed last night, and now I can go to the pub without you hanging on my coattails," she said, flashing him a smug grin.

James' jaw dropped open and his pupils dilated. "W…What?" he said, almost tripping on his own boots.

"Yes, the Commissioner asked Chancellor Lewis if the law could be changed to allow women to go into pubs, bars and taverns unaccompanied by men, and they voted it in," Clara confirmed, striding ahead, puffing out her chest, head tilted back.

James slapped his cheeks, his mouth still open.

"I'd clamp that shut if I were you, you might swallow a fly," she said and laughed at her own joke. "Anyway, I think we're here," she said, knocking on the door of a tin shack that had some dried posies hanging from a pole protruding from the corrugated roof.

A slit appeared in the door, followed by two large frightened brown eyes that darted about up and down the street.

"Are you the Law?" a female voice said.

"Yes, we are the police. I am Detective Overton and this Detective Bronze," Clara said, flashing her badge. Clara stepped aside and James showed the girl his badge too.

"You'd best be coming in from the cold," the girl sighed, stepping aside and letting them in.

Inside there were dirty pots and pans, a bed roll, a tin bath, a few dirty clothes and a bedpan. There were also wooden beer kegs, probably used as chairs. Her face was dirty and tear stained and her eyes were red. The girl produced a lantern from somewhere and lit it, then she hung it over their heads from a hook.

"You're Hetty Thorpe, right?" Clara said, frowning into the gloom.

The girl nodded.

"And you have information regarding Violet Taylor?"

"Yes. Me and Violet was friends. We worked together. The rags said she'd been murdered. Is that true?"

Clara took a deep breath.

"I regret to inform you, Miss Thorpe, that the papers are correct," Clara answered softly.

"Oh my gawd. Poor V…Violet," Hetty trembled.

Clara lightly touched Hetty's shoulder.

"Was it a good friendship, did you know her well?" James said.

"Yeah, we knew each other since six years old. Been working with her for ten years," Hetty replied, sniffling and blowing her nose on a dirty cloth.

"Do you know of anyone who would want to hurt her?" Clara said.

Hetty wrung her hands. "Mr. Phips used to knock us about if we didn't steal enough for him, but I don't think he would ever snuff someone," Hetty revealed, shaking her head.

"Has her behaviour changed lately? Clara said.

"Her brother went missing and she was very concerned. They were tight. He was older and he looked out for her. She would spend hours searching for 'im, never givin' up. Then he shows up out of the blue, swaggering about like a posh git. Decked out in fancy clothes, swannin' about like he owned the fuckin' joint or somein'." Hetty snorted.

"Was there anything else unusual about him?" James asked.

Hetty shivered and rubbed her arms, then she took a sharp breath.

"He would only meet Violet at night," Hetty said, covering her mouth with her hand. "He's turned into one of them fuckin' leeches, ain't he?"

She sucked on her bottom lip in deep thought.

"We don't know that yet," Clara responded.

Clara thought, My God, she's so thin. I wonder when she last had a decent meal.

James moved closer to the lantern, took out his steno pad and a pencil.

Whilst he flipped through the pages, Clara took off the glove on her right hand and lightly touched Hetty's bony shoulder.

"Violet's brother, Andrew, Isn't it?" James said, pencil poised.

"Yes, that's im'," Hetty replied.

Clara's eyes rolled over, like a shark waiting to attack and the trance started. Seeing through Hetty's eyes, she watched a young man with long white blonde hair and sinister red eyes push Hetty to the ground and mouth "GO!"

And now the picture is complete. The face she had seen at the murder scene was Andrew Taylor. Clara backed away from Hetty, cleared her throat and put her glove back on.

He must have cared for her, loved her even. He didn't want to feast on her, but his thirst was too unbearable, and he couldn't control it, so he killed his sister. Maybe he didn't even mean to kill her. I think the vampire council is right. He didn't have a mentor to guide him. This is bad, very bad, indeed.

James finished scribbling on his pad, but before he could open his mouth, Clara said, "Were you romantically involved with Andrew Taylor, Miss Thorpe?"

Hetty pulled her shawl closed.

"You pigs have got a fuckin' nerve, pokin' yer snouts in other people's shit. You probably get off on it, you perverted pricks," Hetty growled, folding her arms over her chest and looking away from Clara.

Clara held up her right hand and said gently, "Miss Thorpe, please try not to be alarmed. We are trying to catch a dangerous killer. We don't want him to kill again. Any information you have will be greatly appreciated."

Hetty faced Clara in the dim light, the flame highlighting the profile of her pretty but dirty face.

After Hetty had unfastened her arms, she thrust her hands into the pockets of her black dress. She puffed out her cheeks, raised her eyebrows and looked at Clara with large rounded eyes, then she slumped down on one of the beer kegs, letting her arms flop at her sides.

"I hadn't thought about the killer killing again," Hetty said, staring at the floor, her voice no more than a whisper. "Yes Andrew and I had a thing for each other, then he fucks off and leaves me. I'm not some kind of a mug, I tell ya! Then he waltzes back into my life all la-di-da and full of fancy words and shit, expectin' me to take him back. Well, you can think again, fella. I was worried sick. I fought I was losin' me mind."

James said, "Did he say where he'd been? Did he mention anyone?"

Hetty shook her head. "Nah, he was wittering on about Agreeable Solutions or somein'."

Clara and James looked at each other.

"They are in your street now," Clara said.

"Well, they can piss off. If Andrew is their best advert, I ain't buying. He was so kind and considerate before he went messin' with 'em. Now he's all airs and graces and flappin' about like a bat or whatever the fuck they get up to."

"Have you seen him lately, and do you know where we might be able to find him?" James pressed.

Hetty tapped her index finger to her lips. "I saw him a few days ago in the north quarter. He was sitting on a slate roof, his hands between his knees."

"What did you do?" Clara said.

Hetty snorted. "I stuck my fingers up, he smiled and dissolved into black smoke," she shivered. "Gave me the willies, it did. Vampires, who the fuck do they think they are anyways?"

"Thank you for your time Miss Thorpe, you've been very helpful. Good day," James said, doffing his topper, with the goggles still attached to the rim.

" 'Ere, how bout that 200 knicker? My palace could do with tartin' up."

"I am terribly sorry, but police officers are not allowed to give or receive money in exchange for information. If your evidence leads to a conviction, visit the police station and they will make sure you receive your reward," Clara said.

"I figured as much. Well, good luck. I 'ope you catch the bastard."

"I hope so too," Clara said, gesturing to James to leave.

As they walked away from the slums, three more Agreeable Solutions carriages clattered down the cobbled streets, sending an icy chill down her spine.

Neither James nor herself said anything until they reached the busy marketplace. Carts loaded with different produce rattled past on the cobblestones. Stall holders shouted at pedestrians as they hurried along. Bells from fishing boats dinged as they pulled into the harbour. A sea breeze wafted towards them, carrying a briny scent that mingled with the smell of cooked meats and baked bread.

Clara smiled with relief but James broke their silence.

"Do you think she's telling the truth?"

Clara nodded. "I am utterly convinced."

"You used your voodoo shit on her, didn't you?"

"I did, but I didn't see you object, for once," Clara said, a smug grin on her face.

James breathed out a large sigh. "Mitigating circumstances, I guess."

"You guessed right, Detective Bronze."

James half smiled. "Which building do you think Andrew Taylor was sitting on?"

"Well, seeing as every building in our beloved capital, Lario..." she gestured to the larger city "...has a slate roof, it doesn't give us very much to go on."

James pondered this for a moment, then he proffered, "Not necessarily. He may have been scrutinising the city, taking in the view. Somewhere he had a good vantage point."

"The old palace, or also known as, The Institute for Supernatural Friends " they said in unison, pointing at each other, then they laughed. James's smile faded first, then he cleared his throat. "We'd better take our places, the presentation is about to start."

Clara nodded, and they threaded through the crowd and made their way to the front of the stage.

A tall, well-manicured bearded man wearing a three-piece suit that included a tailcoat, walked nonchalantly onto the stage twirling a black cane in his hand. He stepped up to the silver microphone and announced heartily, "Good afternoon, ladies and gentlemen. My name is George Dawson. Welcome to the Agreeable Solutions Great Give Away."

The crowd erupted with shouts and applause.

Beaming from ear to ear, Dawson waited for the crowd to settle down before he continued.

"We are a privileged people, living in an exciting time. Some homes have electricity and most street corners have public telephone boxes," he paused as the crowd celebrated again.

"What would you all say if I told you our revolutionary goggles enabled you to make and receive phone calls without ever needing to visit a phone box ever again?"

There were gasps from the crowd and people talked amongst themselves.

"And that's not all ladies and gentlemen. You will be able to make calls for the same price as a pint of beer."

The crowd thrummed with deeper anticipation.

Dawson smiled at his audience like a preacher at a revival rally.

"Now who wants a new set of goggles?"

People clambered over themselves trying to be first in the queue.

Peter Harris took the mic from Dawson. "Please form an orderly queue, there are plenty of goggles to go round."

After the Commissioner had spoken, a line of burly policemen surrounded the stage, hands resting on their night sticks.

Folks started to settle into an orderly routine after that.

Finally, Clara and James received their goggles and after they put them on, they received a phone call.

"Hello?" they both said.

"Ah, thank goodness my little trick worked," Horace said, sounding relieved.

"Horace, what a pleasant surprise. What can we do for you?" Clara said, sounding puzzled.

"I don't know how secure this line is. Come to my workshop where I'll explain everything."

"Okay, we'll catch a cab and meet you there."

"Jolly good, see you in a jiff," Horace said, then he hung up.

When they arrived at Horace's workshop, he asked them to hand over the goggles. After that, he scanned them with a cylindrical tube with a blue light on the end that emitted a buzzing sound.

"There. I am now totally satisfied that they aren't tracking you," Horace said, pushing his half-rimmed glasses further up his nose.

"I am totally confused. Who's tracking who?" James quizzed, furrowing his brow.

"Agreeable Solutions have placed tracking devices on all the goggles. I have reconfigured the software inside the goggles, to keep out anything harmful from attacking you."

Clara slapped both of her cheeks, her mouth open. "What kind of harmful things are we talking about here?"

"If you look at it logically, the human brain or the brain of any living thing, is actually a computer. A computer needs to follow a program. Let's say you are walking down the street and a stampeding horse is running towards you."

"I'm not sure I am following here. What have horses got to do with these goggles? James said, showing his palms and shrugging.

"Sorry, Detective Bronze, let me explain. Basically, your brain would perform a series of complex scenarios and hopefully guide you to safety. A computer can also perform hundreds and thousands of tasks in milliseconds. Computers can be reprogrammed."

"Wait, are you suggesting that Agreeable Solutions are going to send messages to our brains to make us do things against our will?" Clara questioned, rubbing her eyes.

"Is this stuff even possible?" James said, cocking his head.

"Theoretically, yes. I don't want to take the risk."

"So that's why you called us here. Are you going to have the entire police force hand over their goggles to you?" Clara pressed, leaning forward and sliding her chair closer.

Horace sighed and Adamar spoke this time. "We have reason to believe that some police officers are working for Agreeable Solutions or at least are sympathetic to the cause."

"You're talking about inside men," James said.

"That kind of thing, yes," Adamar agreed.

"We really don't know who we can trust at this point. We know we can trust you two and the Commissioner for certain. We believe there are more, but we hope they will come to us." Horace said.

"Well, I don't trust detective Overton," James snorted.

"Yes, you have told me many times and to my face. At least I know where I stand with you, Detective Bronze."

Horace gasped. "I am utterly flabbergasted that you feel that way about Detective Overton. I trust her implicitly."

"What, even with your life, Horace?" James sneered.

"Especially with my life. Golly, I had absolutely no idea there was so much animosity between the two of you. I really hope you can work things out."

"Yes, I think you are good for one another. Two parts of the same well-oiled machine," Adamar added.

"Anyway, enough about our childish spats. I have been thinking about these goggles. Public phones and domestic appliances receive messages through telegraph poles. How do the goggles send and receive phone calls?"

"I am glad you asked. Satellites ." Horace said, a broad smile on his face.

"Satellites?" What are they and what do they do?"

"They orbit our planet, Remina, high above the atmosphere and receive a phone signal and transmit it to the recipient."

"Wow. I can't believe how fast technology is moving. Are we even ready for such things as advanced as this?" Clara said, shaking her head.

Horace sighed. "I don't think we are ready at all. I think this technology is very dangerous indeed."

Children of Tarnuz

Chapter Seven: Unseen Dangers

Silvery moonbeams highlighted the steps to the vampire council building. Clara clenched her leather gloved hands into fists, then she relaxed and climbed the steps. When she reached the top, she knocked on the large doors and waited. As if by magic, the doors swung aside by themselves and Clara's mouth dried up and her stomach tightened.

The three vampires sat on their thrones and smiled as Clara stood before them. Clara had put on what she called her "Confidence suit" which consisted of a dark blue velvet coat, a white ruffle blouse, black leather trousers and thigh high black lace up boots.

All three vampires were stroking kid goats again.

Fuck it! Why do I always pick feeding time? Maybe they will put them down when they hear about Zintius.

"Ah, so nice to see you again, Miss Overton and so soon too. I trust you have news for us," Raqaknoff said, pleasantly.

"I do have news for you, my lords and lady, but it isn't good news, I am afraid."

Raqaknoff stopped stroking his animal and steepled his fingers.

"I am sure we can deal with it. Please carry on, Miss Overton," Raqaknoff said.

"Please call me Clara. Miss Overton sounds so… clunky," Clara said, shifting her weight on her feet.

"Very well. As you wish, Clara." Raqaknoff replied with a hint of a smile.

Clara cleared her throat. "We are still conducting our investigations, but the evidence is still pointing to some kind of synthetic genetic mutation, turning people into vampires. We believe this is administered by an injection."

"We could probably get hold of this injection and have our scientists analyse it," Velorina volunteered.

"Yes, that would be great, but please be extra careful. I can't have this coming back on me." Clara said, biting her lip. "I am certain Horace and Adamar will provide a thorough analysis when they acquire a sample. I would be more comfortable if they had a look at it first, they are employed by the police after all. When they have finished conducting their studies, I will make a sample available for you too."

"We are vampires, careful is our middle name," Dimitri said, with a flourish of his hand.

Clara drew a deep breath, then exhaled. "We have come into contact with a vampire named Zintius, and seeing as he's not part of your council, I am guessing he is unknown to you. Commissioner Peter Harris thinks he could be dangerous. He is the managing director of Agreeable Solutions."

All three vampires put down their goats and sat bolt upright in their thrones.

"We haven't heard that name in over 500 years. The Commissioner is right, he is very dangerous indeed. He is incredibly powerful and the last we heard, he was asleep, healing from the wounds we gave him in the

Children of Tarnuz

Vampire Wars. Somebody must have performed the awakening ritual. This is serious, very serious indeed." Raqaknoff said, wringing his hands.

Clara coughed again. "How is it you weren't aware of his presence? I thought you had a telepathic connection."

The three vampires shifted in their seats and then Raqaknoff responded, "He is a vampire lord. An ancient being from a bygone age. People worshipped him like a god. He has the ability to manipulate people's thoughts and feelings and if he doesn't want to be found, he can sever the telepathic link to other vampires. Clara, he has to be stopped and I think whoever summoned him is in very grave danger indeed."

Clara felt dizzy and stumbled backwards, but before she hit her head on the cold stone floor, a strong breeze made her hair flutter and a high backed chair appeared at the back of her legs, followed by Velorina stroking her cheek. Clara sat down.

"Here, drink this," Velorina said, offering Clara a glass of water.

"Thank you," Clara smiled, taking the glass and drinking from it. The liquid was cool and refreshing, but her hand trembled.

"W…what am I supposed to do, Velorina? How do I defeat a powerful vampire overlord?" Clara said, her body shaking violently.

Velorina stroked her hair. "You're not alone. We will do everything in our power to stop him," Velorina said tenderly, her doe-like red eyes pleading with her. She looked like she was on the verge of tears.

Clara's eyes welled up and then she said very quietly, "Are there anymore vampires like him that are just as powerful, or is he the last of his kind?"

Velorina took Clara's face in her hands and looked into her eyes. "He is the last," she said, letting Clara go and disappearing and reappearing on her throne.

Clara set her jaw and tightened her muscles. "I will rise to the challenge. I know that Zintius is dangerous. I will stop him. I must leave now. I have a lot to think about."

"Of course. Can I take you anywhere?" Dimitri volunteered.

"Thank you for your kind offer, Dimitri, but I need time alone. The cab journey will do me good."

"As you wish. Is there anything we can do for you?"

"Yes, there is. We are looking for Andrew Taylor . He has long, white-blonde hair and red eyes. I think he is an Agreeable Solutions vampire, and the police want to talk to him. He's my prime suspect in the murder case I am investigating. He was last seen hanging around the old palace, aka, TIFSF"

Dimitri nodded and then looked at the floor. "None of us have detected him in our thoughts, which suggests he has the same abilities as Zintius."

Children of Tarnuz

Clara froze and blinked rapidly. "Dimitri, what does this mean?"

Dimitri sighed. "If someone wants to make a vampire, they need the blood of a host."

"Are you saying…" Clara's whispered words trailed off.

"I am saying that Zintius is the host," Dimitri said, finishing her sentence.

***

"I find these goggles to be truly magnificent," Eme said, taking off her Agreeable Solutions goggles and placing them around the rim of her black topper. "What I don't understand is Horace's paranoia about them."

"Sometimes paranoia can mean the difference between life or death," Clara -

Eme wore a ruffle blouse with a peacock design on it, silver jeggings and laced up brown thigh high boots. Edwin was also present, and he was dressed in a navy shirt, with a dark red cravat tied at his throat, grey trousers and black ankle boots. Clara was still wearing her confidence suit. They all sat at the round table in Clara's dining room. It had been an arduous day, and Clara needed the company of her friends. A fire blazed in the hearth casting shadows on the maroon walls. Behind the table was a row of sash windows, which overlooked the garden, orchard and stables. Horses could be heard softly neighing. A walnut drinks table was pressed up against the other wall and next to that was several book shelves.

Eme continued, frowning at Clara and leaning closer. "You make it sound like you think the silly old fart's delusions are justified. I am surprised you are so resistant to change. If someone hands me a new gadget, I can't wait to get to grips with it. And if it has switches and buttons, I'm all over that shit. The more the merrier."

Clara and Edwin laughed at their lovely uncouth friend. She was tonic for the soul, and that's why they loved her.

"Eme, ordinarily I would agree with you wholeheartedly, but this could be a poison chalice. A random vampire slips onto

Tarnuz undetected and starts handing out goggles. Aren't you just a tiny bit suspicious?" Clara proffered, putting her glass on the table.

Edwin finished his drink and placed his glass on the table too. "I'm sorry, Eme, but I'm in agreement with Clara on this one. I am grateful that Horace is looking out for us. I have always valued what he says, and if he thinks these goggles are dangerous, I believe him."

"I think his extra security will keep us safe," Eme nodded, twisting her empty wine glass in her hand.

"Would you both like a top up?" Clara asked, rising from the table.

Eme and Edwin thrust their glasses towards her. Clara went over to the drinks table and came back carrying two bottles of red. She popped the cork on one and poured three more glasses.

"I find these satellite contraptions completely fascinating, don't you? I hung on every word Horace said when you recounted his speech on how they work," Edwin said, raising his eyebrows.

"I was just glad I didn't fall asleep," Eme revealed.

Clara snorted. "You have never had a head for science Eme, have you?"

Edwin barked a short laugh. "You're more of an ignorant consumer, which I find delightful," he said, leaning over and kissing Eme on the lips. Eme closed her eyes and sighed, but Clara cleared her throat and they sat back in their own seats again.

"I find satellites fascinating too. To think that there are these devices flying around in space sending and receiving everyone's telephone calls, is mind boggling. But I think we have allowed ourselves to be blinded by science," Clara said.

Edwin nodded. "Zintius and his organisation are messing with volatile beings which could lead to dire circumstances."

"What do you think we should do?" Eme asked.

"Well, we don't just have vampires, werewolves, changelings, elves etc. at our disposal, we have a dragon family too," Edwin boasted, gripping the lapels of his tailcoat, sticking out his chest.

"Are you proposing a war, Edwin Buckle?" Clara said, gazing intently at him.

"If that's what it takes to thwart the plans of the evil horde, then so be it," he said, drinking from his wine glass.

"I hope to high heavens that it doesn't come to that," uttered Clara, her stomach twisting at the thought.

Eme now stood behind her and placed her hands on her shoulders. "You and the police force will stop it before it gets out of hand. I am sure of that."

Clara put her hands on her own shoulders and gently squeezed her friend's fingers.

"I sure hope so," Clara said, feigning confidence.

***

Children of Tarnuz

Detective James Bronze stepped onto the pavement outside the Lario State University and paid the cab driver.

"Fanks Sir. 'Ave a great day," the driver said and with a flick of his reins, steered the two black horses into the traffic.

James ran his hand over the rim of his topper, took a deep breath, and held his cane high, then he marched up the steps of the campus building.

When he pushed open the glass panelled door, he thought he'd stepped into the lobby of a plush hotel. It had a cream coloured marble floor, a large oak concierge desk and a crystal chandelier hung from the ceiling. To the right of the desk was a large staircase, populated with professors and students making their way to lectures.

A grey haired woman with round spectacles, wearing a light blue blouse, with LSU emblazoned in gold on her left breast pocket sat behind the desk talking on a candlestick shaped telephone. James waited patiently for her to finish her conversation. Eventually, she hung up and looked at him curiously.

"Yes, may I help you, sir?" The woman said, with a voice that sounded like she had a plum in her mouth.

James cleared his throat. "Good day to you, madam. I have an appointment with Professor Oswald Brownlow."

The woman frowned. "Can I ask who wants to see him?"

"Detective James Bronze," James said, flashing her his badge.

"Oh, okay, Detective. I sincerely hope it is not anything serious."

"Oh no, nothing like that. We are looking to throw a 21st Birthday Party for an old student of his. I am trying to find addresses for her old roommates."

"How lovely. Let me give him a buzz," she said, pressing a button on a speaker box in front of her.

"Hello?" a well-spoken male voice said from the speaker.

"Err, Professor Brownlow. I have a Detective James Bronze to see you, sir," she said, releasing the button.

"Ah, yes. I have been expecting him. Send him right up, Mable," Brownlow said.

"Very good, sir. I will send him up," she said, turning to Bronze. "The professor will see you now. It's the third door on the right."

"Thank you, Mable," James said.

"You are most welcome. Good day to you."

James climbed the staircase and passed a female student with a black spiky Mohawk and a nose chain that reached to her ear. She had black eye makeup, and wore a black leather waistcoat, ripped jeans and black Docker boots.

She smiled sweetly.

James opened his mouth, but couldn't find the words.

He walked a little further and came to a door with frosted glass and the words 'Professor Oswald Brownlow' embossed in curved cursive on the glass. Making a fist, he lightly rapped on the glass.

"Do come in. The door is open," the professor said.

James opened the door and saw a round faced bespectacled man, in his fifties. He had brown tousled hair. The professor wore a green corduroy jacket, a yellow shirt and a mustard coloured cravat with a black question mark pattern on it. The professor was alone. The office had a desk with files neatly stacked at one end, a typewriter and a green editor's lamp. Behind the desk was a bulging bookshelf. There were lots of books on providentias, one was entitled 'The Psychology of A providentia'. The room smelled of coffee and old books.

"Coffee?" The professor asked, raising his eyebrows.

"Yes, please, professor."

"What would you like? Espresso? Cappuccino? Flat white? Black?"

"Err, cappuccino please?"

"Coming right up," Oswald said, opening a compartment at the bottom of the coffee machine. Cool air rushed out of the cupboard that was lit with a single rectangular bulb. It had three shelves. The top shelf had a plate with a sandwich and an apple on it, the middle had fruit on it and the last one had dairy products on it. Oswald took the milk from the bottom shelf and smiled at James, who was staring at the cold cupboard with wide eyes and a slack jaw.

"It's a refrigerator or fridge for short. It keeps food cold, therefore keeping it fresher for longer," Oswald said, filling the espresso machine with milk. He placed two large cups under a pipe which hissed as steam came out and filled them with coffee, hot milk and water.

"Would you like chocolate on top?"

"Yes, that would be lovely."

Oswald sprinkled chocolate on both mugs and placed them on saucers with a biscotti on each and handed James his drink.

"Help yourself to sugar if you want it."

"No, that's fine, thank you."

"So I understand you want to find Clara's friends for a surprise party. Is that correct?"

James wiped the froth from his mouth with his handkerchief. "Yes, that's right."

Oswald smiled again. "Splendid. What a delightful idea. There are only two girls still in Tarnuz. The others have either died or moved away."

"Died? How sad," James said, taking another sip of his coffee. It was delicious and he envied Brownlow's espresso machine. He wondered if he could get one somewhere.

"Yes, quite. Very sad indeed. Typhoid I am afraid," Oswald admitted, staring at the wall above the coffee machine, cup poised in mid-air.

He's a providentia too. James thought, noticing Oswald's gloved hands.

I wonder if the sweet professor was Clara's favourite lecturer?

You intrigue me, frustrate and delight me, Clara Overton.

"Could you tell me the names of these ladies, please?"

"I can do better than that," the professor said, opening a drawer in his desk and handing James two address cards. One was for an Annabelle Beard and the other was for a Polly Napper. Both addresses weren't far from the Lario market.

"Thank you, professor."

"You're welcome, Detective Bronze."

"I am not here in an official capacity, so please call me James."

"Very well, James it is."

"Were Clara, Annabelle and Polly close?"

"They hung out with a wider circle of friends. Why do you ask?"

James finished his drink and placed it on Oswald's desk. "There's nothing worse than planning a surprise party and inviting the wrong people. Imagine if all the guests were people you hated," James said, snorting. A part of him hoped they hated Clara.

Oswald chuckled. "I now understand your thought process. I don't recall them having a massive disagreement, so I think it'll be fine to invite them."

"What was Clara like as a student here?"

"She was popular, very academic, quiet at times, outgoing when she wanted to be. A bit of an enigma really."

"Did she have any problems with her abilities?"

"No, I don't believe so. Clara was well adjusted to her gifts. She was more of a mentor to the other girls. She had a mastery of her craft"

James dipped his chin and nodded.

"I mean no offence by this, James, but you ask a lot of questions for someone who claims to be Clara's boyfriend," Oswald said, raising one eyebrow.

James shuffled in his seat and ran his hands on his thighs.

"We haven't been courting very long. Just over a month in fact."

"I see. It's impossible to know everything about a person in that short space of time. I think it's a very sweet gesture, throwing a surprise party," Oswald said, raising his cup to his lips with a twinkle in his eye.

James tugged at his collar and cleared his throat. "Did she ever use her powers to...err...get a higher grade in her tests?" He blurted out the words and pulled his elbows tight to his sides.

Oswald's face darkened for the first time.

"I wish you hadn't asked me that, Detective."

Children of Tarnuz

Chapter Eight: Civil Unrest

Lucius Silas Flint fastened his belt around his dark brown trousers and smoothed the collar on his dark blue shirt. He sat on the easy chair next to his bed and laced up his boots. Laying on the bed was his bowler hat and goggles. After he had scrutinised the goggles, he secured them around the rim of his bowler.

"I am surprised you accepted those things," Hannah Flint, his wife, said, tipping her chin at the goggles, her light blue bustle dress swishing as she came into the bedroom.

"Yes I can see your point. They were handing them out at the factory. Jedidiah Lewis insisted we have them. Besides, I can coordinate meetings on the fly with The Workers Liberation Front. Shortly after he handed them out, TWLF served him with strike action."

"Aren't you worried they might be listening in?"

"I suppose that is a possibility, but nobody thought that would happen when we got the telephone."

Hannah chewed on her lip. "That is true, but an unknown company shows up out of the blue and starts giving out goggles to everyone, aren't you just a little bit suspicious?" Hannah quizzed, twirling a strand of her long blonde hair around her finger.

Lucius ran his hand over his brown beard.

"Nothing untoward has happened yet, but if you want me to, I'll have someone look into it," he said, getting up and holding Hannah's clasped hands.

Hannah nodded with a smile. "I'd like that, Lucius."

"How long do you think the strikes will last?"

Lucius sighed, paced the room and bridged his forehead with his hand.

"It all depends on how long it takes Jedidiah's people to get around the negotiation table really."

"I don't want it to go on for too long. I know you will receive full pay from TWLF, but it doesn't stop them sacking you."

"If they do that, I will have my day in court."

"I just worry about the example it sets Elijah. He's our only son and such a sweet, good-natured child."

Lucius stood with his hands on his hips and glared at Hannah with flinty eyes. "I thought it would be obvious, my dear, that it shows him the importance of standing up for what he believes in."

Hannah sat down at her white vanity unit and brushed her hair. "I just hope that this doesn't get violent. Last time, the judge ruled in your favour."

"And rightly so. The guy attacked me, I retaliated, it was self-defence."

"Yes, but I know how desperate people get when they are hungry or they can't afford a bill. My father took his own life." Hannah began to sob.

Lucius placed his hands on her shoulders and massaged them gently. "I understand your concern and your compassion is boundless. It's what I love about you, but if we don't make a stand for democracy, who will?"

"I think everyone should have a say, and I am praying for a day when women can vote, and I believe that everyone should be paid a fair wage for an honest day's work."

Hannah looked over her shoulder at her husband through rheumy eyes and clutched his hands. "I don't want you to lose sight of the people you are trying to help. You will continue to receive pay whilst the debates are raging on the streets and in boardrooms. People on the front line will be deciding to either pay a bill or go without food."

Lucius took one of her hands and placed it on his cheek, then he kissed it. "Shush, don't worry, my darling. I will do everything I can to remain humble. You and Elijah remind me every day how lucky I am and I don't want to lose that."

Hannah got up, smiled, ran her fingers through his hair above his ear and kissed him on the lips.

"You're a good man, Lucius Silas Flint, and I know you want to do the right thing. Just be careful. These are dangerous times we live in."

Lucius kissed her back. "Don't worry my sweet, I'll be fine, and it'll all work out for the best. Now where did you put my lunch?"

"Wait one moment," she said, holding up one finger and disappearing downstairs. A few minutes later she handed him his worker's lunchbox. Originally, it was an old tobacco box, a tool of the trade.

Lucius smiled at his wife. "Thanks," he said, giving her a kiss. "I must get to work."

"I'll see you tonight. Love you," she called after him as he walked down the stairs.

Elijah was sitting at the kitchen table eating toast for breakfast. Lucius tousled the boy's brown hair and kissed him on the top of his head. "You be a good boy at school today, you little scamp."

"Oi, who are you calling a scamp?" Elijah grumbled, screwing up his face.

Lucius laughed, blew him a kiss, and as he was going out the door and said, "See you tonight, love ya!"

Lucius walked down the alleyway at the back of his house. When he turned the corner, he saw a skinny man with a hooked nose and five o'clock shadow. He wore a peaked cap, black jacket and matching trousers and boots. He leaned casually, against a wall, taking a drag on a roll up. It was his second-in-command, Harry Brown.

"How's it going, Harry?"

"Aw right, Lucius. How 's the family, guv?" Harry said, his gravelly voice as coarse as sandpaper

"Ah, you know. Hannah's worried about the industrial action. Elijah's as cute as ever."

"She's a woman. It's her job to worry. Keeps em' on their toes, don't it? That's why we keep them sweet."

"Yeah, and you've had plenty to keep sweet over the years haven't you? What's this, wife number three now?"

"Four, but who's counting," Harry laughed, it sounded more like a phlegmy wheeze than a laugh.

"I don't know how you have the energy, one woman is enough for me. I see you haven't given up the smokes."

"A man ain't no man without his vices. When was the last time you had a smoke?" Harry said, stopping and giving Lucius a sideways glance.

Chatty workmen passed them by on the way to their shift at the factory. Black smoke bellowed out from the chimney. Some children jumped in puddles, whilst others wheeled hoops along the pavement, occasionally hitting them with a stick. Dirty cats growled or hissed at each other as they fought over scraps in metal rubbish bins.

"It must be about six months now, I guess."

Harry rolled another cigarette, placed it to his lips and lit it. "I wish I had the willpower."

"Willpower to give up smoking or women?"

Harry flipped Lucius the V. "Fuck you, Flint."

They both laughed and walked through the gates of the sheet metal factory, their first port of call that day.

As they walked into the factory, it smelt of oil and the protective coating of the steel. Large steel plates were winched into place and loaded onto a machine. Rollers fed the metal through rollers where it was cut. When the materials emerged at the other end, men smoothed out the burrs. A bell rang and production stopped.

A short bald man in a brown pinstripe suit stood on a platform above the factory floor and cleared his throat. "Gentlemen, representatives from your union would like to speak to you today. I would like you to know that you have my full support. I would like to see fair pay and better working conditions for you all. I would like to welcome Lucius Flint and Henry Brown from TWLF to the platform."

Some men banged machinery with wrenches, others whistled or cheered. Lucius and Harry climbed onto the platform and stood next to the man.

Lucius looked at the crowd and then he said, "Thank you, Trevor. I wish every foreman was as obliging as you. Can TWLF count on your support on the picket line next month?"

"I will be there. I have worked my way through the ranks, and so I know what it is like to work by the sweat of my brow," Trevor declared, clasping his hands together and pumping his arms. Cheers and rapturous applause erupted in the factory, which lasted for a few minutes before he signalled for calm.

Lucius continued, "I am sure every man is working here to the best of his abilities. Dealing with the hand he has been dealt. I think you'll agree, there needs to be investment into the business. Better and safer equipment. None of this patch it up and make-do- nonsense. Only last week the factory had to be closed because someone was killed. That's not good enough."

There were shouts and clapping from the factory workers.

"Decent pay, a safe working environment, and reasonable hours aren't too much to ask for are they?" Lucius called out.

"No they aren't!" the crowd yelled in agreement.

"So TWLF can count on you to down tools on 12th Dem and stand up for your rights, yes?"

"Yes!" the crowd roared.

"Thank you for your time. Harry and I will see you on the picket line," Lucius said, and then he and Harry climbed down from the platform and walked amongst the crowd. Some of the mob patted them on the back, others shook their hands, some voiced their support.

"That was the easiest factory," Lucius smiled, tucking his shirt back into his trousers.

"Yeah, I'm expecting a bit of push back from the others, boss," Harry said, sparking up another rolly. "Wot's the next one on the agenda, guv?"

Flint sucked in air through his teeth. "The cotton mill. A much younger workforce."

"Yeah, I heard it's run by dirty little tikes."

"Yes, they still employ children. They need them to crawl amongst the machines and clear jams and blockages. I am afraid they might use intimidation and bully boy tactics."

"We won't know til' we gits there, boss."

"No we won't, Harry, no we won't."

Lucius hailed a cab, and within ten minutes, they were on the other side of the slums nearest the river. When they entered the factory, the air was hot, humid and thick with cotton dust, making Lucius and Harry cough. Deafening machinery made it impossible to talk. Children with dirty faces gazed at them with frightened eyes, then looked away. A fat, scowling man, wearing a white shirt, gold waistcoat with black buttons, a topper, black velvet britches, thigh high white socks and black patent leather buckled slippers, signalled for the machinery to stop. Taking off his hat, he revealed sweaty blonde hair plastered to his scalp, and he wiped his forehead with a dirty handkerchief.

"This is the third time this week you have failed to unclog the machine," he growled, pointing a finger at a cowering blonde lad. "Yer ain't worth nowt. Wait in the office for another beating."

After the boy had climbed the stairs, Lucius approached the man, offering his hand for him to shake. "Howard Donohue, I am Lucius Flint, head of TWLF. I wondered if I could talk briefly to your workforce about pay and conditions."

Donohue sneered at Lucius's hand, scratched his blonde sideburn, then gave Lucius a weak handshake.

"Say what you want, but half of them can't even speak. Make it quick, mind. Time is money, and I have a boy to thrash."

"Thank you, Mr. Donohue. You are most kind."

Flint cleared his throat. "Ladies and gentleman," he said and regurgitated the sales pitch from the previous factory.

After he had spoken, the young employees stared at him. They were pale, skinny creatures, with dark circles under their eyes. Flint thought about zombies and felt a lump form in his throat.

Lucius thanked them for their attention, then he left with Harry.

Harry took a deep breath then puffed it out again. "That was a hard sell, guv."

Lucius sighed and threw his hands in the air. "I don't even know where to start with those poor little fuckers, Harry." He bridged his forehead with his hand and shook his head.

"We could push for an investigation, boss. See if Donohue is legit."

"You're talking about factory reform. I know that parliament is talking about it, but that's all they do, talk."

"That's why TWLF was formed, innit? We're the ears and eyes ain't we, guv? The boots on the ground."

"Yes we are, but I am afraid more people will be hurt or killed working in these places. Fuck!" Flint said, kicking a dustbin.

Harry placed his hands on Lucius's shoulders. "We can't give up, boss. We owes it to the workers, see?"

"Yes and you have given me an idea. I think we need to put pressure on the government about factory reform."

Harry smiled, then the two men hugged. Flint pulled away and wrinkled his nose.

"Harry, can you smell burning?"

Harry sniffed the air. "I think I can, guv."

Lucius looked around and saw a large building on fire.

"Harry, I think the paper mill is burning," he said, staring at his friend with wide eyes and his mouth open.

***

"You did what?" Clara said, her eyes blazing.

Clara and James were sitting in a deserted cafe on the other side of town. People chatted and read newspapers. The aroma of freshly brewed coffee and pastries wafted through the establishment. Every few minutes, the espresso machine hissed as baristas made drinks for the thirsty clientele. News of the paper mill hadn't reached the detectives yet.

"I wanted to find out if my suspicions were true about you?"

"And are they, Bronze? Are they?" Clara said, talking through gritted teeth and jabbing her finger in James' chest.

"What the fuck, Clara. That really hurt!"

"Just be grateful I don't break your fucking nose. You've got a nerve poking around in my past like that." She turned and looked out of the window and crossed her arms. "I tell you what, Bronze. Shall I invite you over to my house and open my knicker drawer, so you can have a good old sniff around in there too?"

"The professor was very accommodating. He was genuinely annoyed that I asked if you had cheated in…"

Clara held up her hand. "Save it, Bronze. I'll make sure your transfer comes through quicker now. Just you mark my words."

Before James could respond, their goggles buzzed on the table and moved towards each other. Both detectives put their respective goggles on. Peter Harris's face appeared on their screens.

"Overton, Bronze. There's been a riot at the paper mill. The whole damn thing is on fire. Get over there and take some statements."

"On it, boss," James said and both detectives hung up.

"We have to move fast. Let's flag down one of those new steam taxis. Just because we have something of uttermost importance, doesn't mean I'm finished with you, Bronze. We'll pick up this conversation later."

Bronze nodded, and they both paid and left.

Once they were out on the street, they flashed their badges at the first steam taxi they found and sped to the blazing paper mill.

When they arrived at the scene fire crews were successfully tackling the blaze. The air was hot and humid and reeked of burning paper. Sooty faced people gripped fire blankets tightly around themselves. Some of the folks were sobbing, others were being questioned by the police. Flames rose higher in the air, buoyed by the strong winds. Charred paper drifted in the air like autumn leaves. Another fire crew arrived and began fighting the flames. An ambulance crew carried a groaning man covered in brick dust on a stretcher. A bloody bandage was wrapped around his head.

A hysterical woman broke free from the police cordon, yelling "Oscar, are you okay?" Tears ran down her face and her bottom lip quivered.

"Louisa, am I glad to see you," Oscar said, holding up his swaddled bloody hands. Louisa clasped them.

"Are you hurt, and are you going to be alright?"

"I'm a little banged up, but I'll be okay,"

Louisa snorted a laugh.

"He will be okay, madam. He looks worse than he actually is," one of the male paramedics said. "You can ride with us in the ambulance if you want."

Louisa nodded tearfully. "Yes, please. That would be wonderful," she sobbed.

Clara and James moved to a crowd of onlookers and showed their badges.

"Anyone see what happened?" Clara said.

A red haired man with a moustache and wearing a peaked cap, raised his hand.

"If you would be so kind as to step over here, sir," Clara said, gesturing to a safe area away from the gawping crowd.

"I just want to ask you a few questions, sir. Can you tell me your name, please? Clara said, flipping open her steno pad.

"Andy, Andy Norton."

Clara wrote down his name. "Very good, Mr. Norton. Can you tell me what you saw?"

"Well, as far as I could tell, it looked like a picket line to me. People holding signs, fair pay for workers, that kinda stuff, ya know?"

"What were folks doing?"

"Standing around, smoking, telling jokes, singing protest songs. They had lit a fire in a metal barrel to keep them warm. Nuffin' out of order, really."

"How did the blaze start?"

"The foreman of the paper mill confronted them and asked them to go back to work."

"Would you say that this was a wildcat strike? I am sure I read in the paper yesterday that TWLF weren't due to strike until next month."

The man nodded. "The foreman, Frank, accused them of being wildcats and threatened them with legal action."

Clara scribbled as the interviewee shared his observations.

"What happened next?"

"Barry, a tall, muscly man, punched Frank, and the two men tussled on the ground knocking over the fire barrel. The flames spread quickly and everyone scarpered."

"Did you see anyone else? Were the men speaking to someone else before Frank arrived?"

"No, not that I know of. I work in the sheet metal factory, I buy me paper and use this route as a shortcut. I normally wave to me drinking buddies, and then carry on my merry way.

"Could you identify Barry, Frank and the other men if you were required to?"

Andy took off his cap and scratched his red hair. "I am sure I could."

Looking over Andy's shoulder, Clara saw Lucius Flint and Harry Brown of TWLF talking to bystanders.

"Thank you, Mr. Norton, That will be all. If the police need you for anything else, the station will contact you."

"I hope I have been helpful, detective," Andy said, securing his cap on his head.

"You have been exceptionally helpful. Thank you again, Mr. Norton."

Andy doffed his cap and walked over to someone he knew and engaged in conversation.

Clara strode over to Flint. He saw her and walked over to her. Out of the corner of her eye, she saw Bronze talking to Harry Brown.

"Mr. Flint, I'm Detective Overton," Clara said, showing him her badge.

"Hello, detective. Terrible scenes here. Absolutely shocking. How can I help you?"

"Yes, diabolical scenes. After interviewing a witness, I have reason to believe that this blaze was the result of a scuffle over a wildcat strike. Do your members normally act in this manner?"

Flint sighed. "Wildcat strikes are uncommon, but have been known to happen from time to time. I want to make something entirely clear: I do not condone what has happened here today. I don't believe actions that threaten lives or incite violence achieve anything."

"Is it your belief that these men acted independently of TWLF?

Flint took off his bowler hat and ran his fingers through his brown hair. "Yes, that is exactly what I am saying. Having said that, I can see why this has happened. These men are desperate and I think they lashed out because they were frustrated."

Clara nodded thoughtfully. "Do you think these men could have been coerced into industrial action?"

"I suppose that could happen, yes. What are you thinking, detective?"

"I am not at liberty to divulge that information, Mr. Flint. It's part of our ongoing investigation."

Flint leaned closer. "If you find out anything, detective, I would like to be kept in the loop. Here's my card." Flint handed her his business card with the TWLF logo printed on the top in red and white.

"Thank you, Mr. Flint. As soon as I have any further information, I will let you know."

Flint put his bowler back on his head and doffed the hat. "Thank you detective Overton, I look forward to hearing from you. Now, if you'll excuse me, I need to conduct some investigations of my own, I need to speak to my members." And then he walked in the direction of men holding placards.

Clara turned to see Bronze escorting a muscly man in handcuffs, whom she assumed to be Barry, into a police wagon. Bronze tapped on the side of the wagon with his cane, and with a jolt it pulled away, heading in the direction of the police station.

After Clara and Bronze had interviewed a few more witnesses, they picked through the debris. Bronze saw something tossed in the bushes that grew alongside the factory.

It was a can of Dyes Oil, the familiar logo of a blue whale blowing oil from its spout clearly visible on the tin.

"It looks like the fire had a little helping hand." James said, holding the object aloft.

Chapter Nine: Not All the Lost Are Saved

A waxy moon hid behind wispy clouds as Dimitri soared towards the old palace ruins. Amongst the ruins, stood the IFSF building, like a beacon of hope. Scaffolding and polythene covered another section of the site. A light breeze ruffled his hair and his clothes, he closed his eyes and smiled. Drifting towards the crumbling spire, Dimitri opened his eyes and saw Andrew Taylor.

"I knew you would come. I saw it in a vision," Andrew said, with an even, clear voice.

Dimitri said nothing. I had nothing, no visions, no dreams, no signs. You hid all of them from me. You weren't even a murmur on the breeze and that's frustrating.

Taylor smiled and inhaled deeply. "I have power over other vampires. How exciting!" He chuckled and turned into a black vapour and disappeared through the broken windows of the spire, his cackling laughter ricocheting off the walls below.

Dimitri turned into tendrils of smoke and wafted to the ground floor. When he rematerialised, a shimmering blast of energy hit him in the chest, making him slide back. Opening his hand, he fired a pulse back at Andrew, sending him crashing into a pillar that crumbled and fell on him. Dimitri arose, debris and brick dust falling off him as he stood. Pieces of masonry and clumps of dirt clung to his hair, cloak, trousers and boots. His white shirt was grey and grimy.

"I don't want to fight you, Andrew. You need help. You have been through a dramatic transformation with no one to guide you. Vampires normally have a mentor. Let me be your mentor."

"I don't need you," Taylor roared, launching into a lightning fast flying kick, knocking Dimitri into the back wall of the palace, winding him. Once again, Taylor turned into black vapour and disappeared up the spire like fumes climbing a chimney breast. Dimitri flew up the spire and slammed down on the roof, making some tiles slide off and shatter on the ground.

"Ah ya," Taylor said, throwing a punch. Dimitri blocked the blow and flipped Taylor onto his back, then he pinned him to the ground.

"Why did you kill your sister, Andrew?"

"The thirst was uncontrollable. It was either her or Hetty. Hetty and I were in love and we were going to get married. I scared her off to protect her, but I needed to feed, so I chose Violet instead."

"So you hadn't fed since they turned you?"

Taylor shook his head. "I had felt hunger before, but nothing like this. This was new, I felt so angry, so desperate. And now I am without my sister and I have probably lost my fiancée too."

Dimitri got off the boy and pulled him to his feet.

"That offer of help is still on the table if you want it."

"The law is after me. I'm wanted for murder. I doubt even you or the entire vampire council can protect me," Taylor said before leaping high into the air and impaling himself on the spire's spike.

"Andrew, no!" Dimitri yelled, then flew up to Taylor's twitching, bleeding body.

Taylor coughed up blood. "I can feel my body regenerating itself. If you cut my head off, I will die right?

Dimitri nodded.

"I don't want to live like this. They will either give me the chop or they'll run tests on me. Please, set me free," he looked at Dimitri through watery, pleading eyes. Dimitri drew his Nimchar from its scabbard and cut Taylor's head off, which bounced twice and landed in the gutter. Blood spurted from Taylor's neck like a geyser and his body twitched and convulsed, then went still. Dimitri gathered up Taylor's broken body and retrieved his head, then he laid both of them in the graveyard. After that, he placed an anonymous phone call to the police and flew back to his family.

***

Bentley Pelham's heart thudded in his chest as he ran through the alleyways of Lario. The pack was getting nearer and he could hear panting and claws clicking on the cobblestones.

Think Bentley, think! Maybe if I hide on one of the ships on the harbour, they won't find me.

Bentley turned left into the marketplace, saw a ship called *The Green Griffin* with its gangplank down and ran up it. Searching frantically, he found the hull stairs and sprinted down them. An aroma of beer, rum and farts filled his nostrils and the sound of snoring sailors rattled his ears. Hammocks hung from the beams and swung with the momentum of the rocking, creaking vessel.

After rummaging in his jacket pocket, he pulled out a small metal rectangular object with a steel edge. He opened his mouth and swallowed the device.

Concentrating hard, he looked in the gloomy darkness, trying to find somewhere to hide. And then he saw it. A gold lock and key glowed in the dingy cabin. It was a chest. Bentley turned the key in the lock and climbed in and closed the lid. For a moment, nothing changed, then there was the sound of a low growl. Clinking claws and the sound of sniffing replaced the low growl. Bentley could hear his pulse in his ear and he hoped the wolf outside couldn't. Sweat trickled down his spine and he rubbed his clammy hands on his trousers. A few minutes later, the cabin was filled with the sounds of more clattering claws and snuffling. Shortly after that, Bentley thought he heard the sound of bones snapping, joints cracking and skin stretching. And then the lid on the chest lifted and two yellow eyes glared at him. Two strong arms pulled Bentley out of the chest and placed him on the hull floor.

"Look what we have here, lads. The spy we have been tracking." The voice belonged to a huge black haired man with bulging muscles. Balling up his fist, he punched Bentley in the stomach, and Bentley fell to his knees, coughing. "Kill him lads and all the sailors."

The pack howled and a wolf leapt at Bentley knocking him backwards, then it ripped his throat out.

***

Police had cordoned off *The Green Griffin*. Cops glanced suspiciously at Clara and Bronze as they approached. Clara stared at them blankly and showed them her badge. Bronze did the same. After clearing their throats and shuffling their feet, the officers apologised and let the two detectives through. Clara reached into her pocket, took out the methanol rub and put it under her nostrils. Without saying a word, she held up the tub for Bronze and he took it and applied it under his nose.

"You look like shit, Bronze."

"I've had a long night. An anonymous tip came in after you left the station. I was writing a report and took the case."

Clara snorted. "You're such a martyr, Bronze."

Bronze moved close to Clara's ear and whispered, "Andrew Taylor's body turned up at the palace ruins last night. It had been decapitated."

Clara gasped, her hand flying to her chest. "Any clues to who may have done It?"

"Nimchar fibres were found on Andrew's neck. It was a generic blade, nothing special about it. One wound was interesting though," Bronze said, snapping on latex gloves.

"You can stop whispering in my ear now, Detective Bronze."

"Sorry."

"You were talking about this interesting wound."

"Huh, oh, yeah. The victim had been impaled and then had started to heal again. Fascinating."

"Not really, that's a standard healing process for a vampire."

"Unlike you, Overton, I don't fraternise with leeches."

Clara snapped on her own latex gloves, but continued to stare at him. Don't bite, Clara, it's what he wants.

"Let's take a look at the crime scene. I can't tell you how grateful I am for the methanol today. If we didn't have it, the stench would be horrific."

James nodded and chewed his lip.

Blood dripped from corpses hanging from hammocks in the hull, and torn body parts were strewn everywhere. Claw marks were etched into the wooden floor and dead men's faces. Every now and again Clara caught the odour of blood, beer, rum and she felt bile crawl up her throat. After looking around the scene, Clara noticed a male corpse wearing different clothes. Taking off her right glove, Clara saw a gold glow around the man's mouth. Leaning over, she touched his lips. Her eyes fluttered and she went into a trance. She watched the man take something out of his pocket and swallow it. She let go of his mouth and put her glove back on.

"I think I found why this gentleman was murdered, James. He swallowed something they wanted."

When they stepped onto the dock, Clara felt like she was being stared at. She turned and looked straight into the eyes of a hooded figure. With black leather gloved hands, the person pulled down her hood and smirked at Clara.

What the fuck? Abigail Price. She turned to say something to James, but when she turned back, Abigail had gone, like a wraith on the wind. After agreeing to meet James at The Arch Tavern, Clara made her excuses and went back to the police station.

When she had told the clerk what she wanted, she sat down at the microfiche with a large mug of coffee and loaded the film onto the reels. She flicked through the images and found a photo of Abigail's parents holding a baby. Her father wore a light suit, a dark bow tie and black and white brogues. His elaborate moustache sat above his smiling mouth. Her mother wore a white bustle dress and smiled at the camera through tired eyes.

Clara skipped on to the Smeardon case. A picture of a six year old looked at her feet and not the camera. She was surrounded by police officers and her scowling mother wagged an angry finger at the law.

Clara skipped forward and something caught her eye.

"Lario protégé wins scholarship for pharmaceutical degree," read the headline, followed by a photo of Abigail Price. The article was four years old, but the photo was definitely Abigail, complete with a smug smile.

Clara continued scanning but her search was fruitless.

Clara puffed out her cheeks. "Where the fuck did you go, princess, and why have you come back?

Clara shut off the machine, gave the film back to the clerk and thanked them. Once she was on the street she hailed a cab home.

Chapter Ten: Confessions

"Well, I bet that cost you a pretty penny, Overton." James said as they walked down the narrow stairs of the cellar bar, opened the door and sat at a table.

He was wearing a brown pinstripe suit, a light blue shirt and brown brogues. Clara wore a midnight blue flapper cap, dress and shoes. Soft lights illuminated the dark wood panelling, revealing a few tables and chairs, a bar and two doors, male and female toilets.

Clara stared at him blankly. "William drives a hard bargain."

James smirked. "It doesn't help that he hates your guts, either."

A door behind the bar opened and a young barmaid with a blonde ponytail, wearing a bandeau ruffle blouse shirt and a long black skirt and boots, emerged.

Clara approached the bar. "Can I have a bottle of tequila and twelve shot glasses please?"

"Certainly, coming right up," the barmaid said.

Once the order was complete, Clara thanked the barmaid and returned to the table with the shot glasses and tequila bottle on a tray.

"So, why have you brought me here, Clara?"

Clara poured two glasses, a sly smile forming on her lips. "I don't know about you, but if I go to a massacre, I like to get blind drunk. Besides, I find alcohol loosens the tongue. I think you have some explaining to do, Detective Bronze." Clara drank her tequila, turned the glass upside down and slammed it on the table before adding, "I am glad Commissioner Harris gave us some compassionate leave."

James drummed his fingers on the table and then he said, "I wanted to see if you were legit, Clara," he said, drinking his shot and slamming down his glass.

"And what did you find?"

"I found out you're clean."

Clara huffed and shook her head. "So are you still going through with your transfer?"

"No, I don't think I will."

"What if I said I didn't want to work with you anymore and I had requested another partner?" Clara said, downing another shot and slamming down her glass so hard the table shook.

James's shoulders drooped and he nodded slowly. "I understand. I have been difficult to work with."

"Do you think? I have found you to be rude, condescending and utterly unpleasant."

"Whoa, don't hold back, will you."

"The time for manipulation and mind games is over, James. I am seeking honesty and truth from you. Fuck, I don't even know if I can trust you. If you can't trust your partner, who can you trust?"

James hung his head and looked at the table and said very quietly. "I am nothing special. I come from a very humble background. I don't have magic and everything I have worked for has been a struggle. You are remarkable, Clara, in every way. When I was first partnered with you, I felt like I had inherited great wealth."

Clara raised her eyebrows, widened her eyes and touched her throat. "Are you trying to tell me you're in love with me?" she said.

"You always seemed so distant, aloof. I didn't think you would want to date a man like me, so I decided I would make you hate me instead."

A slow smile spread across Clara's lips. "I don't know if I should be flattered or insulted, James."

The barmaid cleared their used shot glasses away and replaced them with clean ones, then she lit the fire in the hearth and returned to the bar.

For a few moments, neither James nor Clara spoke, and only the sounds that could be heard was the barmaid washing their glasses and the fire crackling beside them.

James lent forward and clasped her hands. "I am in love with you, Clara, I always have been."

Clara withdrew her hands and swallowed hard. "I genuinely thought you despised me. This has caught me completely off guard."

"I understand if you would like to work with another partner. I am like a baby elephant in a plate shop." James smiled

Clara barked a laugh, then she set her jaw and fixed him with a flinty stare. "I will give you the benefit of the doubt. You are aesthetically pleasing, but your heart is as black as coal."

"OOF! At least I know where I stand now."

"I say what I mean and mean what I say."

"I can't argue with that. It's another thing that is attractive about you."

Clara flashed him a half smile and held up her index finger. "Can you promise me that your clandestine investigations into me are over?"

"Scouts honour," James said, holding up three fingers.

"Were you even a scout?"

James's hand flew to his chest. "Of course I was," he said, his voice going up an octave.

Clara giggled, then covered her mouth with her hand. "Please don't do that too often. You sound like a stuffed pig."

"Now that's just rude," James huffed, folding his arms across his chest, tightening his lips.

Clara's smile disappeared and she narrowed her eyes. "In all seriousness, I need to know that I can trust you implicitly."

She reached for her goggles, called Eme and then Edwin and asked them to join them. She pulled down the goggles and looked over the rims at James with a flat gaze.

James pulled at his collar with his finger and cleared his throat.

They made idle chit-chat as they quaffed more tequila. Twenty minutes later, Eme and Edwin clattered down the stairs. Eme wore a lilac flapper cap and dress with Edwin sporting a black tuxedo and spats. They hugged and kissed Clara and sat opposite the two detectives. As if on cue, the barmaid arrived and handed them a menu each.

"Hi, my name is Jenny. Can I get you anything to drink?"

"Two bottles of red please," Eme said, before anyone else could order.

"I'll bring it right over," Jenny said and disappeared behind the bar.

Eme scanned the menu and then peered over it at James. "So you're the son of bitch that Clara has to work with every day."

James cleared his throat. "Err, isn't that a little harsh,"

There was a crackling sound as a needle was placed on a record. A slow garbled sound came from the acoustic horn, like an orchestra tuning up and gathered speed as Jenny cranked the handle. When it reached full tempo, the sound of a swing band filled the air. Eme made Charleston hand movements, her feet shuffling under the table.

James swallowed hard and glanced furtively around the table.

Edwin scrutinised James and beckoned him with his first two fingers. James lent forward and so did Edwin. Edwin spoke into James's ear. "Forgive Eme. She shoots first and asks questions later. She may be uncouth, but I echo her sentiments. Clara is very dear to us and we don't want to see her get hurt."

James sighed. "I promise you I will make it up to her."

Edwin snorted. "You've got a lot of work to do."

James held his hands up in surrender. "I am out of options. It's Team Clara for me all the time from now on."

"Well, if you're a friend of Clara's, you're a friend of mine," Edwin said, raising his empty wine glass.

James raised his and the two men clinked their glasses together.

"Here's your drinks," Jenny said, returning to the table with their wine.

"Would you like to try the wine, sir?" Jenny said, looking at James.

"Yes, I would."

Jenny nodded and uncorked the bottle and poured a sample into James' glass.

"That is excellent. Thank you, Jenny."

"Very good, sir," she said and poured everyone a drink. "Are you all ready to order?

"Four steaks and chips, please. With onion rings, peas and peppercorn sauce," Clara said enthusiastically.

Jenny raised her eyebrows, her eyes wide with wonder.

"We all agree," Edwin said.

James opened his mouth to protest, but the others scowled at him before he could speak.

"How would you like the steak cooked?"

"Medium rare, please," Edwin said.

"The food will be about 20 minutes. Is that okay?" Jenny said, collecting up the menus.

"That's fine, and please bring two more bottles of this fine red," Clara said.

"So, tell us about yourself, James," Edwin said, draining his glass and refiling it.

"Growing up was tough. We were very poor. Sometimes we would only have a slice of bread and a pint of beer. Other days we would go hungry."

"So, you resented Clara because she was rich. Is that it?" Eme snarled.

James wiped his clammy hands on his trouser leg. "Seeing as I have decided to be honest with Clara, I will be honest with you too. Yes I did resent her wealth."

"Then you should know that Clara's father founded the Overton Foundation for the poor. It was designed to give poor children an education and a future. A foundation that you may have benefitted from," Eme remarked, lowering her chin.

James slid his chair back and it screeched on the wooden floor. "Ah, yes. I wouldn't be here now if it wasn't for the Foundation."

"Then I think you owe Clara an apology, don't you?" Eme added, tilting her body away from him.

"I am going outside for some fresh air and a smoke," James said, going pale and feeling sick. He walked up the stairs and left.

"He's not such a hot shot detective now, is he? What a prick!" Eme concluded, taking out her silver cigarette case and cigarette holder. She fitted a smoke to the holder and lit it.

"I think you've both made your point. James and I have been to a horrific crime scene, and he has as much a right to good night out as I do. Just cut him some slack. Anyway, I think I have a way to get through to him," Clara said, looking at each of her friends in turn.

"What do you have in mind Clara?" Eme asked, letting out cigarette smoke.

"That's on a need to know basis and you don't need to know," Clara chuckled, tapping Eme's knee under the table. Eme flashed Clara a sultry smile.

The door to the cellar bar opened, followed by the sound of James's footsteps.

James retook his seat at the table, a half smile on his face.

Jenny came to the table with their food. She was accompanied by a male waiter dressed in a white shirt and black trousers.

After the servers had given them their meals, Jenny said, "Enjoy your food."

"Thank you," they all said.

The steak was tender and delicious.

"What made you choose the police force, James?" Edwin said, furrowing his brow.

"I have seen so much injustice and I wanted to change that."

"What about the in… aw," Eme said, as Clara kicked her under the table and scowled at her.

Edwin nodded thoughtfully. "What do you think about all the industrial action and the civil unrest?"

"I sympathise with them. If I wasn't a policeman, I would probably be joining them on the picket lines," James admitted, putting another piece of steak in his mouth.

"How would you change things?" Eme said.

James gasped. Has the bulldog backed down?

"I would give them what they want. They work long hours in appalling conditions for very little pay. What kind of a life is that?" he said.

Eme leaned back in her chair, blew out another stream of smoke and stared at him thoughtfully.

"What a lovely vision you have, but reform doesn't happen overnight," Edwin said, cutting into his steak.

There was a scratching sound as the record was replaced. A slow jazz ballad replaced the swing track. Jenny came and added another log to the fire before placing the dessert menus on their table, then returned to the bar.

"I think if the rich business owners can be convinced people are more important than profits, then we're halfway there," James commented.

"How would you do that?" Clara said, joining the conversation.

"I think the fat cats are blind. They are worlds apart, and they don't know how their workers live. If they could visit the slums and see the struggles of these families, maybe they would understand."

"You are assuming that these people have a heart," Eme said.

"Yes, that is a bold declaration," James said, smiling, making the others laugh.

"I don't want to be naive about this, some of the CEOs are so cold-hearted, they are almost beyond redemption. I believe that the majority of these people would be compelled to action."

"What about the rest of them?" Clara said.

"Well, they would need somebody with special persuasive powers to help them see the error of their ways," James said, smiling at Clara.

"You've changed your tune, James. The way you carried on, it sounded like you wanted all the providentias burnt at the stake," Clara said.

"Let's just say I've come around to your way of thinking."

"There aren't many of us left now. Eme and I are a rare breed these days."

"Professor Brownlow said there are at least two other women who could help. Annabelle Beard and Polly Napper. There were some good things that came out of my unauthorised meeting," James revealed, averting his gaze from the group.

"I haven't seen Annabelle and Polly for two years. Where are they living now?"

"Not very far from here, actually," James said, reaching into his pocket for the address cards and handing them to Clara.

"I'll look them up. It'd be great to see them again. Thank you, James. You're not all bad."

"I am trying to make amends with you, Clara."

"Well, It's a start."

"Are we sticking with the chocolate fudge brownie?" Eme said, not looking up from her dessert menu.

"If it isn't broken, why should we fix it?" Edwin said, smirking.

Clara nodded her agreement. Edwin caught Jenny's attention and she came over and took their order.

After they had eaten their puddings, they asked Jenny to put on jazz dance tunes and the four friends danced.

After dancing for a while, they took a break at the table.

"I am a bit danced out now. But I do know this funky open mic night bar if you're interested?" James suggested.

"Okay, lead the way," Clara said.

Outside the bar, they flagged a cab and made their way to The Broken Piston.

When they stepped onto the pavement, the bar was in full swing. A jazz band was belting out a fast dance tune, and they could hear the sound of dancing feet and enthusiastic shouting. Stepping through the door, they saw people with coloured hair, waistcoats, pinstripe trousers and docker boots. One woman wore a topper, a black ruffle blouse, a pink tutu, red and black stockings and docker boots.

A bare chested man in red trousers breathed fire. High above, a male trapeze artist hung upside down from his legs and caught his female partner as she spun through the air.

Dwarf acrobats flipped and caught each other, forming a human pyramid.

A grey haired man in a red suit stepped onto the stage and grabbed the microphone.

"Ladies and gentlemen, please welcome Andre Lagoona, the master of the Theremin."

Everyone clapped and cheered as a man with brown curly hair and clothed in a tailcoat and white gloves stepped forward. Andre stood in front of what looked like a lectern with a chrome pipe sticking out of it. He waved his hand in front of the pipe. A sound like a whale giving birth bellowed from the instrument. Clara covered her ears and left the building.

When the others realised Clara wasn't with them, they came and found her on the street.

"What's up, Clara?" James said.

"If you call that stimulating entertainment, you're welcome to it," Clara said.

"Well at least we know what a whale sounds like on dry land," Eme said, and they all laughed.

"Look to be completely honest, I'm pretty beat. Could you take me home please, James?" Clara said, yawning and covering her mouth with her hand.

"Sure." James raised his hand and hailed a cab. A carriage stopped and pulled alongside them.

After they had all hugged, James and Clara took the cab home. Opening her purse, Clara found a pill and dry swallowed it.

James's eyes widened and his jaw went slack. "Clara, what the fuck?" his eyes blazing.

"James, it's not what you think. The pill I have taken is medicine. It's a trance inhibitor. I plan to kiss you and touch your face with my bare hands. I can't do that if I don't take this pill."

"Really? What would happen if you didn't take it?"

"I could become overwhelmed by all your emotions, thoughts and memories. I could end up in a mental institution. This drug will prevent that from happening."

James rubbed his hand over his stubbly chin. "I had no idea your ability affected you so drastically."

"It's a blessing and a curse. You could say it's Fate's way of keeping me humble."

"Grim, but fascinating."

Clara nodded. The carriage pulled to a halt outside her house. They got out and James thanked the driver and paid him.

Clara opened the gate and they went into her house.

After they took off their shoes and coats Clara led James to the dining room and she poured them both a brandy. When James received the drink, he swirled it around in the glass.

"Have you lived here for a long time?"

"All of my life. This house has been in my family for 300 years."

"Wow. It has to be haunted, surely?"

Clara laughed. It was a pleasant sound and it made him feel warm inside.

"I haven't met any ghosts, only vampires. Do they count?" she said smiling, the flames from the fireplace reflecting in her eyes.

"If it moves like a ghost, acts like a ghost, it's probably a ghost. I think they definitely count."

Clara moved closer to him. "Do you want to know an interesting fact about me and vampires?"

James raised his eyebrows. "Sure, why not?"

A smile whispered at her lips. "They can't read my mind."

James opened his mouth and clapped his hands to his cheeks.

"My goodness, you are quite the enigma, Clara Overton. I must protect you from those who may seek to harm you. If your abilities are somehow replicated, they could be weaponized."

"The only weapon I am interested in is the one between your legs," Clara said, stroking his groin and feeling his penis twitch.

James touched her cheek with his hand and breathed in through his nose, then he kissed her sultry lips. Clara returned the kiss, then she pulled away and took off her tights. James took off his jacket and Clara ripped off his shirt revealing his washboard stomach and she licked her lips. James took off his trousers. Clara slid down the straps on her flapper dress and let the outfit glide to the floor: she was completely naked. James took off his boxer shorts, and then Clara pushed him onto the rug by the fire. Clara straddled him and she gasped when he entered her. He caressed her perfect breasts and she moaned with pleasure. James stroked her hair and then back, then he squeezed her pert bottom. A few minutes later they came.

Clara got off him and dressed again. "I am beat, let's go to bed."

"Do you want to carry on with this upstairs?"

Clara looked at him flatly. "When I said, let's go to bed, I meant to sleep."

"Oh, right, of course you did. Okay, that's fine."

***

A light breeze, sunshine and bird song woke James. He groaned as he sat up. The space next to him was empty.

Clara must be up already.

After James had found his trousers, he slipped them on, yawned, moved his head from side to side and padded down the staircase. Pausing on the stairs, James thought he heard something and strained his ears to listen. Music. A smile crossed his lips, and he continued in the direction of the sound. As he reached the dining room, the door was open just a crack and he peered in. Clara had her back to him. She was dressed in a white blouse, black leggings and the flapper shoes from last night. She was doing the Charleston dance. James smiled to himself, used the toilet on his right and then went back to bed, still smiling.

"So that's how you keep fit. I am going to have to improve my dancing skills if this is going anywhere. You're so mysterious, Clara Overton."

He took off his trousers again and climbed back into bed. Within minutes he was snoring.

Sometime later, he opened his eyes and saw a note on the elaborate bedside table. He unfolded it and read.

Dear James,

I had a truly wonderful time last night, but please don't be there when I get home.

I have a lot to think about.

Dalton will make you breakfast.

Clara.

James crumpled up the note and threw it on the floor in disgust.

He dressed and went home, skipping breakfast.

***

Sun streamed through the conservatory windows at Edwin's house. The conservatory had a black and white tiled floor, a few bamboo chairs and exotic plants. Clara and Eme sat at the dining table with a breakfast spread in front of them. Edwin was feeding his Caladrius, which sat on a perch in a cage, nestled between the foliage. Edwin cooed softly at the white bird, which responded with coy movements and soft bird song.

I am glad I bought that bird for him. I know it can heal wounds, but I wonder if it can heal mental scars too? Clara thought as she watched Eme smother her white toast with marmalade.

Clara helped herself to two slices of buttered white toast, sausage, bacon and scrambled eggs.

"So, where's lover boy this morning?" Eme said, crunching on her marmalade toast.

"I left him in bed sleeping."

Eme stared at her mid chew and Edwin turned around and looked at her, a smirk on his face.

Eme pressed her lips flat. "Well, I hope this is a providentia thing and not an "I am scared of commitment "thing". She folded her arms and clenched her teeth.

Why is she getting so bent out of shape? We shared one drunken kiss, that's all. And then Clara realised, a slight smile on her lips. She's in love with you, or she thinks she is. A sigh escaped her mouth and she carried on smiling, then she stopped.

"Well, someone's happy," Edwin said, sitting down at the table and spreading marmalade on his own toast.

"No-one's happy after a one night stand. They just think they are. It's all infatuation," Eme scoffed, revealing a mouth full of sausage and egg.

"What do you think, Clara? Do you think there's a future in this, will you see him again?" Edwin said, leaning closer and smiling.

"I left him a note and told him not to be there when I got back."

Eme threw up her arms, palms open. "I'll say it again, Clara, is it a commitment thing or a providentia thing?"

Clara took a deep breath then let it out again. "providentia. It's a providentia thing." She nodded as if she needed to reassure herself.

"Are you sure?" Eme said, also leaning closer.

"Yes, I am absolutely certain. I took a pro-inhibitor last night. I didn't want to touch him and feel everything he felt. All the pain and anguish, the hurt, the loss. All of it. It would have been a sensory overload and I am not ready for that." She shook her head.

"Pro-inhibitors are the standard practice for us providentias when we want a bit of jiggy," Eme declared, standing up and dry thrusting, a large grin on her face. Edwin laughed despite himself.

"Besides, darling, you couldn't stand this man yesterday. What changed?" Eme said, raising her eyebrows.

"There's just something about him. When I am ready, I will search his thoughts. I need to understand him better. Find out what his motives are."

"Most people do that before they sleep with them," Edwin mused.

Clara's fingers touched her parted lips.

"I wouldn't have expected you to judge me, Edwin."

Clara needed to think, so she ate her breakfast.

Edwin waited for Clara to finish eating then he said, "Sorry. That was completely out of character for me. You think James is genuine, and that he honestly believed in what he was saying last night?"

"Yes, I do. I saw a different side to him. You should have seen him. He was racked with remorse and guilt. He didn't have any cards left to play."

"You don't believe he'll go digging in your past, looking for skeletons in the proverbial cupboard?" Edwin said, tilting his head.

"No I don't Edwin. He looked defeated, and I got the impression he wanted a fresh start."

"Are you going to give him a fresh start?" Eme asked, taking a puff from her cigarette holder.

"I think so. I can't see why not."

"Then I think you need to put your supernatural to use, sooner rather than later." Eme said, blowing out more smoke.

"I think you might be right," Clara said, nodding.

Before anyone else spoke, Clara's goggles vibrated on the table.

After she had picked them up, she peered through the lenses and saw James's face.

"It's him," she said, talking out of the side of her mouth, holding her hand to her cheek.

"Well, don't keep the poor bloke waiting. Answer it," Eme hissed.

Clara slipped the goggles on. "Hello?"

"Clara, it's James. I hope I didn't upset you last night. It was a pretty stressful day. I thought maybe we could go for a ride and talk it over?" Clara moved the goggles to her forehead.

"He wants to see me today, so we can have a chat," she mouthed the words to her friends, so James couldn't hear. They nodded and made shooing gestures.

Clara slid the goggles back onto her eyes.

"That sounds great." Out of her peripheral vision, she could see Eme and Edwin smiling and giving her enthusiastic thumbs up signs.

"Meet you at the glade, say 12 P.M.?"

"Great, see you then."

"Fantastic, looking forward to it."

"I better go home and have a shower."

"Knock him dead, kiddo," Eme said.

"Have a lovely time sweetheart," Edwin said.

"Excuse me a second. I need the little girls' room," Eme said, leaning over and kissing Edwin on the forehead.

"Are you using the upstairs bathroom?"

"Always."

"I don't get it."

"The mirror is bigger and I fix my makeup better."

"There's a mirror in the downstairs one that's just as good."

"Just humour me."

Once she was alone, Eme looked in the mirror and shook her head from side to side. Her features changed and she was faced with the image of Abigail Price and she smirked at her reflection.

***

Rays of sunshine filtered through the trees when Clara arrived at the forest entrance. James looked handsome in his riding gear, sitting up straight on his chestnut mare.

Children of Tarnuz

Clara was riding the gentle giant, Thunder, her loyal black stallion. She wore her confidence suit although she didn't feel confident at all.

James smiled at her as she approached. "Not only did you show up, you're on time. Thank you, Clara."

He's being nice to me! This is weird, I wonder if I will ever get used to it?

"I am happy to be here."

The horses trotted slowly along the woodland path. A slight breeze blew through the trees, sending cascades of autumn leaves to the floor. Red, green, yellow and lilac leaves carpeted the ground. A purple squirrel ran up an oak tree, stopped, glanced at Clara and James, then scampered up into the canopy above.

"Did you see that?" James said, pointing in the direction of the squirrel.

"I don't think you venture into the woods very often do you?"

James shook his head.

"I thought as much. The purple squirrel is very common here. They get their colouring because they live on purple acorns."

"Wow, how fascinating!"

James changed the subject. "How do you feel after the massacre?"

"I wasn't expecting that. I am trying to put it out of my mind. providentias have to do that very quickly, it's a coping mechanism."

"Is that the label you have given yourself?"

"It's the label we were given centuries ago. There aren't many of us left now, we're practically extinct."

James stopped his steed and looked at her. "How come? What happened?"

Clara sighed deeply. "I know that vampires can't read our thoughts, which makes us a danger to them. Our trances reveal someone's true nature."

"What, like my heart being as black as coal?"

Clara barked a short laugh. "I didn't mean that. I was angry. Wouldn't you be angry with someone who had been poking their nose in where it didn't belong?"

"Fair comment. I am truly sorry about that. I just want a fresh start with you."

"And I am giving you one, but if you fuck up again, you will be getting a new partner."

James held up his hands in surrender. "You'll get no argument from me."

"Good. I am glad we understand each other."

Both riders pulled on their reins and the horses stopped chewing on grass and carried on walking.

"Anyway, you were saying."

"providentias have always had a bad reputation. Some would use their abilities for good, solving crimes, finding a diagnosis of an unknown illness or disease. Others used their powers for bribery, corruption, blackmail, theft. Any crime really."

"So, the pitchfork gangs rounded them up and burnt them at the stake, like they used to do to mages?"

"Pretty much. Things started to improve when Queen Hanifa and King Stefano passed laws to enable free movement for all people and beasts. Apart from my father, I know four other providentias and one of those is dead now, too."

"Yes, Professor Brownlow said she died of typhoid."

Clara pinched her lips together. *I need to let this go and give him the benefit of the doubt.*

"I wish I had powers."

"A poor boy with powers? It would be a treacherous mountain to climb."

"It might not be that bad. If I could heal people or something."

"I can only speak from my own personal experience, and if you were a providentia, you would develop a love-hate relationship with it."

James pondered this. "Hmm, now that is interesting. What are your main gripes with it?"

"My sense of touch is severely limited. I have to wear gloves all the time, otherwise I might have a sensory overload."

"Yes, you mentioned that in the carriage last night."

"Sorry, forgive me for repeating myself."

"It's fine, Clara. carry on."

"Thank you. It's not so bad in remote places like this. The humanoid interaction with nature is minimal, which is beneficial."

"So, you aren't affected by wildlife then?"

"They are just animals. They do what they need to do to survive, although I did see an elf spider the other day that scared the shit out of me!" Clara said, shivering. I think I don't like spiders. I never really thought about it before, probably because I haven't seen many. She felt goose flesh creep along her arms and she rubbed them with her gloved hands.

James gasped, his hand flying to his chest. "You saw an elf spider?! I heard they are rare."

"Incredibly rare."

"Yes, but I think your response was totally justified. I would have been scared shitless too."

A stream could be heard running through the forest. As they approached, the trees thinned out and the ground was a little flatter.

"This looks like a good spot," James said, dismounting and taking picnic food and a picnic blanket from his saddle bags. He laid out the blanket, sandwiches, cheeses, cold meat, crackers and a bottle of sparkling white wine. The horses ambled over to the stream and lapped at the water.

After James picked up the wine, he pulled the cork and poured it into two glass flutes, and handed one to Clara and they chinked them together. "Cheers," he said, smiling.

"Cheers," Clara echoed. Thank God he didn't toast us. It's a bit early to start saying things like that, it's only our second date! If things go well, how are we going to work together? Clara chewed her lip and hoped James hadn't seen her.

"Help yourself to some food if you're hungry," James said, waving his hand over the food.

"Thank you." Clara selected a cucumber sandwich and started chewing. Her stomach growled. She giggled and touched her lips with her fingers.

"I am terribly sorry. I appear to have a tiger in my tummy!"

James laughed and Clara chortled again.

"It's quite alright, Clara. You're clearly more hungry than you thought."

"Judging by my stomach, I am positively famished."

"It certainly seems that way. I wanted to talk to you about the massacre. What do you think that thing was that Bentley swallowed?"

Clara swallowed, then she said, "We won't know for definite until Horace has analysed it, but I am hoping it has some kind of evidence that Agreeable Solutions are conducting experiments."

"Experiments? What sort of experiments?"

"Mixing human DNA with vampire and werewolf DNA. Something along those lines."

James puffed his cheeks and shook his head. "Whoa, that's heavy!"

"We have no proof of this, I am only passing on the speculation from the vampire council," Clara said, tapping her foot, her eyes flitting around the area.

"Clara, you look worried."

"I am petrified. If the vampire council are correct in their assumptions, we are all in danger. Every man, woman, child, beast, everyone in Tarnuz."

"I appreciate you letting me into the secrets the council has shared with you, it means a lot. But I sincerely hope they are wrong."

"I vehemently agree with you James, but I don't think they are wrong. A powerful vampire lord, Zintius, is the managing director of Agreeable Solutions and the council couldn't detect him."

James widened his eyes and gave her a double take. "Wait, what? They couldn't detect him?" James drained his drink and promptly poured himself another. "How is that possible? I don't know a huge amount about vampires, but one thing I do know is they have a telepathic link."

Clara nodded. "They do, but he is an ancient vampire overlord who blocks telekinesis, therefore rendering him undetectable."

"I don't like the sound of those odds."

"Hmm, they seem insurmountable, don't they?"

"Yes, they do. Here's to the end of Tarnuz," he said, raising his glass with a wolfish grin on his lips.

Clara sniggered and touched her lips again, then she clinked her flute against his. "I wouldn't be surprised if the dragon council calls a meeting at some point. They are the highest authority in the land, after all."

"If that does happen, this is very serious indeed. Do you think they will call us in early from our compassionate leave?"

"I doubt that very much. If we decided to return to work early, we would be subjected to a psych workup. We would also be subjected to that after our two week compassionate leave is up anyway."

"I take your point," nodded James.

"Are you really that bored that you want to go back to work?"

"No, but this is an exciting and terrifying point in the history of Tarnuz."

"I wouldn't rush back just yet as there have been a series of horrific and tragic murders that we have investigated, but its two isolated incidents. I don't mean to be cold or callous, but unless there is a national state of emergency, I think we should take all the time we need. Have you had any flashbacks, visions or night terrors?" Clara said thoughtfully.

"No, not yet. Have you?"

"Not that I am aware of, but it has only been a couple of days."

James nodded. "So tell me a bit about yourself. You have a lovely figure. How do you keep in shape?" Clara smiled at the compliment and welcome change of topic. "Thank you. I dance every day. Sometimes I play tennis with Eme or Edwin."

Clara blushed, her emerald eyes flashing with excitement. "Perhaps you could join us for mixed doubles?"

"I would like that. Apart from riding, what other hobbies do you have?"

"I come out here to practise archery with Commissioner Harris."

"Yes, you two do seem pretty close."

"He was my father's best friend and became my legal guardian when dad passed."

"Ah, that explains it. I am not much of a dancer."

"I noticed that at the cellar bar last night."

"Oi, cheeky,"

Clara tittered. "I can teach you how to dance if you want."

"I would love that."

"What about you? How do you keep yourself fit?"

" Oh, you know the usual stuff: go to the gym, I do a bit of boxing. Sometimes I go for a run."

"Where do you run?"

"Normally around the city and the harbour. I have apprehended many criminals doing that."

Clara clucked her tongue and shook her head. "Always on the job, eh?"

"Something like that, yes."

"I tend to turn a blind eye to that sort of thing after my shift has ended."

"What even if it's something serious?"

Clara scrunched up her face. "Of course not, but a lot of the serious stuff happens when I am tucked up in bed, as I am sure you are all too aware."

"I hear you. The life of a detective, I am afraid."

Clara nodded and put some cheese on a cracker and ate. "I am having a lovely time, and I am starting to see that you're not really unpleasant at all."

James barked a short laugh. "Thank you very much. A backhanded compliment is better than no compliment at all, I guess."

"I'll drink to that," Clara said, smiling and raising her glass. They tapped glasses once more.

"Sometimes, bitterness and rage fuel my thoughts and actions. I am working hard to control it, but there might be the odd relapse," confessed James.

"Well, I am a big girl now, I think I can handle it," she said, closing her eyes, leaning forward and kissing him on the lips. Suddenly she went into a trance and so did James. Pulling away, they both jumped up. James held his hands out like a frightened cat, ready to spring into the air.

"I think I had a trance."

Chapter Eleven: A Bad Choice of Friends

Elijah Newton Flint pulled his long black coat tighter around his body and fastened up the top button. Fog crawled along the ground like a poisonous snake ready to strike. Straightening his goggle clad topper, Elijah made his way through the dusty cobbled streets at the back of his school. Every day, he took the short ten minute walk from his house to school, normally with friends, but they had chosen to stay for the football club today. Elijah wasn't sure how he felt about football, so he decided he would go home and think about it. After he had turned a corner, he saw a scruffy, skinny male chimney sweep, about his age, eight, eating a red apple. The boy took another apple from his pocket and offered it to him. Drawing closer, Elijah tried to take the apple, but the boy laughed and ran away. Startled, but intrigued, Elijah gave chase. The boy ran down an alleyway that led to the slums, his maniacal laughter echoing off the walls. A chill crept up Elijah's spine and his blood ran cold. A voice inside him said, This feels dangerous, go home.

Nevertheless, Elijah carried on pursuing the boy and the apple he craved.

The boy, still laughing, came to a corrugated metal fence with barbed wire on the top. Sliding through a gap, the boy disappeared.

"Wait, wait for me," Elijah called after the boy, gasping as he squeezed through the hole.

Turning a corner, the boy entered the burnt ruins of the paper mill. A bonfire blazed in the centre of the floor, and children of various ages huddled around it, stretching out tiny, shivering fingers. A tall older boy wearing a bowler hat, a long black overcoat and jeans rolled above his boots, poked the fire with a long stick. Apple boy joined the circle of children and Elijah stood next to him.

"Jonas, my name is Jonas. What's your name?" Jonas said, handing Elijah the apple.

"Thank you," Elijah said, taking a bite from the fruit. It was sweet and crunchy. Juices slid down his chin as he chewed. "My name is Elijah," he said, with his mouth full.

The taller boy sniffed the air. "I smell fresh blood," he said, whirling around, a sneer splitting his lips.

"That's Tallon, he's our leader," Jonas whispered in Elijah's ear.

"Come here, boy. Let Tallon sees yer'," Tallon said, beckoning with a crooked charcoal stained finger.

An Invisible hand shoved Elijah forward. Tallon approached Elijah with slow deliberate steps, his hard, red eyes scrutinising him. Tallon's lank, collar length, dirty blonde hair fluttered in the night breeze. Seizing Elijah's arm, he pulled him closer, making Elijah's lips quiver and his eyes water. A cruel smile replaced Tallon's sneer as he lifted Elijah's chin, then traced the side of his face with the back of his hand.

"You're a pretty thing, ain't yer? You'd be popular in prison," Tallon said, his tongue flicking in and out of his mouth, like a reptile tasting the air. "What's yer name, pretty boy?"

"E..Elijah N…Newton Flint," he stuttered.

"Flint, you say," Tallon said, crossing his arms and stroking his stubbly chin with his right hand.

"This changes everything. Your ol' man is the head of TWLF."

"Y…yes, yes he is."

"Well, I am so glad we have met. We work the graveyard shift, see. The sun plays 'avoc with our skin. We don't gets the same privileges as the day staff. Lower pay and shorter breaks. Yer' dear ol' dad is all about better working conditions. Do yer' fink he could help us?"

Elijah nodded frantically. "I…I'll set it up."

"Good. Now here's a little gift to show how generous I am," Tallon announced, clicking his fingers. Someone threw another red apple which he caught in his left hand without turning his head.

Tallon bent down to Elijah's level and gave him the apple. "Now run along and bring daddy here. We have a lot to discuss. Oh, and, Elijah Newton FLINT, make sure your father comes alone."

Elijah nodded again and felt his crotch moisten.

Rising to his feet, Tallon announced, "Let him through."

The children parted and Elijah ran through the gap and all the way home. When he reached his back door, he quietly turned the key in the lock and carefully shut the door. Gingerly, he walked up the stairs. He could hear his parents talking and the soft clink of a cup and saucer. Opening the door to his bedroom, he took out a fresh school uniform, clean underwear and socks. After he washed and changed, he went and knocked on the drawing room door.

"Elijah, is that you, sweetie?" His mother called.

"Yes, mum. Can I come in?"

"Of course you can, son," Lucius said.

Elijah stood in the centre of the room, took off his topper and wrung his hands on the brim.

"I...I have made some new friends, father, and they need your help."

Lucius and Hannah looked at each other.

"Slow down, son. Take it easy," Lucius said in a soothing, placating voice.

"Okay. They want to meet with you. They are new workers at the factory. Nights," he said. "Bad conditions, not many breaks, poor pay."

"Elijah, darling, come and lay on the chaise lounge," Hannah offered, taking him by the hand and leading him to the couch. Elijah lay down. Hannah went to her husband and whispered, "Take your gun. I know it's your job to help workers, but Elijah seems pretty shaken up. I think these people could be dangerous."

Lucius touched Hannah's bicep lightly. "Don't worry, I never leave home without it," he replied, walking over to the gun cabinet and taking out his clockwork laser gun. After he cranked the handle, he slotted it into his belt holster.

"His name is Tallon, Dad. He's the leader. I met Jonas first, he was just outside of the slums," Elijah said, sitting up, then lying down again.

"Thanks, son. I won't be long, Hannah. Love you."

"Love you too. And, Lucius, be careful," Hannah said, twisting her hair.

They kissed and Lucius left.

Shortly after Lucius departed, he heard a crow caw. He looked up and saw the bird hopping on a wall above him. It studied him, then cocked his head to the side.

"What are you doing out this late, little fella?" Lucius said.

The crow cawed again and looked intently at him.

"Look, perhaps I'll see you again. There are some people who need my help. Bye for now," Lucius remarked, giving the animal a quaint wave. After walking a little further, a dirty male chimney sweep approached him.

"Are you Mr. Flint, Elijah's dad?" The boy said.

"I am. And who might you be?"

"I am Jonas. Follow me. Tallon is expecting you."

"Lead the way," Lucius said, unclipping his holster.

Eventually, they came to the corrugated metal fence.

"Mr. Flint, you might have to remove the panel. I fink yer' too big for the gap."

"No problem," Lucius said, grabbing the fence panel and grunting as he lifted it aside.

Both of them stepped into the ruins of the paper mill. The bonfire lay smouldering in the centre. Shadows moved above him and he could hear sniggering children. He turned around and saw Jonas run away.

"Wait, Jonas, come back. What's that smell?" Lucius said, sniffing the air. It smelt of tar and oil, and he could hear a bubbling sound. Looking up, he caught a glimpse of a tall figure in a black overcoat lifting a vat filled with hot, bubbling liquid. As quick as a flash, Lucius drew his gun and fired, hitting the figure in the shoulder. The figure fell off the building and crashed to the floor below. Simultaneously, Lucius screamed as hot tar cascaded over his head and torso, steam rising from his sizzling body. He convulsed for several agonising seconds, then lay still.

Chapter Twelve: A Common Cause

Ten days after the massacre, Clara and James were cleared for active duty. They'd received an invitation to Dragon Mountain. During their hike up the peak, visibility was poor as they joined the mountain path. After rooting through her bag, she found two miners lamps. She gave one to James and the other she fastened to her topper and switched it on. James did the same.

They carried on walking in silence for another hour, and then James said, "So Vywrath finally wants to see us." He paused for breath as they climbed the steep mountain path.

Clara stopped on the soil trail just above James, fumbled in her rucksack, producing a water canteen.

"Cheers," he said, taking the bottle.

As he gulped from it, Clara said, "I was hoping this day wouldn't come, but I think it was inevitable."

James lowered his drink slowly and wiped sweat from his brow with the sleeve of his brown mourning coat.

"I think things have taken a very serious turn," he proffered.

Clara pinched her lips together and nodded.

"Who do you think will be there?" James said, making a frown she couldn't see. The wind dropped and it started to snow. Clara buttoned up her full length navy blue velvet overcoat, took out snow chains from her rucksack and fastened them to her boots. When she had finished, she gave a pair of chains to James. He thanked her and secured them to his boots.

"I think the vampire and werewolf councils will be there, Commissioner Harris, a member of the shifters alliance, the elven eldership, and a bunch of dwarves."

James snorted. "You make it sound like the start of a joke."

Clara spun around. "Believe you me, this no joking matter," Clara grimaced, turning around and stomping off.

Tentatively, James followed her, grabbing tree roots and gritting his teeth. He heaved himself up with a grunt. Clara's lithe figure carried on climbing and he tried to focus on the path ahead.

"So goodbye fun and romantic Clara, hello again grumpy and aloof Clara," he said to himself. After he caught up with her, he said, "I am sorry. I was enjoying our time together too. It feels like it was cut short, rather abruptly."

Clara smiled and touched his cheek with her leather glove. "I enjoyed it too. What is puzzling me the most, is your trance. I'm pretty certain Horace will be there. I don't want to manipulate you into anything, but it might be worth having a blood test."

James opened his mouth, but Clara held up her hand. "Now, bear with me. I would like Horace to test for providentia genes. That's the only way I can see how you had a trance."

He rubbed his chin. "Do you think that when we had sex, it awakened something in me?" He tilted his head to the side.

"Yes I think there's a distinct possibility that providentia DNA may be lying dormant in your blood."

"Ha-ha! This is amazing," he yelled, picking her up and spinning her around. She drummed her small fists on his shoulders playfully and giggled.

"Unhand me, you clumsy oaf," she said, and they both laughed. He put her down gently.

"I take it from your excitable behaviour you'll agree to testing?" Clara said, a slow smile building on her face.

"You betcha kiddo!"

"Kiddo? Really?" C'mon, We're almost at the top, race you."

And she set off at a brisk pace leaving James for dust. Snow dust. After they had reached the top of the stone steps, Clara rapped on the heavy oak doors, inscribed with words written in an ancient dragon language. Suddenly, there was a large creaking noise and the doors swung back on their own. A wind picked up and blew icy snow into the chamber. As instantly as they stepped inside, the doors closed behind them. Clara and James stood in a large room carved out of rock. Sconces lined the walls and a large banqueting table was in the centre. Behind the table was an enormous hearth with a blazing fire. All of the delegates that Clara mentioned were seated at the table. On either side of the hearth were spiral staircases. Vywrath and Kiada, his partner, padded down the left staircase and their son down the right . Clara and James froze in awe as the three dragons entered the room. "Welcome, welcome," Vywrath said, his rich, velvety deep voice echoing off the cavern walls. It was a voice filled with wisdom and a hint of danger. "Detective Overton and Detective Bronze, thank you for joining us. Please take seats with the other delegates. "On behalf of myself and the dragon council, I would like to take this opportunity to say that this is neutral ground. Whatever feuds you may

have, I must respectfully ask you to leave them outside of this building. Now, I will hand you over to Raqaknoff, leader of the vampire council."

There was a round of applause and then Raqaknoff stood and motioned for calm.

"The vampire council had reason to believe that the recent murder of Violet Taylor was committed by her brother, who was a genetically engineered vampire."

Some of the delegates gasped and others muttered. Vywrath stamped his foot making the chamber shake and the commotion stopped. "Councillor Raqaknoff, please continue," Vywrath said.

"Thank you, Councillor Vywrath. Horace has run extensive tests on samples taken from them and Pelham, and they have a common denominator. I'll hand you over to the werewolf council."

A tall man with wavy brown hair, yellow eyes and a brown beard, wearing a black wool coat with gold buttons, stood up.

"I am Delmor of the werewolf council."

More claps came from the other representatives.

"I can concur that a rogue pack attacked and killed Bentley Pelham. Nothing to do with my pack at all."

Commissioner Peter Harris raised his hand.

"Police Commissioner Peter Harris, please stand," Vywrath said.

"Thank you, Vywrath. I was given reliable intel that Agreeable Solutions were behind these bizarre experiments on children and young people. My source was successfully turned into a werewolf with no side effects. It turned out he had werewolf DNA from a great grandmother."

James and Clara looked at each other.

"He said that Zintius, the managing director of Agreeable Solutions, used him as a poster boy which sealed the deal with the Birkians."

Raqaknoff raised his hand.

"Thank you, Commissioner Harris. Raqaknoff, please take the floor," Vywrath said.

"Thank you Commissioner Harris, Vywrath. Zintius is a very old vampire overlord who, up until recently, was in hibernation. We were totally unaware of his return because he had blocked our telepathic link.

Aarlon, the elven leader, raised his hand.

"Aarlon, would you like to share?"

"Yes, I would, Vywrath. My elven community has developed a toxin that disrupts vampire brain waves. Theoretically, this should make Zintius visible to other vampires."

Raqaknoff turned to Aarlon. "I hope you aren't planning on using it on the vampire council," Raqaknoff remarked, giving the elf a flinty stare.

"Relax, councillor. I understand the gravity of this situation. Tarnuz is a peaceful country. We have no intention of going to war with you or anyone else."

"From what I can tell, the only person hell bent on war is this Zintius character," Begnas the dwarf said.

"Don't you see?" Niq, a red haired female shifter, dressed in oxblood leather cat suit said. "This is an old shapeshifter trick. Put an imposter in a community and convince them all to fall on their swords. Being a shifter myself, I know how they work."

"Are you saying this, Zintius, is a shifter?" Delmor said.

"Not necessarily, just employing some of our tactics. If you go to war, why not borrow from your enemies?"

"All this talk of war is making me nervous," Peter Harris said. "My job as a police officer is to keep the peace and protect the public."

"With all due respect, Commissioner Harris," Niq interjected. "Why did you allow this untested drug to be rolled out in the first place?"

Harris sighed heavily, his mouth turned down. "Patrick Spencer threatened to replace me if I didn't comply."

The VIPs chattered amongst themselves. Vywrath held up his front paw again and everyone stopped talking.

"Carry on, commissioner," Vywrath said.

"I felt that if I objected, he would remove me and put one of his puppets in my place. I think that the security of Tarnuz would be at stake, and I didn't want to take that risk."

"Yeah" the audience said in unison and clapped for the Commissioner.

"Patrick Spencer can be a stubborn and difficult man. I think you acted on behalf of the whole country, Commissioner, and I applaud you for it. Peace is the answer, not war. That's why I have called you all here today," Vywrath said, pacing up and down.

"It is our job to keep the peace," Kiada said. Her voice had an authoritative, yet gentle quality to it. "That's why our door is always open. We are not just relationship counsellors you know!" Everyone laughed. Kiada bowed her head. "Unfortunately, the dragon council has fallen foul to Agreeable Solution's diabolical plan. Targem, our son, was rendered unconscious a few weeks ago. When he awoke, he had a puncture wound on his neck."

The guests murmured and gasped. Some covered their open mouths with their hands.

"If they can get to the dragons, then no one is safe," Begnas said, looking at the nodding and muttering crowd.

Kiada cleared her throat. "We haven't detected any foreign dragon activity and Tergem has made a full recovery. If we are faced with adversity, we will retaliate."

"We need to take the fight to them. I am interested to know how we would administer this toxin that Aarlon mentioned," Clara said.

"That would be simple. All elves are a crack shot with the bow. We coat our arrows with it and lure him to the blossom forest."

"You'd have to give him a reason to come," Begnas said. "If there's food and beer, I am there!"

The room erupted with laughter.

"I have an idea. We have The Festival of Life in two weeks' time. Normally, the elves celebrate it on their own, but everyone is welcome."

"What does this festival involve? I am sure there's a bit more to it than beer and food," Niq said, looking blankly at Begnas.

Aarlon continued. "It's a celebration of life in all of its diversity. Traditionally, it is something for children to enjoy. Kids visit different stalls and adults dressed as dwarves, shifters, dragons etc. tell stories about the creature they are portraying. This year, we could mix it up a bit and have the actual different races and creatures there."

"And hope that Zintius bites," James said, with a smirk on his face.

Everyone groaned, some shook their heads, and others rolled their eyes.

"This sounds like a lot of fun, but incredibly risky," Niq proffered, shuffling in her seat.

"It'll be fine. I'll have undercover police officers all over the place," Peter Harris said.

Human servers came and stood behind the guests.

"We have been talking for quite some time," Targem, Vywrath's son said.

"You must all be very hungry. If you would all like to find comfortable chairs around the chamber, the servers will put out plates of food and drink. Feel free to mingle whilst the table is prepared."

Everyone stood and found alternative seating or stood around chatting. Servers approached guests offering red, white, or sparkling wine, beer, and spirits. James and Clara choose red wine, then they searched for Horace amongst the crowd, but Adamar had found them first.

"So great to see you again, detectives. I sincerely hope you have put aside your grievances," Horace said, raising his eyebrows.

"You could say that," James said, holding out his hand. Clara took it, rested her hand on his shoulder, lifted her leg behind her and kissed James on the cheek. Then she looked bashfully at Horace and Adamar.

Horace and Adamar grinned at each other.

"I am very pleased for you both," Adamar said, shaking their hands.

"Ah, this is absolutely splendid news," Horace stated, clapping his hands together.

Clara bent down to Horace's level. "Listen, James and I have discovered something. Can we talk to you in private? And make sure you have your medical bag with you."

Horace's eyes widened. "Sure, whatever you need, Clara. If we take one of the staircases, there are plenty of rooms on the upper floor."

"Okay, Horace, you lead the way," Clara said.

Horace nodded and they followed him. When they reached the top of the stairs, they walked on white marble floors decorated with red dragon murals. On the left wall was a large bank of windows and on the right were countless luxurious bedrooms. Electric chandeliers illuminated the hallway. After peering into two occupied bedrooms, they found the third empty. All of them filed in and locked the door.

The room had a super king size four poster bed with red velvet drapes with gold trim, a large walnut wardrobe, an ornate white vanity unit with gold adornments and red velvet high backed chairs. Red velvet curtains hung next to the windows.

"So, what was it you wanted to talk to me about?" Horace said, resting his medical bag on one of the chairs.

Clara chewed her lip. "James and I made love, and on the following day, we kissed and both had a trance."

Horace tapped his lips with his finger. "This is remarkable, truly remarkable."

"Yes, whilst trances are commonplace for me, as far as we know, James has never had one."

"We were wondering if I was like the boy Commissioner Harris mentioned. That I had a providentia stream in my DNA, some kind of genetic throwback, as it were."

Adamar stroked his beard. "And you want Horace and myself to run some tests to find out?"

"Yes, if you could, that would be frightfully useful," Clara exclaimed.

"Fascinating, utterly fascinating. Okay, so, James, could you roll up your sleeve please?" Horace said, snapping open his brown medical bag from which he retrieved a syringe.

After taking blood samples from James, he placed the vials into his bag.

"We'll have the results for you in two days. We'd better get back to the meeting, as they'll be wondering where we are. Oh, one more thing I need to mention. Did you hear about TWLF leader Lucius Flint?"

"We were still on compassionate leave, but I remember reading about it in the paper. That guttersnipe, Antony Wright, covered the story. Flint was boiled alive in tar. Tragic, very tragic," James said, putting his hand on his forehead and staring at the marble floor.

"Yes, very sad. I have a smoking gun for you. The body they found wasn't Flint's. I examined it, and I was told to look the other way," Horace revealed, sighing deeply.

The two detectives stared at each other with slack jaws.

"So, who's body is it?" James said. "Or, more importantly, where is Flint's body, or is he still alive?"

Horace held up his hands, palms up. "You're the detectives, you figure it out."

"Don't worry, we will," Clara said, poking her tongue out.

Horace chuckled. "One last thing before we re-join the others. Whilst you were both on compassionate leave, reports were coming in about Agreeable Solutions vaccine carriages going missing," Horace conveyed, holding up a tiny metal box. "This is a tracking device that is rigged up to your goggles. Prime the device like so." Horace pushed a button. The gadget beeped and a red LED lit up. "Press the button on top of your goggles to sync with the device. Plant the appliance on a carriage and you should be able to track it on the display in your goggles."

"Thanks Horace," Clara said.

"Why are these carriages going missing?" James said, furrowing his brow.

"That's what we need to find out, but these vehicles carry drugs and medicines. That type of thing would fetch a fortune on the black market," Adamar said.

"Right, I really do think we should get back to the meeting now. Besides, none of us have eaten yet," Horace said.

When they re-joined the meeting, the delegates were discussing The Festival of Life. Clara, James, Horace and Adamar filled their plates and listened intently whilst they ate.

"We need to ask someone if they would like to be the bait for Zintius. It pains me to say that, but we need to have something to lure him with," Aarlon said.

"Well, anyone could be a target apart from the vampires and the werewolves. They have already attacked and killed people, so we can assume they already have test subjects for those species," Dimitri said, speaking for the first time. "I also think it is safe to say, Zintius is the vampire test subject. None of the vampire council could detect him, suggesting the telepathic link was severed."

Representatives murmured and whispered to each other.

"Any one of us could be an attractive proposition to Agreeable Solutions. We are all blessed with unique powers, abilities and magic," Niq said, gesturing around the chamber.

Clara swallowed her food and pushed her plate away. "Vampires can't read my mind or detect me. If they had providentia DNA, their vampires wouldn't be the only species that go unnoticed, it could be anyone."

"It would also mean they could move around during the day," Delmor said.

"It's settled then. I'll do it. I'll be your tethered goat," Clara said.

Chapter Thirteen: Upcycled

Lucius Flint groaned and rolled his head to his left and tried to open his eyes. His left eye opened fine and he saw a bright light overhead and the outline of a figure swam into view. Blinking hard, he tried to open his right eye, but nothing happened. Blackness.

"Have I lost my right eye?" he yelled, thrashing around on his bed, feeling the leather straps tighten around his wrists as he did so.

"I can't feel my legs. Where the fuck are my legs?"

As his good eye focused, he could make out the kind face and smile of a young woman with long brown hair. She was wearing a lab coat, a blue shirt and a stethoscope hung around her neck.

"I am Doctor Albi Lurcock. But you can call me Albi if you want. You had a very nasty accident, Mr. Flint. You have indeed lost your right eye and both your legs have been amputated."

"Look, the only person I want to call is my wife to let her know I'm alright. And my boy, Elijah, I want him to know that daddy loves him," he whimpered numbly, his lip quivering and his eye filling with tears.

Albi smiled and stroked his hair away from his forehead. "Shush, all in good time, Lucius."

And then Flint saw her produce a syringe and felt a slight prick in his forearm. His eyelid grew heavy. Blackness.

***

"He's coming round," Flint heard Albi say.

Flint blinked. Both eyes seemed to work. His breathing sounded different like his face was covered with a diving helmet. Blinking again, his eyelids made a clicking sound.

"What's going on, and what have you done to me?" Flint said.

He tried to move, and as he walked, he heard the sound of pneumatic pistons, ticking and metal thumping the floor. He turned his head, which made a whirring sound and caught a glimpse of himself in the mirror. Instead of seeing his human reflection, he saw a round bodied mechanical man made of copper and he screamed. Blackness.

I am Tocker, or am I A Tocker?

I am sure I was someone else. TWLF? That used to mean something.

A boy and a beautiful blonde lady. They used to mean something. But what?

He continued to scrutinise himself in the mirror. A round bodied clockwork man, made of copper, with blue glass eyes, and a moustache. He wore a helmet on his head. The helmet had a shallow circular crown with a wide brim around the edge. On his breast there was a name plate "Flint" He didn't know if he was a construction worker or a soldier.

"How are you feeling today, Flint?"

"I am feeling well and ready to serve, Doctor Lurcock," Flint said, his metallic voice surprising him.

"Very good. You will be working on the reconstruction of the paper mill. It is unsafe for human workers, so you and the other Tockers will carry out the repairs. Here is the instruction card."

He heard a clicking sound, then he saw flashing images, his moustache twitching rapidly as he processed the images. Scenes of bricklaying, carpentry and other construction work scrolled past. When the images stopped, he heard the sound of his clockwork keys being wound. He walked over to the building site, pulled the cord on the cement mixer, and its petrol engine sputtered into life.

Grabbing a shovel, he mixed cement and sand mix and added the water. When the mixture was ready, he laid a wall in five minutes, even though he had never laid a single brick before.

Jedidiah Lewis stood next to Doctor Lurcock smoking a cigar, watching Flint and the other Tockers work and he smiled broadly.

"I think you have just solved my employment problems. These machines are indefatigable, and I doubt they will complain about pay or working conditions either."

Lurcock raised her eyebrows. "They aren't without their flaws. They need to be wound up every 30 minutes or so. Maybe you could employ some of the men that used to work at the paper mill to wind them?"

Jedidiah puffed on his cigar a little longer then he said, "That's a splendid idea, Doctor Lurcock. Then everyone's happy."

Lurcock pressed her lips together and avoided his gaze, "I am sure they will be ecstatic about having a job, Jedidiah."

Chapter Fourteen: A Very Suspect Circus

James and Clara travelled in silence as the carriage rolled through puddles on the rain drenched cobbled streets. Staring out of the window, James sighed deeply again. Clara looked in her lipstick mirror and applied plum gold lipstick. She pouted, then snapped shut the mirror, putting it in her handbag.

"I think I should wave a red flag at you, Bronze, because you sound like a huffing bull."

"Can you blame me, Clara, when my girlfriend paints a fucking bullseye on her back," he retorted, his nostrils flaring and his eyes blazing.

"Settle down, man. That festival is an all you can eat buffet for a greedy fiend like Zintius."

"Yes, and you're the fucking main course."

"You don't know that."

"If I was him, you'd be right at the top of my hit list."

"Don't be so dramatic, James."

James gritted his teeth. "You are the best thing that has happened to me, and I don't want to lose you."

Clara smiled bashfully and twirled a strand of her brown hair around her finger. "Do you really mean that?"

"Yes. I don't hate you anymore. I probably never did. I tried to convince myself that you would never love me, so I thought if you hated me it would be easier to handle."

Clara leaned forward and kissed him once on the lips.

"That has to be the most ridiculous thing I have ever heard. Love is stronger than hate, at least it should be."

"I didn't want our relationship to get in the way of the job, so I tried to push you away."

"I understand that. It makes perfect sense, James, but we're still doing the job. People meet through work all of the time. I think you need to have more faith in us as professionals."

James pondered this and tapped his lips with his finger. "I guess you have a point. But I am going to do my best to protect you at the festival."

"I am counting on it," Clara said, leaning forward and kissing him again.

At that moment, the carriage stopped.

"I think it's time to focus on the job," James remarked, opening the coach door and getting out.

James paid the driver and thanked him. The driver saluted him and pulled away.

Clara's boots squelched on the soggy grass as she stepped onto the circus site. Coloured caravans were dotted everywhere, each one displaying the name of the artist who lived there. There was Gusto the Great, Fire Eating Fred, Strongman Stan and many others that Clara tired of reading.

Ten out of ten for originality. But there always has to be a degree of cheesiness, it's what people expect from a circus.

A trumpeting sound made Clara turn her head. A zebra with an elephant's head was pulling at the bars of its cage with its trunk, making the caravan roll from side to side. "Elebra" was emblazoned in vivid letters above the bars. Another larger sounding elebra trumpeted and also grabbed the bars and shook them. A calf joined its parents in the commotion. Clara looked away, pressing a palm to her lips to hold back a cry, then she held up her hand and she started to pull at the fingers on her glove.

Before she could take off the glove, James grabbed her wrist and shook his head. "Today we are cops, not animal rights campaigners," he whispered in her ear. He's right. Focus Clara. I can't read animals anyway.

With moist eyes, she looked up at him, nodding.

As they moved further along the line of cages, Clara saw a tree where a monkey peered out from behind a branch, then another simian face appeared, identical to the first. But then the creature moved and she realised both heads were attached to the same body. The animal screamed and leapt from branch to branch. Chewing her lip, Clara moved on. Just before they reached the next enclosure, they could hear crunching sounds. When she reached the pen, Clara saw an elf spider sitting in the middle of a labyrinth of webs, chewing on a fox's head. For a moment, it carried on eating before stopping and hissing at her, blood dripping from its fangs. Nausea made her gag, her hand flying to cover her mouth. Grabbing her arm, James led her away from the cages. Her breathing was raspy and her eyes bulged.

"Breathe, Clara, breathe," James said.

"Those things..." she croaked. "...are the most evil things I have seen."

James walked over to a tree stump and eased her onto it, stroking the back of her hair.

She lay her head on his shoulder.

"Just take a moment, then we'll go and find the ringmaster."

Clara nodded. After a few minutes, the colour returned to her face and she took out her lipstick and applied some, then added blusher to her cheeks.

I need to focus. I am a detective at the moment, not her lover. James thought.

"Okay, I am ready," Clara said, standing up.

Setting his jaw, James strode over to the elf spider and flipped the bird at the monster. Angrily, the arachnid flung itself at the bars, drool dripping from its gaping maw. A red faced Clara tried to hold back the laugh welling up inside her, but let it go and flipped the bird on both her hands, walking back and forth in front of the cage. Eventually, they stepped away from the tormented fiend and looked at the circus tent.

Slogging through the thick mud, they made their way to the big top. As they entered, they saw a circular floor in the centre and espied the ringleader. He wore a black top hat that had a red and white striped band around the rim. A curled flame stuck out of the side of the hat instead of a feather. He had a curly black moustache, wore a red tail coat, with silver clasps, a waistcoat with red and white vertical lines on it, red trousers and thigh high black patent leather boots. He sneered at them as they approached.

I bet he spends more time glaring than smiling. Clara thought.

Far above them, a female centaur walked on the tightrope with a balancing pole.

Dim lighting shone on the tiered seating. Trainers worked with Elebras, horses and three eyed tropical birds with exotic plumage. A dwarf bounced on a trampoline and completing a pyramid of dwarves, standing proudly with his hands on his hips.

A clown fired a human cannonball through a hoop, who landed in a safety net, waving at an invisible crowd.

"I am Detective Bronze and this is Detective Overton."

"Cephas Augustus Sterling, ringmaster here. Badges, please?" Cephas said, narrowing his eyes.

Both detectives opened their overcoats showing their badges clipped to their belts.

"What brings you here today?" Cephas lowered his head and stared at Bronze.

"We are investigating a series of brutal murders. We have reason to believe they were carried out by a werewolf pack," Clara said.

Cephas flashed Clara a fake smile. "When something unusual or violent happens, let's blame it on the travelling freak show." he hollered, then threw his arms up and turned to face centre stage.

"Do you have something to hide, Mr. Sterling?" James quizzed, raising his eyebrows and focusing on the ringmaster.

Clara shot James a sharp stare and flipped open her steno pad. "I can assure you, Mr. Sterling, my colleague wasn't casting any aspersions about you. We are just carrying out routine interviews. Do you have any new acts that have joined you within the last two weeks?"

Cephas smirked. "What you really want to ask is if I've employed werewolves recently? As a matter of fact, I have. They're a huge success with the public."

"What's different about your werewolves? They move around society as freely as you and I do," pressed James.

Cephas bared his teeth. "They have a heightened sense of smell, five times more than your average werewolf. They are stronger, faster, better."

"Talk me through their act," Clara said, looking up from her notepad.

"All of their enhanced senses are put to the test. Finding a flower in the pocket of an audience member when there are over a 1000 pockets to choose from. Things like that."

"When you say a member of the audience, do you really mean a circus worker posing as one?" James said, putting his hands in his pockets.

Cephas rolled his eyes. "You're quite the charmer, aren't you? How do you ever put up with him?" He said, tutting and staring at Clara. "All of the guests are asked at the ticket booth if they would like to carry a flower in their pocket. Once someone has agreed, they are given a flower and asked to keep it safe in their pocket."

"I am sorry, Mr. Sterling. I know that people are often conned into stunts like this." James said.

"You don't have to apologise for your disdain, Detective Bronze. It's written all over your face." Sterling said, looking him up and down.

Clara cleared her throat. "Would you mind If we interviewed the artists."

"I can go one better than that," Cephas said, pulling a buff coloured cloth off a mirror with casters on the bottom. "This is the truth mirror. Once you gaze at your reflection, it reveals your inner soul, proving to the world that beauty really is skin deep."

"Can you call your werewolves here using your goggles?" Clara asked.

Cephas gave her a curt nod. "Kirnon, could you come to the big top please? Okay see you soon."

A few minutes passed until they were joined by a lithe youth with mousy hair, about Clara's height and build, who was no more than 16.

"What's this all about, Cephas?" Kirnon said, his voice low and guttural.

Sterling turned the mirror towards Kirnon, who stared intently at his reflection. The image rippled like water and then revealed a wolf ripping out the throat of Bentley Pelham.

Turning on his heel, Kirnon fled out of the big top and into the woods. Clara drew her gun and gave chase, leaving James behind.

Dusk had settled, bringing an edgy cloak of darkness in with it. Kirnon had disappeared from view, but Clara could hear the sound of cracking bone, stretching skin and a man groaning as she entered a clearing. Abruptly, the sound ceased. A low growl could then be heard from behind the foliage. Clara saw two yellow eyes followed by a muzzle of a large, powerful wolf, teeth bared and dripping with saliva. Clara knew she had to focus on his mouth, so she distracted him with her hands by raising and waving them above her head. However, he attempted to grab and snatch her leg, but Clara used his momentum to strike a blow on the back of his head. Then she grabbed the scraggy hair above his neck and yanked it back to deftly manoeuvre herself onto the creature's back, forcing him to the ground. The werewolf shook its head from side to side in an energetic frenzy, attempting to snap at her hands. She resisted the fierce struggle, clenching her arms tighter around her adversary's head. Then, she opened her mouth wide and clamped her teeth into his neck. As the werewolf howled in pain, Clara rolled off his back and fired a silver bullet in his side. A tremor rippled through his body and he resumed his human form. Shortly after this, James arrived and they cuffed him.

***

Clara opened the door of the police interrogation room with two coffees. Kirnon was cuffed to a metal pipe fixed to the desk, James sat opposite him. Clara sat next to James and handed him his drink.

"Please state your name for the record," James said, staring at Kirnon's file.

"Kirnon O'Hare."

"Occupation?"

"Sheet metal worker."

"Thank you, have you worked there long?"

"About two weeks."

"Very new employment for you. Weren't you entitled to work there before?" Clara said.

"You should know about being entitled, you stuck up bitch," a red faced Kirnon said, straining at his manacles.

"Careful what you say, pal, as you're already looking at a 25 year bid for murder. You don't want to add insulting a police officer to your rap sheet as well," James said, raising his chin and looking down at Kirnon.

"Fuck you, pig!" Kirnon said, spitting in James's face. Whilst James wiped the spit out of his eyes with his handkerchief, Clara lent across the table and touched Kirnon's shirt sleeve with her bare hand. After the trance took effect, she saw a smiling Kirnon receiving the typhoid jab, then him turning into a wolf for the first time and weeping on his bed in human form. An electric shock shot up her arm and she let go.

"Cut the crap, O'Hare," Clara shouted, closing the file. "Outside, you're a tough, impenetrable, juvenile delinquent. But in reality, you wept like a girl when you metamorphosed into a wolf for the first time. I bet you even pissed your pants."

Kirnon's mouth fell open, his top lip curling back. "You touched me. What are you? Some kind of fucking mage, or somefink?"

"Look, mate, if you give us something, we might be able to cut a deal," James offered, sighing heavily.

"When did you first start noticing the changes?" Clara said.

Kirnon rubbed his chin. "About three days after I had the injection."

"And you didn't experience any other side effects before you received the vaccine? No headaches, heart palpitations, sweating?"

"No, lady, I didn't have any of those things. They only started happening after the jab. Look, I didn't want to kill that man, but I had an uncontrollable rage. I wasn't myself. I didn't ask to become a fucking werewolf, you have to believe me."

Clara took a sheet of paper from the back of the file and her pen from her overcoat jacket pocket and slid them across the table. "We know you weren't a lone operative, there were different sized bite marks on the victims. Write down the names of the people you're working with and I promise we will help you."

"You really mean that?" Kirnon said, his voice trembling.

"Yes, we do. We know of a charity that helps rehabilitate people with special needs and abilities. They will work alongside you and help you adjust to society."

"Lady, you just said it is a charity. What if it runs out of fucking dough? I'll be back on the scrap heap."

Clara snorted. "Hardly. I created it. If it fails, that's because of my own ineptitude. All you have to do is give us the names of those you're working with." Clara said, sliding the paper and pen closer to Kirnon.

Grabbing the pen, Kirnon scribbled ferociously.

***

A thick morning fog had descended like a grey blanket and the air was filled with the sound of factory whistles, fog horns from boats and the rumble of wagons entering the marketplace. Traders unloaded their wares and began arranging their stock for another busy day of selling and bartering.

Clara and James observed the scenes through the carriage window. Every now and again, James' leather gloves creaked as he squeezed his hands on the window frame.

I am pretty certain he wore those yesterday.

"Are you having trances, James?"

James looked at her and held his hands in front of his face, inspecting his gloves.

"Yes they come and go." Clara leaned forward and grabbed his hands, scrutinising the gloves.

"These look like Fit Sew Good gloves. Did Eme make these for you?" Clara asked, frowning.

James nodded. "I felt so confused and frightened when the trances started, and I couldn't stop them, so I asked her to make me a set of gloves. I figured that seeing as you and Eme wore them, that must be the only way to deal with it." He rubbed his hand over his forehead.

"There are other ways, like the night we first…" Clara whistled instead of saying the words.

James snorted.

"But that is not a long term solution," she said, finishing her sentence.

James cleared his throat and pulled at the collar of his shirt. "Are there any long term side effects? Does it affect your mental health for example?"

Clara sighed and wrung her hands in her lap. "I am afraid it can, especially if alcohol is involved."

"What do you mean? Does your ability make your alcohol tolerance level less effective?"

Clara shook her head. "No. When you are drinking, you are more carefree. You may go to the toilet and forget to put your gloves back on. Just a short trip from the toilet to the bar could be an information overload."

James nodded, tapping his finger against his lips, narrowing his eyes. "Have you ever had a psychotic break after a trance?"

Clara puffed out her cheeks. "When I was a child I used to have them. My father spotted it and guided me through the process. I could do the same for you." She took his hands in hers and stroked one of them with her thumb.

"I don't have trances all the time. It might be a fleeting glimpse into a world I don't understand, for all I know."

Clara looked to her right, touching her chin. "It sounds like Horace's call came at the right time. You have a lot of questions to ask."

"I think I do."

"Well, you can ask Horace whatever you want. It looks like we're here," Clara said as the carriage stopped.

Clara and James stepped onto the pavement. Clara paid the driver and with a crack of his whip, he was gone.

Clara rapped on the door, her grey wool overcoat rustling as she did so. Horace answered the door and flashed them a huge smile, rubbing his hands together gleefully. He was wearing the same clothes as last time and Clara wondered if he had a wardrobe filled with identical clothing, so he didn't have to think about what to wear.

"Ah, Clara, James, come in, come in," Horace said, sweeping his hands behind him. "You are just in time to see Adamar's demonstration. When you're ready Adamar."

Adamar walked to the back of the workshop, planted his feet and made a halt gesture. A shimmering force field appeared in front of him. Horace picked up a tankard and threw it at the barrier. It ricocheted off and crashed into the opposite wall. Aiming his clockwork laser pistol, he fired at the magical shield and it absorbed the energy. Horace lowered his gun and Adamar fell on all fours, gasping.

"Well done, well done, Adamar. It won't be long before you can hold off an entire army. The elixir is clearly working."

Clara felt a slow smile build on her lips. "I think I recall Adamar taking an elixir on a previous visit."

Horace nodded. "Indeed. You were present when he took a dose. Now, the moment you have both been waiting for… the results show," Horace giggled, doing a little dance.

Clara and James shook their heads, rolled their eyes and smiled at the eccentric little man.

"Your suspicions were confirmed, Clara. James has the providentia genetic marker."

James went pale and sat down on a chair, took off his topper and ran his fingers through his hair.

Horace massaged James's shoulder and said softly, "Your marker is not as strong as Clara's but could easily be enhanced with an elixir. Judging by your reaction, Detective Bronze, that might not be what you want."

James crossed his legs at the ankles and blinked rapidly, his hands in his lap. "It's just a lot to take in. I have been struggling with a lot of emotions lately. My job, my growing love for Clara and now this."

Clara touched her chest, her eyes welling up. "You love me?"

James turned his head and looked at her. "Yes, I can't deny it any more. I know that couples may realign their hobbies to match the others interests, but this is the next level. It's a lot to take in."

"If a unique ability, power or talent is lying dormant, it needs to be awakened and nurtured. That's why I agreed to let Horace test his potions on me," Adamar said, smiling at his friend and mentor.

Horace smiled back and nodded back at his friend. "I can make you an elixir if you want me to, Detective Bronze, but it would take a few days."

"This is a big step. I need to think about it. Can I let you know in a few days?"

"Of course, Detective Bronze."

"James, please call me James."

"Right you are, James from now on."

"Can we talk about something else, please?"

"Oh, yes, of course," Horace said, tapping on a typewriter with a green screen attached to it. "I have uploaded the coordinates of the Agreeable Solutions vaccine centre to your goggles. Commissioner Harris messaged me asking you to plant tracking devices on their vehicles. Agreeable Solutions has agreed to have the gadgets fitted to their carriages."

"Yes, he mentioned it before we came over. I also told him I didn't want a reassignment or a new partner," James said, smiling at

Clara. Clara looked up at him and smiled back.

"Agreeable Solutions are very concerned that their medicines could fall into the wrong hands."

"We have an eye witness in custody that is prepared to testify that an Agreeable Solutions vaccine transformed him and his colleagues into werewolves," Clara revealed.

Horace sighed. "When you carry out a routine inspection of the carriages, get me some vials of the vaccine. We need to start joining the dots."

***

A foggy day turned into a foggy night as Clara and James sat in a steam carriage staring through their goggles.

"I can't help feeling a bit daft sitting in this contraption waiting for something to happen," Clara said, drumming her fingers on her seat.

"I think it was kind of Horace to lend us his prototype. If something goes down, we'll be there in half the time."

Clara watched the red blips on her goggles that represented the A.S. carriages thread their way through the remaining slums. "I suppose there is that. I have been thinking. William, at The Arch Tavern said something about looking into the metal foundry. People were going in and not coming out."

"That's not true, though, is it? We have a suspect at the station who was working at the metal foundry and he's very much alive."

"No, this is something different. Did you see the photos of Jedidiah Lewis and Dr. Albi Lurcock posing with a mechanical man in the papers?"

"Yes, I did. Do you think these things are connected, Clara?" asked James.

Clara stared into the distance. "I don't know, but my providentia senses are tingling."

"There's an easy way to find out. Those mechanical men, Tockers, are rebuilding the paper mill. We could go down there and you could grope a few robots so we'd have a better idea on what's going on down there," James said, smirking.

"I don't go around groping people and especially not machines. Just because I am providentia, it doesn't make me a sexual deviant," Clara said, huffing and folding her arms.

"I was hoping you were at least kinky." Clara bunched her lips and slapped his cheek.

"Aw! What did you do that for?"

"I am not some common strumpet that you can pick up from a street corner, James. Enjoy spanking your monkey tonight."

James hung his head, and rubbed his stinging face. "Wait, I think one of the carriages is heading off course."

Clara focused on her screen. One of the red blips had taken a detour, heading towards the forest. Before Clara could say anything, James switched to normal vision and set the biting pointing on the accelerator, shifted into first gear and the contraption moved off towards the forest. Whilst James was driving, Clara turned on the headlights. The carriage rattled along the bridge next to The Arch Tavern and James accelerated. Eventually they reached the forest and saw the carriage in front of them.

***

Raymond Forger steered the Agreeable Solutions carriage around the fallen oak tree blocking the road, taking the vehicle deeper into the dark woods.

"That was a serious bump. I'm going to ask Raymond about it," Arnold said.

"Okay," Dorothy said.

Arnold pushed down the window and called out to Raymond. "Raymond, that was quite the bump back there, old chap. What on Remina is going on?"

"Sorry, Guv. Bloody tree blocking the road, I had to make a detour."

"Okay, no problem my man. Crack on."

Arnold slid up the window again and sat down.

"A large tree was blocking the road, so Raymond is taking a detour in the woods." Arnold said.

"Oh, okay I hope it won't take too long," Dorothy said.

"I hope so too. I am looking forward to having that drink with you."

"Well, what can I say? You ground me down!"

Arnold smiled. "You won't regret it, I promise."

"I hope you're right, I was planning on washing my hair."

"Oh, Dorothy, you are such a tease."

"Whose teasing? I am being serious."

"Come here," Arnold said.

Giggling, Dorothy slid over and sat on Arnold's lap, then they kissed.

Outside, Raymond was negotiating the tree roots and uneven ground. Suddenly, the horse became agitated, shaking its head and neighing loudly.

"Wot's got into you, you daft old mare?"

Before Raymond had time to react, he was torn in two, his legs still sitting on the box seat.

"What the devil is going on?" Arnold said, pushing down the glass pane and sticking his head out of the opening. Strong, but small arms pulled him from the coach. Arnold felt sharp teeth sink into his neck, followed by sucking sounds. Something was fastened around his wrists and ankles, pinning him to a tree. His body convulsed as he struggled to free himself. Twisting his neck to look at his assailant, his eyes filled with terror as recognised the blonde girl from the slum. The girl's face was as pale as porcelain. Her red eyes were hard and menacing, brimming with death. But someone else had tied him down, he felt the weight of another small person moving about his body. With a hiss, the girl's brother jumped on his chest. The boy showed his fangs, sunk them into Arnold's neck and began to feed. A strange euphoria came over Arnold and he thought about people who suffocated themselves for sexual kicks. Abruptly, the boy stopped sucking, grabbed Arnold's head and ripped it off, making a slurping sound as it did so. Arnold's eyes rolled upwards, his mouth contorted in a silent scream. After this, the boy looked at the head and threw it through the window of the carriage below, forcing a high-pitched scream from Dorothy. Warm urine trickled down her leg and puddled on the floor. Before she had time to defend herself, there was thud on the roof, followed by another. Nothing happened for a beat, then the wooden roof began to splinter. Dorothy saw a flash of the inky black sky then she saw two small smiling vampires, teeth bared, appear in the gap. After they hissed at Dorothy, they jumped on her shoulders and fed again. Dorothy let out a blood-curdling scream.

The engine of the steam carriage coughed and died.

Clara heard the scream. "Did you hear that?"

"Yeah the engine died. I'll go and take a look," James said.

"You do that. I'll go after the carriage."

"Okay, I'll catch up with you in a bit."

When she arrived at the carriage, it was rocking left and right and she could hear the sound of a struggle, followed by muttering. Taking a silver bomb from her utility belt, she primed the device and lobbed it at the carriage. The bomb exploded, with a loud crash, showering the obliterated vehicle with silver dust, which was followed by a banshee-like scream.

"Arrgh," Clara cried, falling to her knees on the damp forest floor and clamping her hands to her ears.

And then there was silence.

Slightly dazed, Clara tried to push herself up. She heard the sound of someone rushing at her. Clara's instincts kicked in and she drew her gun as the creature leapt at her, and a well-timed bullet between the eyes brought it slamming to the ground. But before Clara could take in what had happened, another beast lunged at her, knocking her and her gun to the ground. A small, male vampire pinned her to the ground. His tongue darted out of his mouth and licked her entire face, then he tried to plunge his fangs into her jugular. Wriggling from side to side, Clara freed her right arm and punched her assailant in the cheek, who recoiled. Without thinking, Clara drew a silver throwing knife from her belt and threw it at her attacker's heart. A supernatural scream erupted from his lips as he tried to pull the knife from his chest. With a face full of fear, the monster fell forward and was still. Clara rolled him over, retrieved her knife and wiped it with her handkerchief. Slowly, his face started to change from a hideous blood sucker to a small boy. Clara walked over to the other corpse and saw a small, dead girl. Both children looked alike and she knew she had seen them before. They were the children from the slum the day Agreeable Solutions was giving vaccinations. Clara fell to her knees, raised her hands above her head and screamed, "NOOOOO!"

Hearing Clara's scream, James sprinted over. He held Clara as she wept. James slipped on his goggles and called for backup.

***

Edwin and James made their way down a dark alleyway and some steep steps and Edwin knocked on a door at the bottom. A panel in the door slid open revealing a pair of grey eyes.

"Yes, what do ya want?" a gruff voice said.

"We're here for Madam Chavali's special brew," Edwin said.

The panel shut, bolts were slid across and the door opened.

"Thank you," Edwin said, pushing three sovereigns into the doorkeeper's hand.

After they had walked down three more steps and through an archway, they found themselves in a dimly lit red room. People sat on large rugs or tasselled cushions. A man was smoking a shisha pipe and passed it to another man on his left. Three men played hypnotic, soothing music from their unusual looking instruments. A large red pendant light hung from the ceiling, the source of the dim red glow.

At the back of the room, a black haired, slim, middle aged, dark skinned woman with a maang tikka in her hair, smiled and beckoned them over. She gestured to two cushions in front of her and the two men sat.

"I would like to become a providentia," Edwin said. "I believe you have an elixir that can make that happen."

James fidgeted.

"And what about you, young man? You seem nervous. Madam Chavali has whatever you need," the lady said, smoothly. James didn't know if she was going to slit his throat or sleep with him.

"I would like to be a providentia too," James said, swallowing hard.

"Are you good for it?" Chavali said, holding out her hand.

Edwin reached into his pocket and placed ten sovereigns in her open palm.

Madam Chavali fumbled in her purple robes and pulled out a golden snuff box and gave it to Edwin. Promptly Edwin opened the box and saw two white pills. He thanked the lady, she nodded and they both left.

Opening the door of his shop and then locking it behind him, Edwin cranked his clockwork torch and shone it on the snuff box. James opened the lid and took the first pill. Edwin gave James the torch and took the second pill.

"Now we wait," Edwin said.

"How long do they normally take to work?"

"About ten minutes, give or take. Do you have your gloves handy?"

"Yes, I do."

"Good. place them on the counter. If the trance is too intense, you can just slip them on."

James did as he was told and Edwin placed his gloves next to James's.

Edwin walked around the bookshop and selected two romance books and gave one to James.

"Now, I know for a fact that there is nothing sinister in these books. Both authors were easy going and would regularly meet up. Lots of laughter, eating and drinking, that sort of thing."

"You're sure about this. They aren't going to turn on each other are they?"

"No, not at all. Open the book and see for yourself."

James nodded and started reading. After his eyes flickered, he was in a trance.

Sun shone on a glistening lake and a rowing boat lulled gently on the water. A man's hands were rowing the oars and he saw a pretty young lady twirling a lace parasol. She sat sideways, glancing at the swans swimming next to her.

I am literally watching what the author has written in colour. There are good things about being a providentia after all. I think I should probably say 'yes' to Horace.

After an hour or two, the pills wore off and they sat at a candle lit table at the back of Edwin's shop drinking rum.

"How did your trance go, James?"

"A lot better than I thought. And yours?"

"Very pleasant indeed. It gets complicated when you take it and you make love to an actual providentia."

"Do you both experience each other's pain and suffering?"

"Yes, as well as all the pleasure and the excitement. It's a real mind fuck," Edwin said, taking another swig of his drink.

"I bet it is. So what do you do when you and Eme have sex?"

"Same thing Clara did, probably. Take a providentia inhibitor."

"Are there any lasting side effects?"

"I don't know. Eme and I haven't been seeing each other for very long. I suppose if it was used for long periods of time, a providentia would be just a normal person, whatever that is."

"So, is the plan to take the inhibitor until you really know that person and then stop using it?"

"I have never really thought about it, but I guess that would be the case, yes."

"And what would you do if you were trying for a baby?" James said, frowning.

Edwin's mouth fell open and his eyes widened. "Are you and Clara trying for a baby?"

James screwed his face up. "Nah, we have only just started dating. It was a rhetorical question."

Both men laughed.

"I am not ready to be an uncle yet, even if Clara and I aren't related by blood."

"I know what you mean, Edwin. My dad had a close friend I used to call uncle."

Edwin half smiled. "How did Clara cope with that case today?"

"She was pretty upset, but I think she'll be fine. We can't dwell on things like that in this line of work."

"I understand."

"Anyway, thanks for a great evening. I have made a decision."

Chapter Fifteen: Shattered Flint

People spoke in hushed tones at Flint's wake. Hannah Flint finished talking to a friend of Lucius's, then sipped her tea with trembling hands. Her face showed the strain of the day. She wished she could be back at home in bed shutting the world out, but she needed to honour her husband's memory here.

There had been over 400 folks at Lucius's funeral, but only close friends and family were invited to the wake.

Harry Brown cleared his throat and approached Hannah. "Me sincerest condolences, Mrs. Flint. Lucius was a fine man and a great friend. If there is anyfing I can do, you just holler, ya hear?"

"Thank you Harry, you're most kind," Hannah said, softly.

"You and little Elijah will be taken care of. Lucius had life insurance, so you're mortgage free, and his pension will tide you over for a bit too."

Hannah stared at him for two minutes, then she said, "I am aware of the policies, thank you. I may not carry on living here. I'll need to discuss it with Elijah."

"Yes, of course. And if you need any company," Harry said, moving closer and stroking her hair. "You know where to come."

Hannah's face turned red and she bared her teeth. "How dare you," she screamed, slapping him on the cheek. Harry rubbed his face with a shaking hand and recoiled from her.

"Get out," she yelled. "Get out now, you're no longer welcome here."

A red faced Harry turned on his heel and left.

***

The following morning, a tired and hungover Harry Brown trudged with heavy steps to his favourite news stand.

"How's it going, Ern?" Harry said, to the news seller, handing over the correct change for The Tarnuz Times.

"Awright, 'arry. Looks like you made the front page." Ern said, dipping his chin at Harry's newspaper.

With wide eyes and a slack jaw, Harry stared at an unflattering picture of himself in disbelief.

He took in the headline: Shocking Scenes At Flint Funeral.

Then, with a heavy heart, he took in the story:

Head of TWLF, Lucius Silas Flint was laid to rest yesterday. The event was attended by over 400 mourners and well-wishers. Flint was a well-respected and valued member of TWLF and worked hard to bring reform to the factories with better pay and conditions for workers. It was hoped that his deputy and right hand man, Mr. Harry Brown would carry on his legacy, but it would appear his only concern was to woo Flint's widow, Hannah. Brown was observed by this reporter talking to Mrs. Flint before he stroked her hair at her late Husband's wake, which was held at the family home. Mrs. Flint struck Mr. Brown, telling him he wasn't welcome anymore.

Harry threw the paper in the bin and went home.

Sitting at his desk he wrote a note, then made a copy. He put one in an envelope and addressed it to The Editor Of The Tarnuz Times. He placed the original in the inside pocket of his jacket and waited until it was dark. When he was satisfied, he left his house and found a derelict building on the outskirts of the factory district. After he found a suitable spot, he undid his belt, flung it over a ceiling beam and hung himself.

***

Rain drummed on the ground as the detectives walked onto the paper mill construction site. Two storeys up in the burnt out building, a bald, burly man observed a Tocker flail its arms uncontrollably as it lost power. After it had stopped moving, he casually lit a roll up, smoked it, then he prised off the winding keys on the back of the robot and pocketed them.

"'Ere, Guvnor, this metal monster has given up the bloomin' ghost, ain't it?" He shouted down to his foreman, a wicked grin splitting his lips.

Men all over the site guffawed loudly.

Herbert Lurch, the red haired site foreman, tried to find the source of the voice, then he looked up.

"Roy Pike. I m…m…might have known," he said, patting the pockets of his tweed jacket. "This is the third Tocker that has broken t..t..this week."

"Wot can I say boss, they ain't fit for purpose, are they?"

"Yeah, the only thing they are good for is the knackers yard," another man yelled from the site, accompanied by enthusiastic cheers from the other human builders.

"Yes, well, I don't know how to explain this to Jedidiah Lewis," Lurch said, wiping the dripping rain from his face on his brown trousers.

"Well, I guess that's why you're the boss," Roy said, flashing a yellow toothed grin.

Lurch looked at the ground and walked away, muttering to himself, shaking his head as he did so.

Clara watched the whole thing through her goggles and smiled. *That's it boys, you show them! Power to the people!* Subconsciously, she clenched her hand. When she realised, she resisted the urge to pump her fist in the air.

"This is one time I fully condone TWLF," James said quietly next to her.

"So, we are verbalising each other's thoughts now, are we, Bronze?"

James blushed. "Maybe."

Clara locked eyes with him and smiled. "I'm okay with that. Come on, let's interview Herbert Lurch. I almost feel sorry for the poor gentleman."

James barked a short laugh and followed her. The remaining Tockers carried on working as if it was an ordinary day.

That's odd. I thought the rain would make them rust or something, Clara thought.

"Did you see the paper yesterday?" James said, changing the subject as they strode towards Lurch.

"Yes I did. I can't believe Harry Brown would have the audacity to do something like that," Clara commented, shaking her head.

"From what I hear, he was a serial womaniser."

"Well, I think Remina is a better place without him. I hope the next leader of TWLF has the same vision as Flint. Their cause seems pretty hopeless at the moment."

James nodded. "Ned Jenkins sounds like he is cut from the same cloth as Flint. Married, kids, hardworking, honest, a good communicator. I think the future of TWLF is in good hands."

You're actually quite caring, Detective James Bronze.

"It sounds like you know more than I do about all of this. I really do hope they get what they want. The conditions the working class have to endure are miserable. Tarnuz needs change."

"I agree. It seems a long way from the scholars right now."

"Yes, with all of these technical achievements, you'd think we'd be further forward than we are," Clara said, wrinkling her nose.

"I think we all still have a long way to go. Look, I don't think this weather is going to end soon. Let's go and interview the site manager about the criminal damage they reported yesterday."

Clara nodded.

"I am Detective Bronze and this is my colleague Detective Overton," James said, showing his badge to the site manager.

As he was talking, Clara moved amongst the Tockers as they worked. One had shut down and a human worker turned the clockwork keys on its back. Promptly, it stood upright and carried on laying bricks. After she glanced around a bit more, she saw a Tocker that seemed to pause every now and again, as if it was thinking about something. Carefully, she approached it and looked at the metal name tag on its chest: FLINT.

Clara's hand flew to her open mouth and she stepped back, her eyes bulging in her head.

Swallowing hard, she took tentative steps towards the robot and touched his copper body. Immediately, she went into a trance, and saw a deformed Lucius Flint powering the machine from within. Bile crawled up

Clara's throat and the colour drained from her skin.

Quickly, she made her way over to James and jerked her head.

"Thank you for your time, Mr. Lurch. After we have interviewed the suspects we will get back to you. Here's my card. If you think of anything else, give me a call at the station."

Lurch nodded, his eyes darting about in his head. James and Clara walked over to their steam carriage and got in.

"You look like you've seen a ghost, Clara."

"That's because I have."

***

"Now, let me get this straight. You want to go poking around the metal foundry and have a look inside the Tockers to see if there are people controlling them? Have you completely lost your mind, Clara?" Commissioner Harris said, pouring himself a drink from his coffee machine.

"I know it sounds completely bonkers, but I am trying to join the dots here. William at The Arch Tavern gave me a tip off about three or four weeks ago and Horace mentioned the body boiled in tar wasn't Flint's."

Harris sat in his chair behind his desk. "Horace did say that. I read his report. I know that your abilities have rarely been wrong, but we need more proof. I can't get a warrant to search that place just because people might be being abducted and turned into machines. I need more than that."

"How about Clara and I stake out the place. Take a few photos, see if we can get the evidence you need." James said.

Harris narrowed his eyes. "You've got 24 hours, that's it."

"Thank you, thank you, sir. You won't regret this," Clara said.

"You'd better make sure I don't. Now get outta here, the pair of you," Harris said, shooing them away.

***

"I am glad the rain has stopped. Walking two blocks in that weather would have been hell," James said, adjusting the night vision on his goggles.

"If we'd have showed up right on their doorstep, they would have seen us coming and shut up shop." Clara replied, shuffling her legs. Both the detectives had taken up the prone position on a roof opposite the foundry and looked at the comings and goings through their goggles.

"There, at the service entrance," James said, pointing in the direction of the roller door at the back of the building.

"That looks like a funeral carriage," Clara said, taking photos with her goggles, the shutter clicking repeatedly.

Two pallbearers walked to the back of the wagon and slid out a large tray with a body bag on it and then a figure came out of the foundry: Zintius. Clara and James's goggles snapped pictures frantically as Zintius unzipped the body bag revealing a young man's face. For a moment, the vampire froze, but before he could do anything more, he slapped his neck as if swatting a mosquito. He bent down and picked up a small arrow and twisted it between his forefinger and thumb, a scowl etched across his face, then he snapped it in two and stomped back into the metal foundry.

"Did you see that?" James said.

Clara didn't answer. She was looking at a silver haired elf on the roof of the building opposite. A triumphant smile graced his lips as he pulled up his grey hood and vanished.

James followed her gaze. "What were you looking at?"

Clara smirked "I think our elven friends have just made good on their promise. Zintius is now as visible as a rocket on New Year's Eve. I think we have everything we need. Let's get out of here."

"I think you're right," James said.

And they left.

***

"I am so glad to see you today, James," Horace said, injecting a needle into the detective's arm. "Take it from me, you have made the right decision."

"I sure hope you're right, Horace," James replied, rolling down his white shirt sleeve and buttoning the cuff.

"I have a partner in crime, in more ways than one," Clara said, making them all laugh.

"I prefer partners in the prevention of crime."

"Now that I do like," Clara agreed, pointing at James.

"Ah, look at you too. You're so sweet," Adamar said.

"Are we?" Clara and James squealed in unison.

"Yes, you're both adorable. I'd rather that than you at each other's throats all the time," Horace smiled. "So, that's the good news. The bad news is, you were right about the vaccines. I tested several samples and found a batch that contained werewolf DNA, another carrying vampire DNA and the third had shifter DNA."

"Fuck," James exclaimed, kicking a shelf, making it rattle.

"Was it only those species you found, Horace?" Clara said.

"Yes."

"There must be more to it than just making a more efficient workforce. Why would he need so many supernatural beings?" quizzed Clara, gazing at Horace with sudden focus.

"I think there are some other questions you need to ask too. We have evidence that Zintius is the vampire donor but who are the werewolf and shifter donors?" Horace proclaimed, raising his eyebrows.

***

Doctor Albi Lurcock swapped Flint's yellow construction card for a blue marine one.

"Doctor Lurcock, why have you reassigned me?" Flint's robotic voice said, looking up at her with his innocent looking blue glass eyes.

How can I have empathy for him? He is a machine, a robot, an automaton. But I saw him when he first came in. He was still a man then, frightened and alone. And I took his memories, his feelings, all of it. What the fuck have I done? Maybe I am too close to this subject.

"They are running military tests and they want Tockers to be on the front line. I am sparing you that fate. Make your way to the slipway at the back of the foundry. There's a boat with other Tockers on it. It's bound for offshore electrical cable installations. Make sure you're on that vessel, Flint. Now go."

Without hesitation, Flint boarded the craft, turned and waved at her.

She watched the boat slide down the slipway and disappear.

Chapter Sixteen: Where Are The Wolves?

The wheels on the wagon creaked as James manoeuvred it into the small fishing village and stopped. Clara and James wore navy Ganseys, fall front brown trousers and boots. James climbed down from the cart and knocked on the door of the largest fisherman's cottage.

A white bearded man wearing a Breton cap opened the door. "What do yer want?

The man said, looking James up and down. "I'm guessing by your clobber, you're looking for work. Is that your ride?"

"Yes, it is."

"Well, it looks as weather-beaten as a ship in a storm. I be fixin' to leave yer woman on dry land, if I was yer. The rollin' sea be no place for a lady."

"I'll talk to her and see what she says."

"Say what yer' like, be's stickin to me word, I tell ye."

James climbed up next to Clara. "He doesn't want you to work on the fishing trawlers. Says it's no place for a lady."

Clara sighed and rolled her eyes. "There's still a long way to go with equality. It's not so bad, women are known to gossip and I'll be able to poke around without being noticed."

"You might want to drop your posh accent, as that would be the first thing to draw attention to yourself."

Clara looked at him blankly. "Wot's wrong wiv me accent, guv?"

James barked a laugh. "You don't have to lay it on as thick as that, use three words instead of five. Stuff like that."

"Okay, how's that?"

"You literally just said three words."

"Yes, I did," Clara said, playfully punching James's bicep.

"I'll go and ask our new friend if he has a cottage we can rent," he said, exiting the vehicle.

"You might want to ask him what the women do all day too," Clara called after him.

"My wife has accepted that she will need to stay on dry land. She wasn't happy about it, but she will go along with it."

"Aye, nothing wrong with a spirited maid, I tell yer'."

"She certainly has spirit, I'll give you that. I am Franklin Garrett and my wife is Helena."

"Neville Marsh," and the two men shook hands.

"I suspect yer' be needin' digs?"

"Yes, if you've somewhere affordable, that'd be great."

"I have a nice little two up two down over there for six shillings a week," Neville said, pointing at a detached thatched cottage, a short walk from the beach.

"Okay, we'll take it," James said, smiling and offering his hand to shake.

Neville's smile reached his eyes. "I'll need two weeks rent upfront, you get a week back when, or if, you decide to leave."

James fished some coins from his trouser pocket and passed them to Neville.

"Right. Let me gets the keys. I's be back in a jiff."

A short time later, Neville returned and gave James the keys.

"A maid's place may not be on the rollin' sea, but they be very important on land. I hope yours can knit and gut fish." Neville said, tapping the side of his nose and winking.

I don't know, but the plucky thing that Clara is, I am sure she'll learn.

"If you want work, meet me tomorrow at the docks, 5 a.m., sharp."

"I'll see you there," James replied.

Clara and James carried a suitcase each and opened the door to the cottage.

It was a post and beam construction with a low ceiling, exposed beams and a tiled floor.

A table and captain's chairs were in the middle of the room. There was an aga oven, a box shelf with cutlery on it, a window, a sink and a staircase. An open door showed a basic bathroom.

Taking the stairs, they found a bedroom and a ladder to the loft.

"Well at least we have a bath," Clara said.

"What do you think the aga is for?"

"It has many uses, not just cooking, but heating water and the house."

"Do you think you'll be able to cope, coming from a privileged upbringing and all that?"

Clara gave a short laugh. "Just because I come from money doesn't mean to say I wasn't shown how to knit or darn socks.

Dalton was a good teacher," she said, clearing her throat and looking away.

James pulled her close, lifted her chin and kissed her lips. "There's still so much to learn about you, Clara."

"It works both ways. Now, talking about finding out things, the best place to do that is a tavern."

"And thanks to Commissioner Harris, women can walk into pubs on their own now."

Clara wrinkled her nose. "I am not walking in there on my own, I want everyone to know I am married. It saves drunken sailors cracking onto me."

James laughed.

"What's so funny?"

"You said cracking on. I doubt posh Clara would ever use a phrase like that."

"Well, as you can see I'm a fast learner. Now, I would like to get a belly full of beer," Clara declared.

James offered her his elbow and she took it.

Gaslights illuminated their way on the foggy cobbled streets as they passed the market, quaint fishing cottages, closed souvenir shops and other retail outlets. A chilly breeze blew across the harbour, gently rocking the moored boats. The air smelt of brine and beer as they approached The Drunken Mermaid. The sound of sailors singing sea shanties wafted from the tavern as they opened the door. Lanterns glowed warmly on the tables or from the low wooden beams in the ceiling. A bar was on the left, tables packed with merry fishermen and a fire blazed fiercely in the hearth. The tavern smelt of beer, tobacco and cooked fish.

"The name's Rumus, What can I get yer?"

A brown bearded dwarf said from behind the bar. He wore a white rolled up shirt and red braces. On his right forearm was a tattoo of a bare chested mermaid.

"We're new here. What does everyone else drink?" James said.

Rumus chuckled. "Squid ink."

James contorted his face.

"It's not real squid ink, it's the name of an ale," Rumus beamed, reaching under the counter and producing two tin flagons. After he had filled the tankards he set them down on the counter. "That'll be 4 pence, please."

James slid the money over the counter. "Thank you, Rumus."

"If you're hungry, I recommend the fish pie."

"I'm sure we'll order a couple later," James said, looking around the place.

"Right you are, boss."

James and Clara took a sip from their drinks. It was a pleasant black beer with chocolate and coffee notes.

Neville laughed, turned and beckoned to James and Clara.

"Ah, yer made it to The Mermaid. This be where the party's at, every fackin' day,"

Neville said, banging the table, making everyone who sat there laugh.

When Neville had finished laughing, he looked at Clara. "Lily, be me maid. Yer can find her over there, the table nearest the fire," he said, pointing to where several women sat.

"Fanks, Mr. Neville, sir," Clara said, performing a curtsey. James chewed his smirking lip, Clara flashed him a flinty stare, then she strode over to Lily's table.

" 'Ello, Mrs Marsh. I am Helena Garrett, me 'usband, Franklin, and I arrived today. Yer Neville said I could work for yer."

Lily Marsh had a long grey braid running down her back. She wore a grey shawl, black skirt, stockings and lace up shoes. The other women wore the same uniform, like sailors in the navy.

Lily stood up, and slapped Clara on the arse.

"Oof," Clara said, rocking on her feet. Lily and the women guffawed.

"Yer a damn fine catch, me pretty. But can you cuss like a man and hold yer gin?" Lily said.

"I can do better than that. Get me a yard of ale. I'm fixin' to drink yers under the table."

"You're on. Give me yer money, you land lovin' wenches," Lily said, snatching pound notes from her comrades.

Clara felt like the whole pub had gathered around her, whilst they watched this small woman drink two and half pints of alcohol in one go.

People cheered her on, chanting her name, whilst money changed hands. The row in the pub was deafening. Eventually, Clara set down the glass trumpet and belched loudly.

Everyone cheered, some folks banged tables. Whilst others hugged Clara or shook her hand.

" 'Ere's yer winnings, me dears," Lily said, stuffing a large wodge of notes in Clara's breast pocket.

"The first catch normally arrives at 8am. Be at me house by 7am, and I'll show you the ropes."

"Yer house, 7 a.m., got it."

" 'Ere comes yer man, he's a cutie ain't he," Lily said, slapping James on the arse.

"Oof," James said as his legs buckled.

"I 'ope e's sea legs work good un proper. 'E looks a bit green to me. An early morning on the ocean will show us what e's made of, I tell yer."

"Well, it's been great but we must be off home now. I've an early start in the morning. Come on, Helena, let's get to bed," James said, offering Clara his elbow.

***

Clara and James lay in bed by candle light.

"I didn't know you could drink a yard of ale."

"Well, you do now. Eme is a bad influence on me."

"So I can tell. How are you going to explain the gloves?"

"I have a trick up my sleeve. Horace has given me something that will have the desired effect. What about you? you're a providentia now."

"I will take inhibitors whilst I am on the boat."

Clara gasped, then propped herself up on her elbow. "James, you can't do that. It hasn't been tested. You could have a heart attack. Besides, you should have bare hands on ropes and the helm. It's important to know what triggers your trances too. We are undercover looking for werewolves, remember. One or all of them could be on that trawler for all we know."

"Relax, Clara. It'll be fine. But I didn't think about the triggers. I'll bear that in mind tomorrow. Anyway, let's blow out the candles and get some shut eye. We have a big day ahead of us."

***

Children of Tarnuz

Dressing in the dark, James crept out of the bedroom and left Clara snoring in peace.

She snores like a man. It must be all that booze last night. I need to keep an eye on that. It destroyed my father's life, and I don't want it to ruin hers either.

An icy chill gripped the dark, early morning air and James pulled his Breton hat tighter over his ears and jammed his hands into his pockets. Neville saw him when he was still far off and waved, whilst the other fishermen checked nets and stacked lobster pots. The air smelt of brine, fish and seaweed.

James boarded the boat, The Untiring, and Neville shook his hand. "Welcome aboard, me hearty."

"Thanks for giving me this opportunity."

"Yer might change your mind when you've been rocked up and down on the waves, chuckin' yer guts up over the side." Neville laughed, and so did some of the others. One of the fishermen, a black haired man with a side parting and dark eyes, looked away but didn't say a word.

It's the quiet ones you need to watch, right?

"Anyway, let me introduce the lads to yer. Before I do, Jesse, fire her up please?" Neville said to the black haired man.

"Yes, skipper," Jesse said and then disappeared below deck.

"That there is Jesse Moody. Quiet one, keeps himself to himself."

Shortly after that the engines fired up, then idled. The fisherman unfastened the ropes, and then a man with red hair and a beard piloted the ship out of the harbour, cranking the dynamo on the searchlights. A large beam shone on the blue sea and they pulled away.

"The guy piloting the ship right now, that's Ora Lever. Over there, that's Nicodemus Brewer, deckhand like you. We call him Nic for short." Nicodemus, a black man with a green woolly hat, smiled and waved.

"The guy standing next to the lobster pots is another deckhand, in fact, the rest of the crew are. Anyway, that's Harrison Eagleden, 'girl in every port', that one. Must be the blonde hair, beard and blue eyes. Little brown haired tike over there, Newt Popkiss. The other crew members Alan Brock, Amos Palmer, Max Dalley, Luther Iggelsden are scattered about the ship somewhere. You'll meet them soon enough, I am sure."

"I look forward to it. When do we start fishing?"

"Only another hour to go."

"Great. What fish are we hoping for?"

Neville lit his thin white clay pipe and puffed on it before he answered. "Hmm, some cod would be nice."

***

Clara woke at 6 a.m. with a thundering headache and she winced as she slid out of bed and padded down the stairs to the bathroom. She looked in the mirror and her bloodshot emerald eyes stared back at her. Her heart shaped face was pale and her brown hair was a bird's nest. Reaching inside her canvas handbag, she pulled out some headache tablets and dry swallowed them. After she filled a stock pot with water, she boiled it on the Aga and poured it into the tin bath, then she added some cold water too. When she had done that, she tested the temperature with her wrist. After she had discarded her night clothes, she had a strip wash, fixed her hair and then went upstairs and dressed in the fishermen's wives uniform.

She headed towards Neville and Lily's cottage, and a man cheered as she walked passed.

"Yer surely can handle your drink, maid. Yer got my fackin' respect, for sure!"

Clara smiled bashfully. "Fanks, mate."

"Yer welcome. Have a great day."

"Cheers, you too."

Clara rapped the gold anchor knocker on the light blue door of the cottage. She could hear movement inside and the smell of kippers and scrambled eggs. Lily opened the door and smiled. "Come in, Yardie Girl."

"Me name is Helena Garrett, Mrs Marsh."

"We all 'ave nicknames round 'ere. Yer made history last night. I've never seen a woman do that before. Always trying to show the men we're as good as 'em and you succeeded. Hungry?"

"I could eat the 'orse and come back for the rider," Clara said, clutching her growling stomach. And then she said, "Yardie Girl? Because I can drink a yard of ale?"

Lily smiled broadly. "Yer catch on quick, maid. Or should I say Yardie Girl?"

Clara smiled, whilst her belly rumbled again.

Lily chuckled. "I fink yer stomach agrees with yer."

Lily turned to the aga, plated up and set the food before Clara and sat opposite her.

Clara cut up her food and greedily shovelled it into her mouth and she realised her and James hadn't eaten last night. As she was eating, a goose honked, making Clara jump. She stared at the white bird as it waddled up to the glass and pecked on the window pane.

Lily tittered. "Oh, don't mind Gertie. She's harmless, she only wants to say hello."

"These eggs are delicious. Did Gertie lay them?"

Lily nodded whilst she chewed her food and said, "Yes, she's a good layer. I alternate between goose, duck and chicken eggs. That way we's never tire of em."

"I would love to buy some of your eggs. Do you sell mixed boxes?"

"Yer can ave the first box for free. Call it a welcome to the village present."

"Ah, fanks, Mrs. Marsh."

"It's Lily, everyone calls me Big Lil. Are you finished?" she said, her eyes flicking at Clara's empty plate.

"Oh, yes that was amazing. Fank you so much."

"Yer welcome. Would you like a brew?" Big Lil said, as the kettle whistled on the Aga.

"Yes, that'd be lovely."

"Coming right up."

The cottage was a larger version of the one her and James were renting. Clara wondered if they had bought the cottage next door and merged the properties together. Large windows let in the dawn sunlight, and the dewy grass looked like tiny crystals as the birds frolicked on it. Gentle waves lapped against the back garden wall, and the watery sun glistened on the ocean waves.

These people are what makes Remina go round. They are a little rough around the edges, but they don't deserve to be slaughtered by genetically modified werewolves. James and I will do everything in our power to stop that from happening.

Before Clara could think anymore, there was a knock at the door.

Big Lil answered it and the ladies from The Drunken Mermaid walked in.

All of them carried baskets that brought in a fishy aroma to the cottage. Big Lil cleared the table and made tea for everyone, whilst their expert hands gutted the fish.

I am out of my depth here. I can gut fish as well as these ladies, but nowhere near as fast as them.

When Big Lil mentioned last night about swearing as well as the men, she wasn't kidding. Although Clara was no prude, some of the jokes they told made her feel awkward. After a while she acclimatised to it and managed to laugh and enjoy herself.

When all the fish were gutted, Big Lil - who wasn't fat, just very tall - inspected samples from every woman and girl. Finally, it was Clara's turn and she held her breath.

Big Lil looked very serious for a few beats, then a big smile split her face.

"Welcome aboard, maid."

The women cheered and some of them clapped Clara on the back.

"Now, let's show those men who's got the best quality fish!" Big Lil said, pumping her fist in the air.

"Yeah," all the women yelled.

They wound their way through the bustling streets amidst yelling traders.

"Come and get your fish 'ere. Best fish in town," a man shouted.

Big Lil barged through the crowd and grabbed the fish from the man's hand.

"This fish is full of maggots," she said, holding the fish out of the man's reach.

"It has maggots, I tell yer." she shoved him to the ground.

"Big Lil and her girls 'ave the freshest fish in town, not this fackin snake oil salesman."

The crowd jeered the trembling man and threw rotten fruit and eggs at him.

Struggling to get to his feet, the man tripped, then scampered away.

"Come and get your lovely fish. Big Lil and her maids will see you right."

When they had run out of stock, The Untiring pulled into the dock and the crew unloaded the fish. Big Lil and the other women hugged and kissed their men and helped gut the fish. Once all of the fish were gutted the men went to the pub, whilst the women carried on selling in the marketplace.

***

"These eggs are delicious. Where did you get them from?" James asked, putting another forkful of poached egg in his mouth.

Clara had made them both ham, eggs and chips.

"Big Lil gave me the eggs. I bought the ham from the butcher."

"Wonderful, truly wonderful," he said, leaning forward and kissing her. "How was your first day as a fisherman's wife?"

"They are tough racketeers. Big Lil barged a poor fishmonger out of the way and stole his custom."

"Hmm, I think they live by different rules here. It's cultural."

"Don't worry, I'm not busting out my handcuffs and arresting anyone. I just wasn't expecting it, that's all."

James nodded. "They are tough women trying to make a living in a man's world. It's such a shame they have to become like men to succeed."

Clara smiled and kissed him on the cheek. "You believe in equal rights for women, Franklin Garrett?" she said, giving him a sultry look.

"Yes I do. I believe in equality. I think that men and women should receive equal rights, a fair wage for a hard day's work and everyone should be able to vote, too."

"Patrick Spencer has allowed women to go to a bar on their own now. Do you think change is coming?"

James grunted. "I doubt it. He wanted Commissioner Harris to vote for the goggle rollout."

"That's very cynical of you," Clara said, pursing her lips.

"Look, Spencer is in bed with Lewis. All they're interested in is pounds, shillings and pence. If you want to see real change, we need a new chancellor."

Clara looked to her right. "We need somebody younger, a visionary. How about James Bronze?"

James laughed and leaned back in his chair. "I am truly flattered that you think that, but I committed to the police."

At that moment, there was a scraping sound at the front door. Clara and James stared at each other, then James slid his chair back and opened the door.

An old woman with a black and grey ponytail, wizened fingers and a crooked spine, trembled as she placed a steak on the doorstep.

"Beg pardon, sir. We be fixin' to lay these outside every door in the village," she said, scratching her cheek, her eyes darting up and down the street.

James frowned at her. "Whatever for?"

"If we lay these outside, the wolf promises not to attack us."

James rubbed his chin. "Oh, okay thank you."

"I'll just leave it 'ere. Good evening and sorry for the disturbances." She bowed, then hobbled down the cobbled street.

James shut the door and stood with his back against it.

"They are definitely here, then," Clara said.

"Well, one of them certainly is."

Clara nodded. "The question is, is he or she working alone?"

"That is a question we need to find the answer to. If we don't, someone might die."

Clara swallowed. "Did anyone appear suspicious on the boat today?"

"As matter of fact, yes. There was someone that caught my eye."

Clara sat up in her chair. "Go on."

"A quiet, dark haired guy called Jesse Moody. He wouldn't look at me and kept himself busy."

"It's the quiet ones you have to watch, right?"

"That's exactly what I thought."

"Definitely start with him, then."

"I certainly will," James said, yawning and stretching his arms.

"I am beat. Let's go to bed, Clara."

"Okay."

***

Groaning and rotating his shoulders, James got out of bed and dressed in the dark.

Yesterday's clothes were drying over the fireplace.

I don't know how these people live like this, day in and day out. Only having two sets of clothes to wear and maybe a second jumper for Sunday best.

They get used to it, I suppose.

He found his lunch box and closed the front door with a soft click.

What was all that wolf stuff about last night? Fishermen and women are naturally very superstitious, so maybe there's nothing in it, and it's just an old tradition. James shook his head, his boots creaking as he walked towards The Untiring. No, that woman was genuinely afraid. I need to speak to Neville about this.

Breathing on his hands, he rubbed them together and flexed his fingers. His fingerless gloves were useless against the cold. Men stood around drinking coffee from flasks, and then they carried on preparing the boat for the day's catch.

"Arr, came back fer more did yer?"

"My wife and I need to eat."

Neville chuckled. "Well, I's pleased to see yer. We're a man down today. Moody went Tom Dick."

Interesting.

James nodded and clapped his hands around his body and he could see his breath.

"I am sure we'll manage," James said.

"I 'ope so. You're on net duty today," Neville said, pointing his pipe at the nets.

"Aye, aye, captain."

"That's what I like. An obedient worker," Neville exclaimed, barging into him as he walked past and cackling as he did so.

These people seem unhinged to me. What the fuck is wrong with them?

Later that day, James was eating his ham and pickle sandwich in the mess room with Ora Lever.

"What brings yer to these parts, Franklin?" Ora asked.

"My wife and I were looking for work, and we heard the fisheries commission was hiring."

"Well, you seem to know your way around a trawler."

"My father owned one, and we used to fish every now and again to top up our income."

Ora nodded. "It sounds like fishing is in the blood."

"It would appear that way, yes."

"Do you have any family?"

"My parents are dead and I have no siblings. Helena's father died a few years ago. We only have each other."

Ora leaned forward and squeezed James's shoulder. James patted the man's forearm, immediately going into a trance. He saw Ora with his smiling wife and children. His wife was ladling soup into wooden bowls and his son tore off a hunk of crusty white loaf and chewed. They were sitting at a table and a fire blazed in the hearth.

And then Ora pulled away.

It doesn't look like Ora is our man.

James cleared his throat. "What about you? Are you married? Have any kids?"

Ora smiled with his whole face and pulled out a black and white photo from his black wool jacket pocket and pointed at his wife.

"That's Isla, Alfie, aged nine, and Darcy, aged seven," Ora said, his thumb moving from one person to another as he said their names.

Everyone was smiling in the photo.

They genuinely are happy. No one smiles in photos. I wonder why.

"You have a very beautiful family."

"Thank you, me hearty. Do you and Helena plan to have a family?"

James chewed his lip. "We haven't been married very long, three months or so. We have talked about it, so maybe one day if the good Lord allows."

Ora crossed himself. "Amen. May the Lord bless you richly."

"Amen."

I am not religious at all, so I don't know where that came from! I don't even know if Clara believes in God. I'd better ask her.

"I must be getting on, my lunch break is over. Nice getting to know you a bit better, Franklin," Ora said, closing his lunchbox and putting it in his locker.

Other crew members came and went, but James found nothing connecting them to a werewolf.

Jesse Moody. You're the only one left. Maybe I'm wrong and you're just shy and retiring, but your absence is definitely arousing my suspicions.

James took off his woollen hat and ran his fingers through his tousled brown hair.

***

A light shone in Jesse Moody's bedroom window and the silhouette of a man entered the room. James ducked behind the ragstone wall and hoped he wasn't seen. Shortly after that, the backdoor was opened and relocked. Footsteps crunched on the shingle as Moody opened the garden gate and walked onto the misty muddy moors. James waited a minute or two whilst his hammering heart slowed down, then he followed Moody, keeping pace with his target and hiding periodically behind rocks. Eventually, Moody opened a rusty black iron gate that screeched as he pulled the handle and walked to an old barn. James hid behind a bush and waited until Moody had gone inside, then he took tentative steps towards the barn wall. Pressing his ear against the wall, he strained to hear what was being said.

After a few minutes of silence, a voice James didn't recognise said, "I thank you for feeding me, but thanks to Delmor and the werewolf council, I am an outcast. Nothing more than a stray dog begging for scraps."

"I am just grateful that fishing communities are superstitious. If they weren't, I wouldn't be able to feed you at all, Bardulf."

There was another silence and then Bardulf said, "I could eat like a civilised man if you spoke to your boss." He growled softly.

"I am working on it. Some bloke and his wife showed up a few days ago. Neville gave him a job and his missus works with Big Lil."

"Are you saying there aren't any vacancies on The Untiring?" Bardulf snarled. "There must be a lowlife good for nothing on that boat that can disappear."

"There's the boy, Newt Popkiss."

"Excellent. Bring him to me and I will discuss his career opportunities."

***

"What else did they say?" Clara said. James and her were drinking red wine, staring at the fire in their hearth.

James shifted his weight on the couch and recrossed his long legs at the ankle. "That was it. I didn't want to overstay my welcome. Do you think Bardulf is the A.S. donor?"

Clara nodded. "It seems highly likely. I think Bardulf should thank his lucky stars. In the past, Delmor would have had him executed for treason."

"Thank goodness for democracy."

"Yes, but judging by what you said about Bardulf, he doesn't care about democracy."

"What about Newt? He might be in danger."

"We can't do anything about that, James. You overheard something you weren't supposed to. We just have to hope he doesn't come to any harm."

James made a tusking sound and shook his head. "I don't like this, I don't like it at all."

Clara chewed her bottom lip and clasped James's hands with him squeezing hers in return.

"It's like you said, we're not cops down here. We play by their rules."

"Yes, I know, but I don't have to be comfortable with it."

"We'll just have to sit tight. I think Bardulf would have to be pretty stupid to abduct a child."

James rubbed his hands over his face. "I hope we find out sooner rather than later."

Clara met his eyes with a steady gaze and touched his cheek with her hand. "There's no use speculating about it now. Let's go to bed."

***

When James arrived at The Untiring the following day, Neville was talking to Newt Hopkiss and another man.

"I's be understandin' perfectly Robert. I think an education would be great for young Newt," Neville said, ruffling the boy's hair.

Robert smiled and he shook Neville's hand. "Good luck, young un," Neville said, waving at father and son as they walked off.

A few minutes after the Hopkisses had gone, a tall man with curly brown hair and a beard, dressed as a fisherman stood at the gangplank for The Untiring.

"Are you Captain Neville Marsh?" The man shouted through cupped hands.

James felt an icy chill run down his back. Bardulf.

Neville squinted at the man and wrinkled his brow. "Aye, that be me. Ooh's askin'?"

"Jesse Moody said a worker had left you in the lurch today."

Neville stroked his white beard, his eyes wide with wonder.

"Well, I know this is a small village, but news travels fast in these parts. Do you have any experience? You certainly look the part."

"I worked on The Blonde Mermaid for six years. Have you heard of it?"

Neville's jaw fell open, he jerked his head back and cleared his throat. "Err, yeah, big Lewis Corp trawler. Bad news for the little man. It be fixin' to tear the throat out of the small business." Neville spat on the deck.

"I was a victim of the corporate machine. I got laid off. Got replaced by a clockwork toy, we all did," Bardulf said, shaking his head and staring at his boots.

"I ear' yer." Neville took off his captain's hat and scratched his head. "I can give yer a job, but if yer ship mates come a knockin', I ain't got no work for 'em'."

Bardulf held up his hands in surrender. "I am the only one, I swear. The others looked for work elsewhere. Some even left the trade completely."

Neville scrutinised Bardulf for a moment, took out his thin white pipe from his black woollen coat pocket, filled it with tobacco and lit it. After two puffs, he said, "What's yer name, son?"

"Bardulf Fielding," Bardulf replied, holding out his hand to Neville and he shook it.

"Welcome aboard, shipmate. Newt's job wasn't well paid, mind. But sometimes people leave and yer might get promoted, yer never know."

"Thank you so much," Bardulf said, pumping Neville's hand. "I am just grateful for a job is all."

James shuffled his feet and slipped his canvas bag off his shoulder onto the deck.

"Ah, this is able shipmate Franklin Garrett."

James held out his hand and Bardulf shook it. No trance, nothing.

He must be using some kind of inhibitor unless he has the same ability as Zintius? I'll sound Clara out about this later.

"Haven't we met before?" Bardulf said, cocking his head to the side.

Stay calm. "No, I don't think so."

"Oh, I felt sure I recognised a familiar scent," Bardulf said, sniffing the air and gazing at James through hooded eyes.

"My wife buys me an aftershave called Land Ahoy! It's sort of an in-joke."

Stepping forward, Bardulf sniffed James's neck. James swallowed hard and his hands felt clammy.

Finally, Bardulf moved away and flashed James a toothy, wolfish grin. "What a delightful aroma. Where can I get it?"

"I am not sure. I'll ask my wife where she got it from."

"Oh, if you could, that would be truly wonderful. Women are such delicate creatures. She must worry about you going out to sea. It's so common for men to fall overboard in a storm, never to be seen again."

James planted his feet. "Are you threatening me?"

A look of mock horror swept across Bardulf's face, his hand flying to his chest.

"I wouldn't dare do such a thing. We have only just met. Why would I need to threaten you?"

"I don't know, you tell me."

"I beg your pardon, I didn't mean to get off on the wrong foot. Let me buy you a drink tonight. Maybe your wife could join us?"

Clara should definitely meet this lying piece of shit. I wonder if she'll be able to sense something. Her providentia prowess is stronger than mine.

"Okay then," James said with a degree of mock reluctance, "We'll see you there at six."

"I look forward to it."

Jesse tapped Bardulf on the shoulder, and, much to the detective's surprise, the new crew member pulled him in for a hug

At lunchtime, James chewed slowly as he watched Jesse and Bardulf laugh and joke like old friends. Nicodemus Brewer sat opposite James blocking his view.

"Waa gwaan, brother?" Nic said, smiling and revealing perfectly straight, white teeth.

James carried on staring, and Nic looked over his own shoulder.

"You lookin' at the newbie?"

"Yeah. What do you make of him?"

"I think he's just like you and me. A working man."

"Wait til he sniffs you, Nic."

Nic chuckled. "Sniff's me? What are you talking about?"

"He smelled me."

"What like dogs sniffing each other's arses?" Nic inquired, frowning.

"Something like that."

"Did you sniff his arse?" Nic said, letting out a booming laugh and slapping his thigh.

James contorted his face. "Fuck off, Nic. No I didn't."

Nic laughed and grabbed James' shoulder and shook it, laughing loudly. "I gots yer good un proper, didn't I?"

James rolled his eyes. "Yes you did."

"It's fuckin' weird that dogs do that, ain't it?"

"I guess."

Nic's smile faded. "He bothers you, doesn't he?"

James shuffled in his chair. "I am just suspicious, that's all. Don't you think it's a bit odd that Newt's seat hasn't even gone cold, and this guy shows up and takes his place?" he said, frowning at Nic.

"I haven't known you very long, Franklin, but I like you. If you're suspicious, I am suspicious." Nic said, pointing at his chest.

James flashed a half smile. "Thanks, buddy. I appreciate that."

"I'll keep a close eye on dem both," Nic said, tapping the side of his nose as he got up and left.

James stayed seated a moment longer as he contemplated the conversation.

In a strange town where I have very few friends, I need as many allies as I can get.

***

Rumus raised his eyebrows and smiled when James and Clara entered The Drunken Mermaid that night. Business was brisk and people laughed, some spilled beer on the floor. Somewhere a squeezebox wheezed followed by woozy voices warbling the wrong lyrics.

Bardulf saw them, beckoned them over with two fingers, and they sat opposite him and Moody.

"Ah, so good of you to join us, Franklin and Helena, isn't it?" Bardulf said, flashing another wolfish grin.

"I didn't tell you her name. How did you find out?" James asked, folding his arms over his chest.

Bardulf cleared his throat, running his fingers through his thick, dark wavy hair. "Neville told me," Bardulf said, as a waitress placed four flagons of Squid Ink on the round wooden table. Bardulf smiled and paid for the drinks. The waitress thanked him and left to serve another table.

That grin again. He uses it too readily. James thought as an icy chill slipped down his spine.

Clara smiled at the two men sweetly, maintaining eye contact as she sipped her beer.

I don't think Miss Overton trusts them either. Good girl, James thought.

"Do you make it a habit to look up other men's wives?" James inquired, clenching his fist on the table, his nostrils flaring.

Clara touched James's fist lightly, a warm sensation flowed up his arm and he relaxed.

There's more to her powers than she's letting on.

"It's okay, Franklin. We live in a tight knit community where everyone knows everyone else. It would be very easy for Mr. Fielding to find out who I was," Clara cooed.

"Quite. I thought it would be polite to address your beautiful wife by her equally beautiful name."

James wanted to clench his fist again, but Clara's magic touch stopped him from doing so.

He smiled dismissively.

How long will that spell she cast on me last?

"Helena, you do look strangely familiar," Bardulf said, leaning closer to Clara.

"I must 'ave one of them faces, mate," Clara said, laughing nervously.

Bardulf and Moody laughed too.

"No, no, I am sure I have seen you before. You remind me of someone famous or at least a face in the paper." A look of recognition flickered across Bardulf's face, he clicked his fingers, then he pointed at Clara.

"Well I'm blowed! You're the spitting image of that rich copper bitch, Clara Overton!" Bardulf exclaimed, leaning back, flicking the tails of his green tweed overcoat and crossing his right leg over his left knee.

"Well, everyone has their doppelganger, don't they. Who knows, yours could be a wolf in sheep's clothing for all we know," Clara said, taking another sip of her beer, whilst locking her eyes on Bardulf.

Bardulf's grin disappeared, a nerve bunching in his jaw. He interlaced his fingers and twiddled his thumbs, then he smiled again.

"As you say, everyone has a double. Anyway, I didn't come here to make enemies. I came here to earn money and find some new friends. What about the pair of you?"

"We are trying to stay one step ahead of the industrial age. It seems like everyone is being replaced by a machine lately."

"I hear that. I got replaced by a clockwork man a few weeks ago and have been trying to find a job ever since."

"Yeah, Neville mentioned that. A tough break."

Bardulf stared at the table and nodded.

"I don't think Big Lil and the fishermen's wives would allow that to happen here," Moody said, speaking for the first time. The other three stared at him, and James was grateful that his jaw stayed shut.

A few more drinks and a fish pie meal for them all turned the tide of ill feeling into a pleasant evening, or at least the impression of one.

Later that night, James lay in bed staring at the ceiling. "Clara, are you awake?"

"Well, I am now. What do you want?"

"Never mind. We'll talk about it tomorrow."

Clara giggled.

She has such a cute giggle.

"Do you think Bardulf is onto us?"

"That's exactly what I think. He knows my identity."

"What do you think we should do?"

"Nothing at the moment. I think he is fucking with us."

James sighed. "Do you think he will expose us?"

"He might, but if he knows who we are, he probably suspects we know who he is."

"He definitely thinks that. He mentioned that he knew my scent, which is a really weird thing to say."

Clara snorted. "He's just overplayed his hand. Anyone that says that is basically saying I'm a werewolf. He might as well have said; "I howl at the moon and be done with it."

"That is effectively what he is saying. So why is being so blasé?"

"Because he knows we have nothing on him and if he is guilty of murder, we can't prove it."

"Fuck, that's frustrating."

"It is, but we need to try and find some incriminating evidence, catch him in the act."

James propped himself up on his elbow and looked at her in the gloom.

"Do you have a plan?"

"No, I don't think there's any point. If I'm honest, we may as well give up and report back to base. Our cover is blown."

James sighed and laid back down. "Is the great Clara Overton rolling over and admitting defeat?"

"Perhaps I am."

"I don't know what to say."

"All might not be lost. If he goes to Neville with it, the captain will probably laugh it off. Besides, Bardulf can't back up his claims. Unless…"

"Unless what Clara?" James sat up again.

"Bardulf has old paper cuttings of us and shows them to Neville."

James snorted. "Bardulf is on the run. It seems highly unlikely he would have snapped up his scrapbook on his way out of the door."

"So what do you propose we do?" Clara said, propping herself up and looking at her lover.

"I think we stay put and expose this dirty moon howler."

"So keep your friends close but your enemies even closer."

"Exactly! And I am hoping Bardulf is thinking the same."

"So we are staying put?" Clara said, making a frown James couldn't see.

"Yes. But we are in a stalemate and nobody likes a stalemate."

"A wise man once said to me the devil always overplays his hand."

"Well, I hope the devil is Bardulf and not us."

"We are the law, James. If one of us is running with the devil, then we have a problem. Anyway, I'm tired. Let's get some sleep."

"Okay, Clara. Goodnight."

"Goodnight, James."

***

Her blood tasted coppery as he ripped her throat out. Gunshots and the sound of shouting men punctured the silence of the forest. After he listened to the approaching mob, he fled the dying woman. His feet pounded the earthy floor as his four legs carried him away from his pursuers. When he was sure he was far enough away from the angry mob, he slowed down and approached a stream, illuminated by the silvery moonlight. He lapped at the liquid with his tongue. When the water stilled, he gazed at his reflection. The reflection of a wolf. James gasped and sat bolt upright in his bed, his body glistening with sweat.

***

"Here's a penny," Clara said, sliding a coin across the table to James.

"Huh? What's that for?" James said, picking up the money and studying it curiously.

"Your thoughts. You've been staring at the hearth so long, your eggs have gone cold and your bacon is probably turned to rubber!"

"Sorry, Clara. I had a night terror last night."

"I noticed. There was a lot of shouting and thrashing about."

"Sorry again."

Clara smiled sympathetically, stroked James's hand and poured another coffee into his mug. Like an automaton, James raised his drink to his lips, his eyes still fixed on the fireplace.

Clara waved her hand in front of James's face, who's eyes remained glassy, his face rigid like a mannequin.

"James, you can tell me what the fuck is going on, or I can turn the providentia dial up to eleven!"

"Hmm...ah...oh...sorry, Clara. Last night's dream was horrible and it felt so real," James said, rubbing his left forearm and shivering.

"Some dreams can have that effect on you, but, in my experience, a problem shared is a problem halved."

James bit his lip, creased his brow and then he said, "I dreamt that I ripped a girl's throat out, and I was pursued by an angry mob with guns through the woods. It was night time and when I had lost the gang, I drank from a stream. I saw my reflection cast by the moon in the water, and that reflection was a wolf."

Clara leant back in her chair and puffed out her cheeks.

James drew his hand over his stubbly chin and looked at her. "What do you think it means?"

Clara stared at the table. "Truthfully, I think Bardulf slipped something in your drink."

James ran his fingers through his hair. "Do you mean some kind of hallucinogen?"

"That's the best possible outcome, yes."

James leapt to his feet and jammed his hands into the pockets of his grey wool trousers, his eyes as wide as saucers.

"Best possible outcome?" he said, his voice shrill like a pig being slaughtered.

"What are the other outcomes, Detective Overton?" James said, turning to face the fireplace, hooking his thumbs into his suspenders, white shirt rustling as he did so.

Clara swallowed and then licked her lips. "Err, well, erm, you could have been given the werewolf transforming drug."

James whirled around and kicked the coal bucket, spilling coal all over the floor, making Clara jump.

"You're trying to tell me I am might be turning into a fucking four-legged freak?"

Clara's lips and chin trembled and she held out her shaking hand. "That is… a…a… a… possibility, yes."

Oh dear God. I think he has been given the transforming drug. All the symptoms are there.

"Fuck you, Clara. Have a great weekend," he said, pulling his black wool coat off the hook on the door. He opened the door and slammed it behind him.

Clara dropped to her knees and wept bitterly, her body quivering with grief.

***

James cursed softly to himself as the moor merged into the forest. Pulling away thorns, he threaded his way along the twisted muddy path that led him deeper into the woods. Smoke drifted lazily from a hunter's cabin. It was made of mud chunked logs. Long grasses and wildflowers surrounded the building. There was a covered well, wood stump, cut logs and an axe that was propped against the side of the building. A deer looked at James briefly, then disappeared into the undergrowth. An owl hooted somewhere and the rushing of a river could be heard. James ducked behind a bramble bush and waited. The door of the cabin opened, followed by a red bearded dwarf in leather armour and green trousers, carrying a glowing lantern.

"How can I help you?" The dwarf said in a light sing-song voice.

How did he know I was here? I am pretty certain I was standing still, and I'm hidden from view.

James rose to his full height.

The dwarf shone the lantern in James's direction and he grinned. It was a smile that reached his twinkling blue eyes.

"Are you hungry? I have some venison stew in the pot if you are."

Even though James had eaten recently, he did feel peckish.

"Yes, that would be nice, thank you."

The dwarf's smile broadened and he gestured to the open door of the cabin.

"Come in, my man, come in! Make yourself at home. You can take a seat at the table," he said, pointing at the table and three chairs.

A bubbling pot hung from a hook over the fireplace, its lid rattling with the heat.

Dead rabbits, pheasants and squirrels hung from the ceiling. There were rough plywood shelves and a sleeping loft. One wall featured a window with a small wardrobe next to it.

"I am Tufel Marblebane," the dwarf said, bowing with a flourish of his hands.

"Franklin Garrett," James said, offering his hand. Tufel took his hand and shook it.

"What brings you to the forest at this time of night?" Tufel said, ladling some broth into a wooden bowl and handing it to James. After he had done that, he gave him a spoon and tore off a hunk of white crusty bread. Then Tufel sat opposite James, putting his deerskin boots on the table and crossing his legs at the ankles. He took out a pipe, loaded it with tobacco, lit it and smoked. The stew was a rich maroon colour and smelt of red wine and redcurrants. As James stirred the liquid, he could see carrots and button mushrooms. He dipped some of the bread in the food and ate. It was delicious. He closed his eyes, a satisfied smile on his face.

When he opened his eyes again, Tufel was still smiling.

"Oh, I am so sorry, Tufel. Where are my manners? You asked me why I was out here so late. I had a quarrel with my wife."

Tufel toked on his pipe. "What were you arguing about?

James let his spoon rest in the bowl. "Will you promise me you won't laugh?"

"You are my guest. Why would I laugh at you?"

James cleared his throat and shuffled in his chair. "I think I might have been given a transformation drug."

Tufel stopped dragging on his pipe and spoke with it still in his mouth. "That is very serious indeed. What do you think you will transform into?"

"A werewolf."

Tufel chuckled.

James drained his soup and stood up, turning his back on the dwarf. "You said you wouldn't laugh. This was a mistake. Thanks for your hospitality, but I think I'll leave now."

"Sit. Down. You have the wrong Idea. I chuckled because I always thought wolves were cute, until they attack, that is. It's very difficult to tell a werewolf apart from a normal one, but if you know what to look for, you can tell the difference."

"I thought you were mocking me."

"I pass no judgement on man or beast. Everyone is welcome here. If I feel that somebody has been wronged, I will fight to prove their innocence."

Tufel's tone was relaxed and reassuring. James stood again and listened to the soft "puck, puck, puck" sounds of the dwarf's lips on his pipe and the crackle of the fire. After he had sighed, he rolled his shoulders and sat down again.

Tufel lent across the table and patted James's hands. "You can trust me. Perhaps if you told me what aroused your suspicions in the first place, I might be able to help you."

James cleared his throat and the words fell out of his mouth like a waterfall gushing into a ravine.

When James had finished his story, Tufel put some more logs on the fire, prodded the wood with a poker, uncorked a large bottle of dark brown ale and poured the drink into two clay flagons. And then he refilled his pipe and carried on smoking.

"I can always tell when a man is telling the truth."

James drank from his tankard. "Do you think I am lying to you?"

Tufel flashed James a half smile. "On the contrary. No, I don't think you made any of this up. Although, I think you could be a very convincing liar if you needed to be."

"A backhanded compliment is better than no compliment at all, I suppose."

"I am sorry if I have offended you, Franklin. That certainly wasn't my intention. Can I call you James?"

"I would prefer to keep my alias intact if you don't mind. At least until this is all over."

"Of course. I understand perfectly."

Silence fell upon the room for a few minutes.

"I know Robert Hopkiss. We go back a long way. He visits from time to time and he always buys a rabbit or pheasant from my stall in town. It's Newt that stops by the most. He's a bright happy little chap, but something has been bothering him lately. His eyes always used to sparkle but now they are dark and troubled. He doesn't look directly at me anymore, and he shuffles his feet, and sometimes he shudders as if he is remembering a painful memory. Now I know why."

"Will you help me, Tufel?"

"Of course I'll help you. This Bardulf is evil, and he must be stopped before someone else is hurt or killed."

"If I needed refuge, could I come here?"

"Of course. Here, let me show you something."

Tufel beckoned him over, and the two men bent down over a trap door.

"Near the entrance to the forest, there is another trapdoor very similar to this, but it is covered in foliage. Not many people know about it. Remove the foliage, it is enchanted, so it will grow back the moment you disappear down the hatch, covering your tracks. Once you are in the tunnel, the enchanted sconces will light themselves, guiding you to my humble abode."

"Thank you, Tufel," James said, squeezing the dwarf's shoulder.

"I truly appreciate it."

"Now, it's getting late. Your beautiful wife is probably worried about you. You'd better get back to her."

James thanked the dwarf again and left.

It's funny, he thought. If I hadn't stormed out on Clara, then I'd have never met Tufel. We developed a bond straight away. It's hard to know who to trust here, but I think Tufel is genuine. I just hope Clara is alright with me now.

***

The barman lit the candle on her table and placed a bottle of rum and a shot glass in front of her. Clara paid the man. He thanked her and went back behind the bar. After a short ride out of the fishing village, Clara found the bar she was sitting in now. It had six tables, a low ceiling and the walls were decorated with fishing nets, pilot wheels, and plastic fish. She was the only customer, and she liked it that way. When she had glanced over the menu, she ordered the cold meat platter and beer. That was four hours ago, now she needed to think and rum always helped her relax and reflect.

Should I go and look for him, or should I let him blow off steam and come home with his tail between his legs? She barked a short laugh, then poured another thimble of rum and knocked it back. Fuck! I hope it is a metaphorical tale. I don't really want to riddle him with silver bullets. I am beginning to like him, perhaps even love him. She shuddered. Do I love him, or am I at least starting to love him? He's difficult at times, and I think I can trust him now, so that's something. He can be angry at times and occasionally unpredictable, but these aren't reasons enough to throw him to the wolves.

She poured herself another shot, downed it and went to the ladies.

After she had closed and locked the door, she put on her goggles and dialled Horace.

"Clara, how great to hear from you," the old man said, his eyes bleary and his voice groggy.

"I wish I was calling you with good news, Horace."

Horace's smile faded. "This sounds serious. My dear girl. Whatever is the matter?"

Clara's breath caught in her throat and she blinked hard. "Do you still have samples of James' DNA?"

"Yes, I do. Clara, you're starting to worry me. What has happened?"

Clara sniffed. In a crackled tone she said, "Well, technically, nothing has happened yet, but something is beginning to happen."

Horace sighed. "Take your time."

"Well, basically, we have found the werewolf murderer, and I believe he slipped a transformation drug into James's beer," she revealed, taking a succession of quick breaths.

"I see. What makes you believe this to be true?"

"A few hours after the drink, James awoke in the morning. He was pale and distant. He said he'd had night terrors. He dreamt he was a wolf, and that he'd ripped open a girl's throat and armed men were chasing him through the woods. I said that I felt a man named Bardulf, who we strongly suspect is a werewolf himself, had drugged him. He lost his temper and stormed out of the door."

Horace was silent for a beat, sighed and then he said, "These are classic metamorphosis symptoms. I need to work on a vaccine."

"How long will that take?"

Horace sucked in breath through his teeth. "I only have a prototype inoculation, and I have to make more batches."

"How long will that take?"

"Three days."

Clara rubbed her face and pulled at her hair. "That is a very tight window. By the time he receives the vaccine, he will be a fully-fledged werewolf. He could kill in that time."

"There's something else to consider. My vaccine may not work."

Clara wrung her hands and bit her lip. "I had tried not to think about that, but we have to try this drug on someone."

"I agree, but having Detective Bronze as a guinea pig is incredibly risky."

"Horace, I am prepared to take that risk. I think the safety of the whole of Tarnuz is in danger, and I can't allow that to happen."

"Okay, let's roll the dice on this one. I'll be in touch."

"Thanks, what can I do in the meantime?"

"Use James's providentia drugs on yourself and try to get James to take them too."

"I am a fully-fledged providentia, why do I need to be more providentia?"

"Calming James takes a lot of energy out of you. If you heighten your abilities, James will stay relaxed and this, in turn, will slow down the mutation, buying us some more time."

"Okay, that makes sense, but what effect will that have on me? Aren't I sensitive enough?"

"Wearing thicker gloves would be my advice."

"Would the providentia shot help him fight off the werewolf one?"

"The werewolf shot is effectively a virus, and we know that James has providentia DNA, so it would aid his natural immune system."

"Interesting. So we do have a good chance of combating this thing, but are there any side effects?"

Horace ran his fingers through his thinning grey hair. "Heart failure or a permanent change to werewolf."

"So, what would you propose I do?"

"I would give you and him small doses of providentia three times a day and pass your energy onto him to keep him relaxed."

"Should I keep him away from the fishing trawler?"

"Yes, I think that would be a good idea. Did you say that the werewolf was Bardulf?"

"Yes. Yes, I did."

"He is trouble with a capital T. He fell out with the werewolf council a few years back.

"Yes I heard about that. Do you think he is capable of selling his DNA to the highest bidder?"

Horace nodded. "Undoubtedly. When you are as bitter as Bardulf is, one would stop at nothing to seek revenge. He is extremely dangerous. I would advise you and Detective Bronze to stay on high alert."

Clara tapped her lip with her finger. "I'd better get back to the house and see if James is there."

"Right-ho, my dearest girl. And I'd better get on with this antidote. There's not a moment to lose."

"Thanks, Horace, I owe you."

"Don't mention it, my dear. I'll be in touch."

Clara's goggles went black and Horace was gone. Clara pocketed the eye glasses, flushed the chain and went back to the bar and settled up. The barman promised to look after her horse. He said she could collect it in the morning. He called her a cab and she made her way home.

When the cab clattered to a halt outside their small fishing cottage, Clara could see a solitary candle flickering off the kitchen walls. A wave of excitement passed over her and her pulse quickened, she bit her lip, took a deep breath and turned the key in the lock.

After she had opened the door, she saw James sitting at the kitchen table. Half of his face was illuminated by the candlelight, the other half was in darkness. Dark whiskers covered his face and his body twitched, his hands balled into fists as he did so. Clara sat opposite him and soothed him, by caressing his arms with her soft hands, feeling the energy leaving her, watching him relax with every gentle touch.

James closed his eyes, a contented smile on his lips; then he opened his eyes, the smile was still in place.

"Thank you," he whispered.

Clara smiled sweetly and lightly touched his right cheek.

"You're welcome, you're always welcome," she said, softly.

James clasped Clara's hands and his smile faded.

"Have I been infected, Clara?"

"I think you have, James."

At that moment, the candle went out and Clara shivered.

"So, what do we do?"

"We don't give up, I know that for certain. I have spoken to Horace tonight, and he has a cure."

"That's great!" James said, squeezing her hand tightly.

Clara flashed him a half smile that he couldn't see in the gloom. "It could take three days to make, then another three for it to reverse the process."

"Wait, so what you are saying is, I could have a short spell as a werewolf?"

"Yes, but all is not lost. If you stay close to me, I should be able to keep you calm, slowing the process down," Clara said, trying to sound confident.

"But keeping me calm makes you weak, it could even send you into a coma."

"Not necessarily." Clara outlined everything that Horace had told her. Afterwards, James stood up and paced around for a few moments.

"There seems to be a lot of ifs and maybes involved in this plan, if you ask me."

"It's the only plan we have."

"I found an unlikely ally tonight."

Clara's brow creased. "How so?"

James told her all about Tufel Marblebane, the Hopkisses, and everything else he'd discussed with the dwarf.

Clara took a sharp breath and clasped his hands. "Promise me you will go there even if you have the slightest amount of trouble?"

"I promise."

Satisfied with his answer, Clara smiled, lent across the table and kissed him on the lips.

"How do you plan to get Lily and Neville onside?"

"We invite them to dinner and my providentia charm will do the rest," Clara said, smiling broadly.

Chapter Seventeen: Painful Memories

After two days of blizzards, the fishing village was covered in a blanket of snow. Families had gathered at the frozen lake. Children threw snowballs at their parents, made snowmen or skated on the ice. Men sold roasted chestnuts to passers-by, and couples in sheepskin coats walked their dogs along the riverbank. The air was filled with the sound of laughter and the smell of roasted nuts.

"They say this is the worst snow storm we've had for 20 years," James said, wrapping his fingerless mittens around his thermos cup to drink Clara's pea and ham soup.

Clara nodded. "I can't remember the lake ever freezing over like that."

"You won't catch me skating on the ice. You never know if it's thick enough to hold your weight."

A half smile whispered on Clara's lips, she stood on tip toes and kissed James on the lips. "Did you sleep alright, Franklin?"

"Yes, I did. Thanks to you."

"I do what I can."

"Well, keep it up. It seems to be working."

"Do you think the metamorphosis is slowing down?"

"I sincerely hope so. We'll have to wait and see."

"I think that is the hardest part," Clara said, pursing her lips and rolling her shoulders.

James looked out over the lake and nodded. Newt was skating unsteadily on the ice, arms flailing, a panicked look on his face. Newt's father caught him and laughed. The boy clutched his father, his legs splayed out behind him. Robert Hopkiss placed his hands on his son's shoulders and spoke encouraging words to him. Newt nodded and let go of his dad and began skating again.

"That's it, me boy, that's it," Robert said, his hands making a dull thudding sound as he clapped his sheepskin gloves together.

"I am doing it. I am skating," the red cheeked boy beamed, his eyes glowing, his breath visible in the icy afternoon air. Crack.

Suddenly, the ice creaked under Newt's weight as cracks appeared. The boy let out a high-pitched scream as the frozen surface could no longer take the strain, and he plunged into the icy water.

"Newt! I am coming in to get you," a petrified Robert yelled.

James tore off his clothes and sprinted across the lake and dived in searching for the boy.

He darted about in the gloom, the water muffling the pandemonium from the people above.

Newt was a good swimmer and managed to surface, his breath rapid and shallow. Strong hands gripped his shoulders and pulled him free of the freezing water.

James pulled himself onto the frozen lake.

Clara placed a blanket around the shivering boy as the crowd congratulated Bardulf.

James cursed under his breath. He gets everywhere that fucking bastard.

"Get him indoors, keep him warm by the fire and make sure he eats and drinks plenty,"

Clara said, manoeuvring Newt towards his tearful, but relieved father.

***

"He keeps cropping up like a bad smell," James said, as he angrily poked a log in the hearth. He was wearing grey wool trousers held up with black suspenders and a white shirt. Clara was wearing one of his white shirts and nothing else. Her hair was covered in a white towel.

"James, you must try to remain calm. If you don't, you will hasten the transformation."

He returned the poker to its stand with a loud clatter, strode over to the kitchen table and poured himself some wine into an earthen beaker. He gulped it down and slammed the mug on the table.

"I am fucking calm!" he bellowed, breathing heavily, his nostrils flaring.

Clara lightly stroked his arm, and, as she did so, he relaxed and his breathing returned to normal.

"Well, you are now. James, you have to try to fight this. You need to have grace under fire. What are you going to do if Bardulf genuinely threatens you?"

James poured himself another drink and stared at the fire. Two logs collapsed in the flames with a crack.

"You're right. You're always right."

"I wish that was true. Look, let me give you a shot of providentia. You need everything at your disposal to fight this thing."

"If you think it'll help."

"Until Horace comes up with the antidote, this is the only line of defence we have. Now roll up your sleeve."

James did as he was asked, and he winced as the needle pierced his skin. Clara placed a cotton pad on the injection mark and fastened it with surgical tape.

"So, do you want to get all touchy feely now?" James said, taking her in his arms.

Clara looked up at him and smiled. "I have never slept with a werewolf in the middle of a mutation before."

"You've slept with a fully-fledged werewolf, then?"

Clara smiled coyly and twirled a lock of her long brown hair around her finger. "That would be telling."

"You can tell me anything, you know that."

"I can, but there is a time and a place for everything. Are you going to fuck me or are we going to talk all night?"

James reached under her shirt and ripped off her black panties, making Clara gasp. Sliding down his braces and his trousers, he grabbed her around the waist. She straddled him and he entered her.

Lying in bed, Clara traced her forefinger over his nipple and he moaned with gratitude.

"You know we could always just stay in bed and make love all the time until the antidote arrives."

"That would be wonderful, but we are undercover cops looking for a werewolf murderer."

"You're no fun, Helena Garrett."

Clara made an "O" shape with her mouth. "You remembered to use my alias, Franklin Garrett."

"'Never take your eyes off the prize' is my motto."

"Is it? Since when?"

"Since now."

Clara chuckled. "You're so funny. Hardly a prize, though, is it?"

James sighed and turned on his side. "No, I guess not. The prospect of staying a werewolf forever fills me with dread."

Clara moved closer and ran her fingers through his hair on the back of his head.

"I understand that completely. But Horace is a genius, and I am so glad we have him fighting our corner. If anyone can find a cure, it's him."

"You seem pretty confident he'll come through for us."

"I am as sure as I can be, given the circumstances. I don't believe we should give up hope. If we do, Bardulf and Zintius win and we can't allow that to happen."

James turned over to face her and brushed a stray hair from her face. "All the while there is breath left in my body, I will fight this thing. I can't allow myself and the rest of Tarnuz to sink into the abyss."

Clara threaded her fingers through his and smiled. "You don't have to fight this battle on your own. I'll be right by your side, always."

James swallowed hard, his eyes moistening. "This must be the moment I propose to you for real."

Clara pulled away and laid on her back, staring at the ceiling. "Please don't. We hardly know each other. Hell, it wasn't that long ago we hated each other."

"I'm sorry. That was incredibly forward of me."

"Do you think? Look, I don't want to rush into anything. I like you and I think we have something that is becoming quite special, but let's take our time, okay?"

"Okay."

"I don't know about you, but I am pretty tired. Let's get some sleep."

But James was already snoring.

***

The following evening, Clara was putting the finishing touches to the evening meal. James and Clara had invited Neville and Lily over for dinner. Shortly after she had gotten the meal out of the oven, there was a loud rap at the door.

"Franklin, see who that is," Clara yelled from the kitchen.

She heard a rustle of newspaper and a grunt as James extracted himself from his wooden chair and answered the door.

"Awfully nice of yer to invites us o'er for kon like this," Neville said, smiling broadly, as James opened the door. Neville thrust a bottle of brandy at James, who took it and thanked the other man.

"I thought ' yer 'ates us or somethin'," Lily revealed.

"We've been here for over a week now, and we wanted to show our appreciation for giving us both jobs," Clara said, smiling and ladling fish pie onto Neville's plate.

"Ah, me favourite. Fish pie with a mashed potato lid. The white sauce is full of prawns and peas too. I can hardly wait."

"Maybe you should come over here and get Helena to cook yer kon from now on, Nev." Lily said, a scowl on her face.

Neville's nervous eyes flicked at his wife, then he laughed uncomfortably, his cheeks red with embarrassment. "Oh, nothing beats your food, pet."

"Wise man. I knew you'd see sense," Lily said, elbowing her husband in the ribs, making him cough.

Clara flashed them a smile of gratitude as she dished up green beans and carrots.

"It's nice to see you both settling in," Lily said, filling her mouth with food.

"If you think we are settling in, then that is good enough for me. Isn't that right, Helena?" James cooed, smiling at Clara.

"Yes of course. It's always difficult when you travel around looking for work."

Neville nodded thoughtfully. "Do yer move around a lot, yous two?"

James scratched his chin. "It depends. The most we've ever been in one place was six months."

Neville finished his food and pushed his plate away, lit his pipe without asking permission and blew out a plume of smoke.

"That was damn fine food. Thank you, Helena."

"I am glad you liked it."

"It filled a hole," Lily chimed, giving Clara a lopsided grin.

She doesn't like competition at all. I hope I don't end up like that poor fishmonger the other day.

"Would you care for apple crumble? The apples are from a tin I am afraid."

"I freeze my apples, Helena. I wouldn't expect a mere slip of a girl like you to know something like that. I'll have to show yer sometime how we do's it."

"That would be lovely, Lily," Clara said, swallowing hard and tucking a strand of hair behind her ear. *What a patronising fucking bitch. I'd like to wrap this case up pretty quick, just so I can get away from her.*

Clara served them apple crumble and custard. When they had finished, James poured Neville and himself a brandy each and offered Neville a cigar, which he accepted. Both men blew out smoke rings.

Clara washed the dishes in the sink, Lily joined her, tea towel in hand.

"Oh, you're my guest Lily, you don't have to do that."

"Nonsense, child," Lily said, waving a dismissive hand. "I am happy to help. Besides, I think you would benefit from my vast experience."

"I appreciate it, thank you."

Vast experience? It's just washing up. She's doing my head in, thought Clara.

Lily smiled, grabbed Clara's cheek and waggled it. Immediately, Clara went into a trance. A younger Lily silently yelled "Alvin." The veins in her neck bulged, a terrified look on her face. A dark haired man with a thin narrow face and a cruel smile slit a young boy's throat, then turned to vapour and disappeared, dropping the dying boy to the ground. Abruptly, the vision ceased and Clara's head flopped forward.

Lily's face was white and filled with worry. She handed Clara a glass of water.
"W…what just happened, Helena?"

Clara took the glass and gulped down the liquid. Her throat was parched and her breathing was laboured.

"Who was Alvin?"

Lily's hand flew to her chest, her legs buckled and she slid to the floor.

Hearing the commotion, James and Neville ran to see what had happened. A pale-faced Lily lay on the floor. Both men helped her to a chair in the lounge, then James fetched a glass of water. After Lily had finished the drink, she pointed a shaky finger at Clara. "What sorcery is this? She… is… a… witch!" Lily hissed.

Neville grabbed Clara up off the floor by the shoulders and shook her. "What have you done to my wife?"

"Let go of me, Neville, and I will tell you," Clara said, firmly.

"Very well, maid. I'll let yer speak," Neville said, returning to his chair.

"I can assure you both I am not a witch. I was born this way. What I have comes to me as easily as taking a breath. It is both a blessing and a curse. Sometimes, I wish I never had it at all. I am providentia, and I can see a person's future or their past, depending on what they are thinking about at the time."

Lilly snorted. "I thought they burned yer kind a long time ago for witchcraft."

"We were misunderstood, but a few of us survived."

"How do yer use this ability?" Neville quizzed, raising one eyebrow.

"A trance is triggered when I touch something or someone, then I see things. Sometimes they are pleasant things and sometimes they are horrific."

"She asked me about Alvin," Lily said, sniffling.

Neville's eyes narrowed. "What did yer see, maid?"

Clara stared at her boots and shuffled her feet. Then she turned and looked out of the kitchen window before clearing her throat. "I saw a young boy get his throat cut, and when you shook me, Neville, I saw you bury the boy's killer in a shallow grave."

"Yer are a fucking witch," Neville yelled, leaping from his seat, hand raised, to strike Clara. James stepped in front of Neville and twisted the captain's hand behind his back.

"You lay as much as a finger on her, sailor, and I'll break your fucking arm, I swear." James growled, through clenched teeth, applying a little more pressure to Neville's arm, making him yelp.

James released the older man and shoved him back to his seat. Neville sat down, massaging his sore wrist, a scowl contorting his face. "What do you want from us? Money? We barely have a pot to piss in."

Clara shook her head. "We are not interested in financial gain. We simply ask that Franklin and myself work with Lily on land."

Neville laughed sarcastically. "Yer two are terrible blackmailers."

Lily laughed too.

"Bribery and corruption isn't what we are about, in fact quite the opposite," James said.

Clara and James explained everything. How James had become infected, how they had come to work at the fishing village, their real names, the whole lot.

When they had finished, Neville puffed out his cheeks, lit his pipe, toked on it, raised his head and blew out smoke.

"Cops, eh?"

Clara and James nodded.

"So we can trust you, you're not going to turn us over to the authorities?" Lily said, scrutinising the two detectives.

"providentia evidence is not admissible in court. Unless you want to give us a full confession and show us where the body is, we're powerless to do anything," Clara said.

Neville smoked his pipe, as heavy rain and a strong wind battered the kitchen window.

Neville and Lily came clean about Alvin, his killer and their part in his demise. After their emotional confession, a smile creased the old seadog's lips. "We have a deal," Neville said, holding out his hand. James shook the proffered hand and returned Neville's smile. "We have a deal."

"This Bardulf is a dangerous criminal and a prime suspect in an ongoin' murder investigation. You say?" Lily asked, frowning.

"We have to prove it first. But this is where you come in," James revealed, glancing at Neville.

"Okay, how are we fixin' to prove it?"

"I want you to get a copy of one of his fingerprints. If it matches the ones found at the crime scene we can arrest him on suspicion of murder," Clara said.

"What about yer, pet? Yer on borrowed time," Lily said, looking at James.

"I am hoping that our friend, Horace, will come through with the antidote in time."

"Yes, I am hoping that nobody gets hurt in the process, least of all James." Clara said, smiling at her lover.

"I think we can find him some work at the house, even if it means chopping wood," Lily offered.

"I would prefer he did something a little less aggressive, If you don't mind Lily," requested Clara, raising her eyebrows.

"Oh, right. Yeah, of course. I think he'd be alright gutting fish."

"I think a variety of tasks would be fine. If he gets bored, he gets irritable."

James waved his hand to get their attention. "Ladies, I am here. I can hear every word you're saying."

"Oh sorry, dear. I thought you'd nodded off," Clara said, and the two women laughed. Neville turned his red face away and pretended to cough.

"Whatever," James huffed, folding his arms and setting his jaw.

"You'll be fine. We'll look after you, I'll see to that, my dear."

"You don't have to patronise me, Clara."

"Who's patronising? I mean every word I say."

"I am sure you do," James said, turning his body away from Clara, tightening his lips.

"I be fixin' to see this lying, killing bastard brought to justice. I will do everything in my power to assist you in this." Neville said.

"You can count on me too," Lily agreed.

"I have to reiterate that our true identities must be a secret between us. As we mentioned before, we already think that Bardulf is onto us. We can't allow this to get out of hand, it is a matter of national security." Clara said.

"You have our word," Neville and Lily said, in unison.

Later that night, James and Neville were standing outside the cottage, leaning on the wall, smoking cigars and drinking brandy.

Neville took a deep breath and exhaled loudly. "After yer have got yer man, will you turn me and the Mrs over to the authorities?"

"It's your word against mine. I don't have any evidence of your crime. I wasn't even born when the murders took place."

"It was a dark elf that killed him, during their bitter war."

"Then you were protecting your family against an enemy soldier, who was buried in an unmarked grave. Thousands of soldiers ended up like this. If your conscience gets the better of you, turn yourself in to the local police department. Law enforcement officers are stretched to breaking point, I doubt they'll care too much about an old cold case though."

Neville smiled and clapped a large hand on James's shoulder. "You're a good man, Franklin Garret."

"I wonder about that sometimes. The job makes you question every decision you make, and every day you wonder if it's your last day on the force."

Neville took a sip from his glass and smacked his lips. "Not unlike fishing, lad."

James sipped his own drink. "I guess not."

Neville finished his drink, stretched and yawned. "Well, it's gettin' late and we have an early start tomorrow. Thanks for your hospitality, be seeing yer." Neville pumped James's hand, then disappeared into the cottage. James followed him in and they said goodbye to their guests.

***

"Clara, are you still awake?"

"Yes, I am, unfortunately. What do you want, James?"

"Neville said that the murderer of their son was a dark elf. Does that match the description of the person you saw in your trances tonight?"

"Yes, I think so. Why do you ask?"

"Neville told me that Alvin's murderer was a dark elf."

"Did you think he was lying to you?"

"I don't know, maybe."

"I don't think anyone would forget the murderer of their child."

"Yes, that's what I thought."

"We should turn them in to the authorities after this is all over, you know," Clara said, pulling the bed covers under her chin.

"I gave him the choice to turn himself in. I told him if his conscience got the better of him, he should report himself to the local police department."

"What did he say?"

"He didn't answer me. I think he took my reassurance that I wouldn't turn him in at face value."

"Well, I hope he turns himself in, because if he doesn't, I will take him in myself," Clara said, making a show of turning on her side.

***

Icy droplets dripped from the icicles hanging from a gutter. James turned his head in the direction of the sound. As quickly as the big freeze came, it was receding rapidly right before James's eyes, and he couldn't help thinking about what had caused these freak weather conditions.

I wonder if the city smog has anything to do with this. People get sick when the pollution is severe, maybe the environment gets sick too?

"Help, somebody help me," a child yelled.

James's thoughts were interrupted as he looked around and saw Newt dangling from the second storey window of the windmill.

Fortunately, the sails weren't moving. A crowd had gathered below and were pointing at the boy and murmuring to themselves. A collective gasp went up from the crowd as Newt lost his grip with one hand and clung on with his other hand. Elbowing his way through the startled onlookers, James threaded his way to the windmill stairs and ran up the steps. When he got to the top, he grabbed a beam with one hand and thrust his other hand out to Newt.

"Newt grab my…"

But before James could finish his sentence, someone punched him in the stomach and he crumbled to the floor. He clutched his tummy as Bardulf stepped over him and rescued the terrified boy, carrying him down the stairs and out onto the cobbled street below, being met with rapturous cheers and applause from the excited mob.

Wincing and feeling dizzy from the pain, James grunted as he struggled to his feet. After his eyes had adjusted to the light, he thought he heard someone trying to speak and the sound of shuffling bodies. For a moment, he stopped to listen and, stooping down, he gingerly picked his way through the oak beams on the floor and found the miller and his apprentice bound and gagged, both wide eyed and frightened. He slipped the gags from their mouths and cut their restraining ropes with his fish knife.

"Thank you, Franklin. Thank you so much," the miller said, a lithe man with wheat coloured hair, as he rubbed his red wrists.

My, my. Everyone really does know everyone here. Somebody must have told the miller my name because I am pretty sure I have never met this guy before.

"You're welcome. Who did this to you?"

"That new fella, Bardulf. Works on the boats, like yer, sir," the apprentice said, trying to catch his breath.

"What was he doing up here?"

"Well, he was manhandling the boy, he was. Demanded he hang from the winda' so he could rescue 'im. I guess he fancied himself the hero or some shit. A bloody disgrace, if you ask me."

"A bloody disgrace, indeed," James agreed. "Would the pair of you be prepared to testify against this man should the need arise?"

The miller held out his hand. "Help us up, would ya, guv?" James took the proffered hand and pulled the man to his feet. "Cheers, boss. I'd be glad to. That bloke is nothing more than filthy scum. He deserves to get what's coming to 'im."

"I appreciate it. Should the need arise, I will call upon you."

A look of realisation came over the Miller's face. "Wait a minute, guvnor, are you a copper or sumfin?"

James held a finger to his lips. "I would thank you for not blowing my cover."

The miller smiled and pressed his fingers to his lips. "After all you have done for me and the boy, it's the least I can do, boss."

Shouts and insults rose from the angry mob below.

After rolling his shoulders back, James took a deep breath. "I think I'd better face the music. Would you both accompany me downstairs? I might need a character witness."

Before the mill hands could answer, small tapping sounds could be heard against the side of the windmill. Shortly after this, a stone came through the open window that Newt was hanging from only a few short minutes ago.

"I think we'd better get out of here," James said, looking at the miller for support.

"Follow me, chief. I know a shortcut out the back," the miller said, winking and tapping the side of his nose. And with that, he pulled a rusty old lever and a panel slid open, revealing a small door.

"Quick, in here," the miller said, beckoning to James, his eyes wide and full of determination.

James stooped down again and brushed a thick cobweb away. A cool, musty breeze blew up a dark spiral wooden staircase. The miller flicked a switch and a naked bulb came on above their heads.

"Follow me," the miller said, squeezing past James's tall muscular frame. For a moment, James thought he would follow the flour grinder, but then he felt a tug on his overcoat, making him turn around.

"Please, mister. Let's me go first," the apprentice begged, wringing his cap in his hands. "I am afraid of the dark, see."

James looked down at the little child, smiled sweetly, ruffled the boy's hair and said, "Of course you can go first. You have had quite the ordeal today. I'll be right behind you."

"Fanks. Sir, 'ppreciate it."

"You're welcome, lead the way," James said, gesturing to the stairs and stepping out of the way. The miller stood four steps below them, his head turned in their direction, waiting for them to follow him.

Walking in silence, they made their way down the steps, the wood groaning under their feet. The corridor was narrow and

James scraped his broad shoulders against the cold wooden walls.

Creaking from the sails could be heard, and when they reached the bottom, James blinked hard as his eyes adjusted to the bright, wintry sun.

After producing a long bronze key, the miller opened the back door of the bakery.

"'Ow do, Eric. Are yer fixin' to bring me some more flour for baking?" A red cheeked woman with a round face said. She bore a resemblance to the miller.

I am guessing she must be his younger sister.

"No, I haven't had time to make any yet, Nancy. We had a bit of a hostage situation on top of the mill."

Nancy's hand covered her open mouth. "You're kidding me, Eric."

Eric fixed her with a flinty stare.

"I can tell by that look that you're serious, brother of mine."

"Deadly serious. Look, I'll explain later. Give this gent whatever he wants, on the house, and then let him escape by the underground tunnels. And shut that mouth of yours, you'll catch a fly, leave the spiders to do that! Now, if you'll excuse me, I 'ave to deal with the pitchforks." He doffed his cap and left.

"I… err, What can I get you, sir?"

"Four cottage loaves, please. And don't worry, I am good for the bread."

Nancy chuckled. "Eric don't give nuffin away, mate. Make the most of it."

A red faced James sheepishly closed his wallet. "Thank you, miss."

"Nancy. Please call me Nancy," she said, handing him a large brown paper bag containing his baked goods.

He opened his satchel and placed them inside.

"Right, the trap door is at the back of the shop. Come behind the counter, and I'll show you the way," Nancy said, taking a lantern down from the wall. After she had lit it, she handed it to James and he thanked her.

Lifting her dress, she opened the trap door, and dropped a lighted candle down the hole. It landed on the floor, its orange flame flickering off the soil walls, illuminating a wooden ladder.

"Be quick, there's a cool breeze that might snuff out the flame. I don't want you tumblin' in the dark and breaking your neck."

"Right ho. Thanks again."

"Don't mention it. Now go."

James nodded and gingerly climbed down the ladder, one hand holding onto the side rails, the other carrying the lantern. Eventually, his foot touched the bottom and his boot crunched on the tunnel floor.

Sounds more like sand. I wonder if the tunnel leads onto the beach?

James looked up into the trap door opening. Nancy smiled, blew him a kiss and replaced the cover leaving him alone in the darkness.

"I guess it's time to find my way out of here," he said, moving his neck from left to right.

He crouched down a bit and held the lamp in front of him to light his way. A breeze blew down the tunnel making him shiver, and his senses heightened when he heard the scurrying rats. After about ten minutes, he saw sunlight and he sped up to meet it. At last, he was outside in the daylight and he breathed in the salty air and listened to the waves as they crashed against the rocks. "Ha-Ha-Ha," cawed the seagulls as they wheeled above his head and he smiled. He was alive, he was free of an angry mob, and he wasn't being pursued by a werewolf bent on revenge.

Chapter Eighteen: Revelations

A loud thud followed by shouting men disturbed James's sleep and his eyes flickered open.

"Clara, wake up. I think they have come for me!" he said, shaking his lover from a heavy sleep.

"Woah? James, what are you talking about?" Clara said, propping herself up on her elbow and rubbing the sleep from her eyes.

"Listen," he said, holding a finger to his lips.

"We know you're in there, Garrett. And we know what you have done."

"James, get dressed. You know that trap door in the middle of the kitchen floor?"

"Yes, what about it?"

"It leads to the cellar and then to a tunnel and out onto the moors. Get down there and make an escape. I'll distract them and

I'll find you in the woods. You find Tufel and stay there until I come for you."

"But what about you?"

"Don't worry about me. Now go!"

James pulled on his clothes and went down stairs. Clara, who had also thrown on some clothes, opened the hatch in the kitchen, kissed her lover and pushed him down the opening, closing it behind him, and then she slid a trunk on top of it.

"Just a minute," Clara called out, straightening her woollen shawl.

She opened the door and saw an angry middle-aged man holding a torch. Behind him were more angry men carrying torches and weapons.

"What's all this about? It's very late."

"Where is he?" The leader snarled. Clara realised who was addressing her. Alfred Raffkin, the town mayor.

"Where's who?" Clara said, trying to play dumb, hoping to give James more time to escape.

Raffkin scowled. "Don't play innocent with me, Mrs. Garrett. We have come for him. Franklin Garrett, your husband."

Clara looked at the man with wide eyes. "Whatever for? What has he done?"

"See for yourself," Raffkin said, stepping aside and gesturing to her garden. The other men parted and Clara stepped through. Sheep remains lay littered about the grounds and the area smelled of blood.

Clara coughed and covered her mouth.

"There must have been some kind of mistake. Franklin wouldn't do something like this."

Raffkin tightened his lips into a thin line, his face going red as he shook his fist in fury.

"Don't try my patience, Mrs. Garrett. Sergeant Cannon, perhaps you would like to show Mrs. Garrett your warrant for her husband's arrest?" Raffkin said, a smug grin splinting his lips.

"Certainly, Lord Mayor. This is a warrant to search the premises for your husband. He is wanted for questioning with regard to the slaughter of farm animals and the attempted murder of Newt Hopkiss. Please allow myself and my officers access to this building. Any attempt to prevent us from doing so, may result in your arrest."

"This is absurd! I am certain that Franklin is completely innocent, but I know the law and I will assist you any way I can," Clara said, and walked back into the house. She turned the key in the lock and let the officers into her house.

The policemen began tossing furniture and yelled out. "Franklin Garrett, we know you're here somewhere. If you cooperate, we will do our best to make sure you have a fair trial."

"Sir, we moved a trunk in the kitchen and found a trap door. It looks like it leads to a cellar. Most of these houses have a cellar that leads to a tunnel, a way out."

Cannon clenched his teeth together. "If you have helped your husband escape, I will throw the pair of you in the slammer," he hissed, wagging his finger at her.

"Innocent until proven guilty," Clara declared.

Cannon stepped in front of her, his face inches from hers. He smelt of whiskey and cheap cologne.

"Don't you quote the fucking law to me. Aiding and abetting a felon is a criminal offence."

Clara winched, stepped aside and gestured to the opening in the floor.

"Be my guest, officers."

Cannon shot Clara a flinty stare, and he and his officers disappeared down the tunnel.

Shortly after this, there was a rap on the door. Clara opened it and Raffkin barged into the room knocking her to the floor. The mayor spun around, and when he saw the open trapdoor, he said, "This way, lads."

Clara screamed and backed against the stove as man after man invaded her home and disappeared down the gaping hole in the floor, like worker ants carrying a carcass back to their lair.

When they had all gone and Clara was alone, she said, "God help you, my love."

After that, she retrieved her goggles and called Horace.

"Horace, thank God. The village has launched a manhunt for James, and I fear for his life. Can you get here, fast? We really need your help."

"That is very upsetting news, my dear girl. I will be there in a jiff."

Clara sighed with relief and closed her eyes. "Thank you, Horace. And Horace?"

"Yes, Clara?"

"Please bring the werewolf antidote."

***

Silver moon beams lit the quiet forest as a faint, flickering light glowed from Tufel's cabin. James lightly tapped on the door. He heard footsteps and then the door was opened by the dwarf, who beamed, "Come in my boy. We've been expecting you."

James hesitated, then he said, "What do you mean 'we've been expecting you'?"

"Please don't be alarmed," Robert Hopkiss said, rising from his seat, his hand stretched out and eyes wide.

"We believe you, Franklin. You have tried so hard to protect Newt and we thank you."

James sighed and slumped in a chair opposite Tufel. "I need a drink. Have you got any mead, Tufel?" he inquired, staring at the table.

The dwarf slid a tin tankard across the table, uncorked a clay bottle and poured James a drink.

Grabbing the drink, James gulped down the beer ferociously, spilling some of the liquid down his chin.

He slammed down the mug. "More," he gasped and Tufel dutifully refilled his flagon. After he had finished his top up he crashed the beaker down on the table again, wiped his mouth on the back of his sleeve and said, "We are in grave danger and we don't have a lot of time. The whole village is after me. Bardulf slaughtered a lot of sheep and framed me for it. The villagers came armed and baying for my blood, but I escaped and came here."

"That's okay, we trust you and we will protect you," Robert said, nodding at Newt.

"That's not all. Bardulf has given me a werewolf transformation drug. I have tried very hard to fight it, but I fear that tonight will be the night my metamorphosis will be complete."

Newt went pale, gripped his father's jacket sleeve, turned his face into his father's chest and wept bitterly.

"We still believe you will do the right thing, don't we, Newt?" reassured Robert, stroking his son's hair. Newt stopped weeping, turned and looked at James and said, "You're a good man, mister. You have done your best to help and protect me, and I fink you'd do the same if yous was a wolf."

James gritted his teeth and clenched his fists. "I can't be responsible for my actions when I turn into that… that… beast!"

Tufel placed a reassuring hand on James's shoulder.

"I think when you are a werewolf, you will fight the good fight, my friend. You are on the right side of the law; it runs through your veins."

As soon as Tufel finished speaking, there was a knock at the door, and the Hopkisses sat bolt upright in their seats, a look of fear on their faces.

"James Bronze, let's settle this once and for all," Bardulf said.

"What shall I do?" James said, staring at Tufel and chewing his lip.

"Stop stalling, Bronze. Come out all of you, and I promise I won't harm anyone."

"I think we'd better do what he says," Tufel said, fixing James with a watery stare.

I really hope Clara comes through with the cavalry, I need all the help I can get.

James stood up and stretched his arms. "Let's do this."

He opened the door and the others followed him out of the cabin.

Bardulf smiled and opened his arms like a father welcoming his children, making James shudder.

"James Bronze, you are quite remarkable, and yet you resist reaching your full potential," Bardulf said, pacing the clearing as he spoke.

"And what is that supposed to mean?"

Bardulf spun around and emitted a sound somewhere between and bark and a laugh. "Your DNA is incredible. You could be anything you want, not just a werewolf. A shifter, vampire, providentia. My boss is dying to meet you."

"Not only did you drug me, you shared my DNA without my permission? You're a fucking bastard, Bardulf."

Bardulf tutted and wagged his index finger at James. "Language in front of the child."

"Whatever. Who is your boss, Bardulf?"

"I am not at liberty to say, but if you survive this night, I am sure she will reveal herself. You are very useful to her, alive or dead. If you want to defeat me, you will need to transform into a wolf." After he had finished talking, he moved his head from side to side and then there was a sound of bones breaking and skin stretching. Bardulf's nose stretched and turned from human to wolf. When he had finished transforming within seconds that seemed to last a lifetime for the others, he let out a blood curdling howl and in one leap clamped his jaws around Newt's waist and carried the screaming child into the night.

"No!!!" James, Robert and Tufel yelled.

Immediately, James fell to his knees and clutched his chest. His body convulsed and his bones snapped. His cries turned from human to wolf and the change was complete.

"Go and get him, James," Tufel yelled.

James's wolf threw back his head and howled, then he gave chase.

At that moment, Clara and Horace arrived on horseback.

"Where's James?" Clara said, looking at Tufel.

"His transformation is complete, and he has gone after Bardulf. That evil monster has my son Newt. Please bring my boy back to me alive and unharmed, I beg you." Robert pleaded, falling to his knees and grabbing Clara's black riding boots.

Clara looked down at the panic stricken man with steady eyes and a small reassuring smile on her lips. "I promise Horace and I will bring your boy back to you."

"Thank you, thank you so much. Newt means the world to me. He is all I have left."

"Okay, we'll be back very soon. Yah!" Clara said, kicking her horse into action as she and Horace sped off into the forest in the direction of the two werewolves. They spurred their horses on through the tree tunnel. Shortly after this, they heard the wolves and caught sight of their furry behinds. The animals sprinted up a slope to a rocky ledge.

"Clara, you take the high ground, I'll take the low," Horace yelled, taking a downward slope underneath the ledge.

"Okay," Clara shouted over her shoulder.

"Bardulf, let the boy go. He's done nothing to you."

Bardulf turned to face her, his yellow eyes glowing in the dark. He tossed his head sharply, releasing Newt from a vice-like grip, bearing his bloody fangs at Clara. A scream escaped the boy's lips as he tumbled through the air like a ragdoll, his limbs flailing as he fell. Crimson liquid soaked the boy's top as he winced and writhed on the floor. Horace pulled out what looked like a large shotgun and fired it at the forest floor. After he had pulled the trigger, a net with stakes attached to it flew out of the barrel and secured itself to the ground. Newt tumbled into the net safely.

Horace dismounted and offered the frightened boy his hand.

"Here, lad, take my hand."

Nodding, the boy took his hand and Horace helped him down. Horace checked the boy's torso, and was surprised to see the fang marks were barely skin deep.

Horace gathered strips of bandage from his saddlebag and applied them to Newt's wounds. After this, he retrieved an aluminium flask.

"Here, drink this. It's hot chocolate," Horace said, pouring out the liquid into the cup and handing it to the boy.

"Fanks, mister. Can you take me to me dad?"

Horace looked over the child's shoulder at the line of torches coming towards them along with the sound of marching feet.

"I think he's on his way, look," Horace said, pointing at the advancing mob.

Newt turned around and he meet eyes with his father and yelled, "Dad!" Robert ran forward and opened his arms. Newt, adrenaline pumping through his veins, sprinted towards his father. Robert crouched down and hugged his son, careful not to hold him too tightly after his ordeal.

***

Circling each other, the wolves snarled, saliva dripping from their sharp teeth. Bardulf leapt at James and bit into the other's shoulder, making him yelp. Horace joined Clara, reuniting her with her gun that she loaded with silver bullets. As the fight progressed, she struggled to get a clear shot. Writhing wolves snapped at each other, trying to gain the upper hand, but Bardulf had weakened his opponent and was winning the fight. Suddenly, James lunged forward knocking his nemesis backwards and Clara pulled the trigger. A bullet flew from the gun and hit Bardulf in the chest, the momentum sending him over the ledge. With an agonising howl he fell into the net and lay there. By the time Clara reached the ledge to peer over, an unconscious Bardulf was already resuming his human form. The angry crowd stood around looking at the scene. Some of them pointed at the ledge above.

"Make room, make room. Official police business," the Commissioner said as he and a team of his officers pushed their way through to the net.

"Officers, arrest that werewolf on suspension of murder, attempted murder and kidnapping. And that's just for starters."

"Ah, Commissioner Harris. Sergeant Keith Cannon here. I've been conducting the investigation into Franklin Garrett and I.."

Harris held up his hand for silence.

"I've heard about you, Cannon, and how you manhandled Helena Garrett, who happens to be an undercover police officer. How you and your men barged into her home and allowed a whole village to march through her house and turn it upside down."

"Sir, I can explain."

Harris flashed Cannon a small smile and opened his hand.

"Hand it over."

"Hand what over, sir?"

"Don't play dumb with me, Cannon. Surrender your badge, your gun and clear out your locker. You no longer work for the Tarnuzian constabulary."

Raffkin, who was standing nearby said, "Commissioner Harris, I must protest.

Sergeant Cannon was only acting on my orders."

"And your orders are to harass women in the middle of the night, are they? I don't think this is going to go down well with your constituents. When's the election next month, isn't it?"

"Y..y…yes, but…"

"Save it, Mayor. Officers, take Bardulf away," Harris said, addressing his men.

"Yes, sir." They cuffed the criminal and put him in the prison wagon. With a crack of the whip, the cart pulled away, rocking to and fro on the uneven woodland floor.

"And, Cannon, before you go, I would like to know the names of the officers who assisted you tonight."

Cannon handed over his badge and gun, then looked at the commissioner flatly. "Officers, Fuller and Brown, please step forward."

"Yes sir," the two policemen said, walking into the clearing.

"I will expect a full report from the pair of you. It will form part of your disciplinary hearing. Dismissed, both of you."

***

Clara tended James's wounds as an out of breath Horace stepped onto the rocky precipice.

Reaching into his shoulder bag, he pulled out a syringe, uncapped it with his teeth and jabbed it into James's exposed arm. James was near naked, his clothes were torn to shreds in the transformation.

"Thanks, Horace. I hope the antidote works," James said, gasping for breath as Clara mopped his brow.

"Don't mention it, Detective Bronze. The signs look good that you will make a full recovery." Horace looked at Clara. "Now, my dear girl, let me inspect Detective Bronze's wound please?" Clara stood up.

"Thank you." Horace peered over his half rimmed glasses. James's shoulder was sore and blood poured from the bite marks.

After Horace had re-cleaned the wound, he applied a salve and then fastened a large piece of gauze to the gash with surgical tape.

"Here, put these on," Horace said, throwing James a jerkin, black trousers and black boots.

Clara and Horace turned their backs to him whilst he dressed.

"Okay, I am ready. Let's go and face the music." James sighed, trying to stand, but wobbling as he did so. Horace and Clara propped him up, he took a few more steps, then he held up his hand and they stopped. He walked on his own and then he straightened up, walking unaided.

Neville and Lil were talking to Commissioner Harris, who seemed to be listening intently, and James smiled to himself. It looks like their consciences got the better of them.

Still smiling, he looked at Clara. How can anyone hide from a providentia?

"What are you smirking about, Bronze?" she said, elbowing him in the ribs.

"Just how beautiful you are, and how you made Neville and Lil confess."

Clara smiled back. "Fear is probably the greatest motivator, I just helped them realise they needed to do the right thing."

"There she is!" James said, leaning over and kissing her on the lips.

"There Who is?"

"My five word Clara, Aw!" James said, grabbing his boot after Clara stamped on his toes.

"What did you do that for?"

Clara poked her tongue out, smiled and then climbed on her horse.

"I ought to put you over my knee and spank you," he said, gingerly climbing onto his own horse.

"Before we go," Horace said, trotting up beside James on his own horse, "the werewolf DNA in your body will heal your wounds very quickly. By the time you are fully human again, the injury will be no more than a scratch."

After showing Horace his best false smile, James said, "And there's me thinking I would carry the scars of war."

Horace's face darkened. "I wouldn't be too cavalier about such matters, Detective Bronze. The children of Tarnuz have now been fully vaccinated." And with that Horace tapped the side of his horse with his boots and pulled ahead.

All colour drained from James's face, his mouth went dry, as he thought about Horace's words. Does he think a war is coming? He's a mysterious man with indeterminable age. Can he travel through time and space? Has he seen this all play out before? He is very knowledgeable about so many different things. And how is it he is able to magic up all these gadgets out of thin air, seemingly without any prior knowledge? I need to get him alone and ask him all these things. I mean, is he really a friend or do I need to be more guarded around him?

James's thoughts were interrupted by the sound of his horse chewing on some grass and the figures of Clara and Horace disappearing into the darkness.

"Come on, beast, let's get a move on. They are leaving us behind," he said, tugging on the reins. His animal snorted and sprinted up to catch the others.

"I thought for a minute we had given you the nag," Clara said, when he pulled up alongside her.

Horace and Clara laughed.

Chapter Nineteen: Evil Tightens Its Grip

"Is there any truth in what Bardulf said to me about my DNA?" James said.

A week had passed since the showdown between Bardulf and James. Clara and James were sitting in Horace's laboratory with Adamar and Horace.

Horace rubbed his chin. "I think it is perfectly logical to question the claims of a liar, but on this particular subject, Bardulf was telling the truth."

James stood up and paced the room. When he stopped, he put his hand on his forehead. "So what does this mean? Am I some kind of fucking freak cocktail or something."

"Please lower your voice, James, and your countenance is burning. Sit with me my sweet and I will soothe your growing temper. Listen to what Horace has to say," Clara said, patting the red velvet sofa next to her, and pouting her lips.

Don't do that it makes me want to tear your clothes off and fuck you right here. Is she mocking me? Is she turned on? Stop with the mixed messages already! I feel like I am going to explode!

James planted his feet. His hands gripped the sides of his dark hair and he yelled, "I don't know who the fuck I am anymore. I…" he felt a light prick to his neck. He touched the spot, looked at Horace, who still held the syringe in his hand, then blacked out. Clara caught him and laid him down gently on the couch.

"He is still having withdrawal symptoms from the werewolf potion I am afraid," Horace said, sighing. "I recommend he is examined by the police physician to confirm my diagnosis, but I would suspect that he would agree with me."

Clara looked at her partner as he slept and brushed a stray strand of hair from his face, then she planted a soft kiss on his forehead. She took his hand in hers and kissed that too.

"What course of action do you propose, Horace? He is very special to me."

"Well, you can conduct yourself however you see fit, my dear girl, but giving him the come on was highly irregular."

Shit! He saw that. I suppose he did.

Clara stood up ramrod straight and puffed out her chest. "I'll thank you for not lecturing me on my conduct. You are not my father."

"Nor would I ever profess to be so. Your father was a truly great man, whose shoes I would never be big enough to fill. The point I am trying to make is this: James is very fragile in the mind at the moment. He has experienced a great deal of trauma which I believe he is still recovering from."

Clara sighed and folded her arms over her chest and repeated her question "What is the next course of action, Horace?

"Well, Adamar and myself need to explain to him what his DNA map actually means."

"Yes, our good friend at the Institute For Supernatural Friends, Dr. Anneka Stokes, will also help James adjust to the newfound knowledge," Adamar added.

Horace placed his hands on Clara's shoulders and looked her in the eyes. "He will need your support."

Clara snorted. "So will you Horace when he comes around. He's going to be frightfully upset with you for knocking him out like that."

Horace and Adamar laughed.

When he had finished laughing, Horace strapped on his goggles and called Doctor Stokes. By the time James had woken up and had calmed down, the physician had arrived.

Dr. Anneka Stokes was slim, in her late 30's, average height with long curly raven coloured hair and olive skin. She wore a black single buttoned belted blazer and tailored matching trousers and boots. She had an easy smile and a warm disposition.

She introduced herself to Clara and James, they shook her hand, then she took a seat.

Horace flicked on a screen with a remote control and a pie chart appeared. Above the pie chart it said, James Bronze's DNA in black letters.

James clenched and unclenched his fist, then he placed his hand on the table. Clara stroked the top of his hand and he relaxed. A large portion of the chart was coloured red and marked "providentia" that comprised twenty-five per cent; the next largest section of the chart was green, twenty per cent marked "Elf." The next section was brown, marked at eighteen per cent under "Werewolf." The remaining thirty seven was divided up between shapeshifter, dwarf, and mage DNA.

"Now that we have all been formally introduced, I would like to welcome Dr. Anneka Stokes today," Horace said. "She will answer any questions you might have regarding the IFSF. It's important to note that the IFSF is a support network, not just a research facility or a hospital. Trained experts are on hand for advice and counselling. Dr. Stokes will answer your questions subsequently, but first, Detective

Bronze, I want to go through what your DNA markers have told us. Adamar over to you," Horace said, gesturing to the elf and retaking his seat.

"Thank you, Horace. As you can see from the pie chart, your DNA, Detective Bronze, makes for very interesting reading."

James grunted. "Freak chart more like. I don't really care what you're doing here. Thank you for wasting my time," he said, getting up to leave.

"Sit down, James," a red faced Horace hissed, his eyes blazing.

Adamar hunched over, as if he was choking down a sob. When he made eye contact with James, his eyes were watery, his mouth downcast.

James looked away, and sat down again.

"Very well. You've got me," he huffed, throwing up his hands in surrender.

Horace smiled sweetly and handed Adamar a handkerchief.

"Thank you, Horace," Adamar said, wiping his eyes and blowing his nose.

After he had composed himself, he continued.

"I don't think DNA diversity is something to be feared. I believe it is something to be embraced and celebrated."

James looked at the nodding heads of everyone in the room.

Even Clara agrees. I guess I'll just have to hear them out.

"If we have a strong genetic marker, we can enhance that marker with the help of controlled substances. This is something you are familiar with now, Detective Bronze, having taken providentia enhancers for a number of weeks. How do you feel now that the trial period is over?"

James shifted in his seat crossed and uncrossed, then recrossed his black pinstripe trouser legs, his khaki and black spats bouncing on his knee. He flicked at his yellow cravat with his fingers, then he fixed his gaze on Adamar.

"Before I was dosed by the werewolf bastard, I started to acclimatise to providentia powers and abilities."

"How did it make you feel?" Anneka Stokes said.

She had a pleasant low voice, immediately putting James at ease. *No wonder she is a doctor. She has a very caring nature about her. I feel like I could tell her anything.*

"Like it was as natural to me as breathing." Upon hearing this, Clara squeezed his hand.

Horace rubbed his chin. "Detective Bronze, would you be prepared to continue your clinical trial as a providentia?"

"It would mean that your DNA would alter, and over time, you would become as fully fledged as Clara. Is that something you would be prepared to do?" A frowning Adamar said.

"I don't know. It's a lot to consider, and if my DNA is so special, wouldn't I be sacrificing my other unique abilities, effectively killing off a part of me?"

"That is a decision only you can make, Detective Bronze," Dr. Stokes said. "But myself and my colleagues at the IFSF are always on hand to help you reach your full potential."

James tapped his long fingers on his knee.

"Firstly, cut the Detective Bronze crap. Call me James." Everyone chuckled.

"Okay, James it is," Dr. Stokes said smoothly.

Horace and Adamar nodded again.

"Of course, you must be totally certain you want to become a supernatural empath. You may decide that you are more suited to the werewolf way of life." Horace said, leaning closer.

"I think that would be a terrible error with disastrous consequences," Clara said, looking at James and chewing her bottom lip.

"I have to agree with Clara. I do have a bad temper."

Horace and Adamar cleared their throats, Dr. Stokes just smiled.

"Let me give it some thought."

"Take all the time you need. You may need to discuss it with Miss Overton as it will affect your professional and personal relationship," Horace said, laying a reassuring hand on James's shoulder.

"I have a lot to think about, and I would like to talk it over with my friends. I'll be in touch with you all very soon," James said, taking Clara by the hand and then leaving with her.

***

"I think the biggest hurdle you have to overcome is if you really need this. The change does sound permanent to me," Edwin said, without turning around.

He was feeding his bird as Clara, James and Eme were sitting at his table drinking red wine.

"Permanent is not a favourite word of mine. It sounds so…eternal," Eme said, blowing out a jet of smoke. She was smoking from her trademark cigarette holder.

Edwin turned to face his friends. "It's a big commitment James. Is it something you're prepared to endure?"

James put his fingers to his mouth and raised his head, looking above Edwin.

"Well, when I took the providentia enhancement before, I felt a lot closer to Clara, like I understood a little bit of what she has to deal with on a daily basis. I feel that Clara and I have a future, and I want to be in tune with her."

Eme pointed two fingers at her open mouth. "Don't make me Barf. You sound like a love sick teenager. Ha ha! You have only been dating for a few weeks."

"Yes, but Clara and I have known each other for years."

Eme looked at him flatly. "It wasn't that long ago you wanted to transfer away from her. Clara told me all about it. Do you know how many nights she cried on my shoulder after a shift with you? Do you?" Eme pointed at him with her cigarette holder.

"No, sorry. I have no idea."

"It was a lot. I'm doing my best to accept you for Clara's sake, but I am finding it very difficult."

James barked a short laugh. "Eme, listen to yourself. If I'm the love sick teenager, what does that make you? Because from where I'm standing, you sound like a jealous lover to me."

Clara is my weakness, and I know that she is Emmeline Miller's too. Is it wrong that I want to fuck, dissect her, clone her, make her my lab rat, my slave, my concubine. My... my.. my... everything? Damn you, Clara Overton.

You have made me vulnerable and I fucking hate you for it!

Eme looked across the room at her friend.

"Enough! The pair of you," Clara yelled as she stood up and held out her hand for them to stop.

"Eme, I have chosen James to be my lover and want you to accept him as such. If you can't do that, then I am afraid we can no longer be acquainted. James, the same goes for you. If you can't accept Eme for who she is, then we can no longer be lovers. The choice is yours." she looked at James then at Eme.

James pursed his lips and held out his hand. "Truce?"

Eme narrowed her eyes, blew out some more smoke and accepted his proffered hand. "Truce."

Clara smiled. "Well, that is the kind of conclusion I was hoping for." She turned to James.

"This is your opportunity to ask Eme or myself anything you like about being a providentia."

Eme unscrewed the cap from a beer, took a mouthful, then placed the metal top on the table. "Let me show you a little trick." Eme took the cap and spun it on the table. Closing her eyes and holding out her hand, she concentrated very hard until the cap metamorphosed into a tiny silver horse that ran around the table. The others gasped in amazement, all of them pointing at the tiny metallic creature before them.

Eme exhaled and the horse fell on its side, lifeless.

They clapped and cheered and Edwin put his fingers in his mouth and whistled.

"How… did… you… do… that? I know you come from an ancient line of providentias, but I don't have that level of expertise," Clara said, a large smile on her face, her eyes wide with wonder.

Eme gave Clara a knowing smile. "Like you say, it's in my genes."

"Well, if that was the providentia sales pitch, sign me up!" James said, excitedly.

Eme stared at him flatly. "There's more to this life than cheap party gimmicks, my friend."

James took a step back, his hand flying to chest. "So, we're friends now, Eme, is that it?"

"What Clara wants, Clara gets." And I want Clara. Abigail thought. I shouldn't have to keep this pretence up for too much longer now. I pity you, you ignorant fools. You're all stumbling around in the dark. You have no idea how close the end game is now. It's just a matter of days before Lario falls and the rest of Tarnuz will follow. She wanted to throw back her head and laugh maniacally, but that would give her away.

"I know that smirk. You're planning something. Come on Emmeline Miller, out with it," Clara said, clicking her fingers, smiling broadly.

Eme whispered something in Clara's ear. Clara listened intently then a sheepish smile split her lips.

Clara went over to the drawer and pulled out a horse whip.

"Now, hold on a minute. You should have consulted me first before you retrieved that," Edwin said, holding out his hand, a worried look on his face.

"Come on now, Edwin, don't be such a prude," Clara smirked, clinking her wine glass against Eme's beer bottle, both women giggling as they did so.

"We are not mere acquaintances, we are all friends here. There should be no confidential matters between us. James, come and take this crop from me," Clara said, holding out the strap for him.

James scrutinised it in his hands, with a puzzled look on his face. "And, what exactly am I supposed to do with this?"

Clara and Eme chortled again. "You want to be a providentia so badly, big boy, close those big brown eyes of yours and tell us what you see," Eme said, goading him.

James took a deep breath, then he exhaled. Closing his eyes, he gently caressed the whip and he was rewarded with the vision of Eme whipping Edwin's bare bottom.

"What the fuck!" James shrieked, dropping the crop on the floor.

The two women guffawed loudly and rolled on the floor kicking their legs in the air.

A red faced Edwin picked up the whip, grabbed a bottle of brandy and two glasses, put his arm round James' shoulder and said, "I Think we'll leave these two clowns on their own. Let's have a cigar and drink this brandy in my study."

After exhaling a smoke cloud, James leaned back in his armchair and the red buttoned upholstery creaked as he did so. Edwin's study was still and the only sound that could be heard was the steady ticking of the grandfather clock, and it made James feel calm and relaxed. Up until now, he had felt like a coiled spring.

"Have you ever considered it, Edwin?"

"Considered, what?"

"Becoming a full blown providentia."

Edwin swirled his brandy around in his glass before he answered. "I drew up a mental pros and cons list, I had more cons than pros, so I dismissed it."

"Was it as simple as that for you?"

"It wasn't as easy as that, I can assure you. I agonised over this for months before I made my decision. I think I decided I had enough to deal with without having to manage being an empath full time. It would be a colossal undertaking. Does my explanation help you with your decision?"

James drank a bit more of his drink. "I certainly value your opinion, but when twenty-five per cent of your DNA is providentia, it helps one to decide."

"It sounds like you've made up your mind, James."

"Do you think so?"

"It sounds like it to me," Edwin said, turning to face James. "How do you feel when you have the full providentia experience?"

"I feel connected, truly alive, complete."

"I think you need to see Horace tomorrow and ask him to start your treatment."

"I'll drink to that," James agreed, raising his glass for Edwin to clink it which he did.

***

"Okay, that's a wrap, fellas," Dr. Albi Lurcock's voice said in Flint's earpiece.

Flint turned the dial on his blowtorch and the flame went out. He could hear the muffled sounds of movement in the water as the other Tokers extinguished their blow torches, having received the same message he had. The underwater pipeline was finished, which meant the whole of Tarnuz was now connected to the telephone goggle network. If he was still human, he would have felt pride. He didn't feel anything anymore, and the faces he used to see had gone. Day by day, something from his previous life disappeared, or maybe it was erased. He didn't care. He was following the program they had given him that day.

He stood in a line next to two other Tokers and opposite three more. All of them looked the same. The only thing that told them apart were their name badges, which even they couldn't read in the darkness at the bottom of the ocean.

"Please stand still as the retrieval cage approaches," a metallic voice said in his ear. A large claw came down and clamped around Flint and all the mechanical men, forming a cage. A whirr from the winch singled their ascent as it pulled them from the depths of the ocean to the vessel waiting for them on the surface. After an hour, the ship docked, and Flint was greeted by the good doctor herself.

"Well done, Flint, good job," she said, smiling.

"My pleasure, ma'am." Flint replied, saluting her with his clockwork hand.

Alibi watched Flint and the other automatons walk to their storage area and power down for the night.

Doctor Albi Lurcock sighed as the large metal door hissed shut behind her. She turned and looked at herself in the mirror and morphed into Abigail Price.

"I know that sigh. You're letting him get under your skin."

"Thanks for your vampire insight, Zintius. You have no idea what it's like to live inside another person's skin. It affects you, you know. You literally become that person. You live, breathe, and feel them. You are them. Sometimes, empathy sticks around."

Zintius closed the interior design magazine, uncrossed his legs, and pulled his dark overcoat from underneath his buttocks. When he was comfortable, he leant forward and steepled his long fingers.

"Lucius Silas Flint is nothing more than a machine now. An automaton, whose sole purpose is to receive orders and act upon them. He is an experiment, a lab rat."

"What do you see when you look at the lab rats, Zintius?" Abigail asked, turning to face him.

"I see a snack before the main course," he said, laughing coldly, his canines shooting out from the roof of his mouth. "I can see the pulse in your neck. The roar of your heart in my ears is like a beating kettle drum. I am so thirsty it has been a while since I drank," the vampire said, walking slowly over to her, his boots making no sound on the white tiled floor.

Still facing him, Abigail reached behind her and pulled her gun on him.

"And I have the power of the sun in my hand," she said, as the hammer on the gun clicked. "Don't make me use the UV setting on you."

Zintius' evil smile faded. "Just a little drink, please?"

Abigail rolled her eyes. "Wait there, just a second." She unlocked a door on her left and came back with a large white rat. "Here," she said, tossing the animal at her undead sidekick, and it squeaked when he caught it deftly in his hand.

"Thank you," he said, and then sucked the animal dry in seconds. After that, he carried it by its tail and dropped it in the wastepaper basket.

Abigail leaned against the bench and crossed her black trouser legs at the ankles, her back to the mirror. Her white lab coat swished as she did so. She placed her hands on either side of her.

"I think it's important that you understand what we are trying to achieve here at Agreeable Solutions."

Zintius threw open his arms. "Please, enlighten me."

Abigail crossed her arms. "People are not as complicated as everyone thinks. They are driven by desire. A desire to be loved and liked, to succeed, to have the very latest design in fashion, or the next must-have gadget. And do you know what the unique thing is about desire?

Zintius tilted his chin to his chest. "Go on."

"Desire can be created. With the right advertising and a little gentle persuasion, you can sell anyone anything. It's like a junkie chasing their next fix. We manufacture a need so great in someone that our product becomes everything they live for."

"Right, the people of Tarnuz love the new communication goggles. I prefer telekinesis, although your mind is closed to me, Abigail, and I find that disturbing," he said, bearing his teeth.

Abigail flashed him a carefree smile, her fingers idly drumming on her gun next to her.

"How does supernatural DNA factor into the equation?"

Abigail tutted and wagged her index finger from side to side. "All good things to those who wait. I will reveal my plans one step at a time and your part in the grander scheme of things. Your reference to the goggles is great, and I am so glad you brought it up."

"I am glad I could be of help," Zintius said, with a flourish of his hand.

"You see, this is the antithesis of progress. We see a gap in the market, we create a desire for it, and then it becomes the very thing people can't live without."

"And solving the problem of wanting an answer straight away, without having to wait for snail mail. Genius. Almost makes me want to be human again."

"I'll take that as a compliment. It must be so boring living for centuries, and the only desire you have is for blood."

"That and world domination."

"Now that is something we can agree on. Okay, you've forced my hand. The supernatural DNA is the real plan. Imagine a country overrun with feral beasts. It would be utter chaos, complete anarchy. Once everyone has been killed, you and your merry band of vampires can swoop right in and take control. Just leave me a seat at the table."

"Very well, but where will you go when this is all over?"

"Tarnuz doesn't owe me anything. I will expand into the rest of Remina, selling my designer drugs and telephone goggles to the highest bidder."

"So, if people need to score, they have something to call you on. Aren't there enough drug dealers in the world?"

"I can assure you I am more than just a high-tech drug dealer. I have more ideas I want to share with the world. Anyway, let's concentrate on destroying this nation before we think about ruining another one. I just need to deal with that fucking meddling Overton bitch."

"Oh yes, you and her have history together," Zintius said, chuckling.

"Yes, well, the sands of time are about to run out on her."

"If only I had a goblet of blood, I would propose a toast."

"If only," Abigail said, grimacing.

***

Masonry exploded around them as the mini-gun spoke again.

"I recognise the need to use firepower in certain circumstances, but this is utterly preposterous," Clara said, when the firing had stopped.

"Agreed. I didn't even know these things were weaponised," James said, gingerly peering around the remains of a house wall. "I thought they were being used to speed up house building and other manual labour jobs, not be part of the police force."

"I wish to disclose something that Commissioner Harris told me off the record."

Before James could answer he heard the metallic sound of the Toker's feet and whirr of the mini-gun as it drew closer. "Okay, Clara, make it quick," James whispered.

"Chancellor Spencer threatened to cut the police budget if Peter didn't agree to

Agreeable Solutions supplying weaponised Tokers to law enforcement."

James looked at her with wide eyes. "You've got to be shitting me."

"If only I was. I find the whole thing detestable."

"I think we're going to need to carry on this conversation later. He sounds like he's getting closer. We need a plan to take this thing out."

Orders from the top had recommended the Toker go into the slums to flush out vaccinated children. The mechanical man had been instructed to fire a few warning shots to disperse the youngsters. A blind panic startled the kids and like frightened rats deserting a burning building, they scattered all over the city. Small charred bodies lay on the road, their mouths permanently open, revealing sharp vampire teeth, as the sun shone down on them. More masonry crumbled to the floor as man-made structures were now victims of a killing machine. People had left in a hurry, taking just the bare essentials.

Belongings were scattered on the road. An old fob watch lay on the ground, cogs and springs poking out of it. Bits of clothing, jewellery and household items were strewn everywhere. A dirty net curtain flapped in the winter breeze from a first storey window. Underneath the window was a pile of rubble and next to that was a staircase, and Clara had an idea.

"Can you see the remains of that house over there, you know the one with the flapping net curtain and exposed staircase?" James's gaze followed the direction her finger was pointing in.

"Yeah, what about it?"

"We need to lure our clockwork friend over there. You throw a rock to distract him, then I'll sneak over to the ruins."

"This is complete madness. Whatever are you thinking, Clara?"

"You are just going to have to trust me on this one."

James shrugged. Assuming his vantage point, James waited until the mechanical man rounded the corner. When he saw the tip of the brody helmet, he threw a stone to his right. With clumsy, jerky movements, the robot chased after the stone, and then opened fire. Bits of stone and debris flew everywhere. A cloud of dust hung like a thick heavy fog, and rubble fell to the ground like large hailstones during a heavy storm. After the dust had settled, another stone hit the back of the automaton's helmet. He turned around and planted his feet like a sumo wrestler. Huge blue glass eyes scanned the war torn buildings and his copper moustache twitched as he did so.

"Oi, clockwork cock, over here," Clara yelled, waving from the top of the staircase. Click, click, click went the trigger of the mini-gun, but the gun was empty and useless. Angrily, the machine tossed the n aside and waddled up the staircase towards Clara. When it was halfway up the steps, its round body convulsed causing it to become still like an exhibit in a science museum. Pulling the lever on her gun to the explosive setting, Clara aimed and fired. There was a thump sound from the barrel. Jumping to the ground, Clara sprinted away and took cover, just as the robot exploded, leaving behind two copper feet with copper springs still attached.

James ran to the spot where he thought Clara was, looking around trying to find her.

"Psst, James, I'm over her," she said, waving her hand above a pile of rocks.

"Clara, are you hurt?" James said, sounding concerned.

"No, I am absolutely fine."

He walked around the rocks and saw that she was covered in soot and brick dust, but appeared to be unharmed.

Thank God you're alright. My world is so much happier with you in it, Clara Overton.

"Now it would be jolly decent of you if you could help me to my feet, please."

"Sorry, Clara, where are my manners?" He offered her his hand and she took it and stood up.

"Quite, where did your manners go? Did they take a stroll around the lake or something." She pulled her ruffled navy blazer down, brushing the dust off the jacket and her matching walking suit skirt that barely covered her knees. She took out a handkerchief from her blazer, spat on it and buffed her ankle boots.

"You're a fine one to talk about manners, my dear."

Clara looked at him flatly. "I'll pretend I didn't hear that. Now we need to figure out what we are going to tell Commissioner Harris about the robot we destroyed. After that, you can buy me a beer."

"He did say stop the bloody thing, no matter what. That's very cheeky of you, demanding a beer out of me, aww," James said, as Clara gave him a sly look and pinched his bottom.

"Now, that's cheeky," Clara said, giggling.

James shook his head. "Unbelievable, totally unbelievable."

"You wouldn't have it any other way, James Bronze."

They had reached the main road and James hailed a cab.

They stepped inside the carriage.

"Where to, guv?"

"Police headquarters, please."

"Right-ho, mate," the driver said, tapping the reins on the horses. The vehicle lurched forward and they were on their way.

"How are you feeling? You had your first providentia supplement today."

James's red leather gloves smoothed his wine red jacket and trousers. "I haven't had a chance to use my powers yet. I didn't see how they would be useful against a homicidal mechanical maniac," he said smiling.

Clara burst out laughing, then covered her mouth with the back of her own leather gloved hand. Her gloves matched her skirt suit and her ankle boots. James looked dapper in his matching suit, gloves, topper, complete with goggles. His black shoes finished off the look nicely and she wanted him, the flutter in her loins reminded her of that. She leant forward and kissed him passionately, and he reciprocated, taking her in his arms.

After the embrace, she straightened her blazer and her skirt, then cleared her throat, and looked out of the window at the bustling cobblestone street.

"Yes it was definitely fight or flight in the slums," Clara said, coughing, taking out a throat sweet from her pocket and popping it in her mouth.

"Are you okay, Clara? You look a little flustered," James said, smirking.

"Hmm? Ah? What?" she said, fanning her red face with her hands. "I..err.. Have an incredible urge to fuck your brains out, but that is utterly absurd and I can't wait until the shift finishes so I can make good on my promises. There I have said it. Satisfied now?" Clara said, giving him a sultry sideways glance, neatly placing her hands in her lap.

James smiled, leant forward and whispered in her ear. "Do you have any requests when you deliver on your promise?"

A thrill trickled down her spine and she shivered with delight. "Yes, you can leave your hat on!" she said, feigning indifference and looking out of the window again. "We have arrived at the police headquarters." Clara opened the door and bowled up the steps, her hips swaying provocatively, or had James imagined that?

He stood on the pavement, took off his topper, shook his head and scratched his hair.

She is a mystery wrapped inside an enigma, this girl. Everything she does has an element of class to it. Even her bumbling. No, maybe not everything. The little trick with the horsewhip and then lolling about on the floor, there was nothing classy about that at all.

There's so much to learn about being a providentia, too. I think, or I certainly hope, she will be an excellent teacher. That bottle cap horse was something else! Even Clara was speechless over that. I'll have to ask Eme how she did that.

Before he knew where he was, he was knocking on the frosted glass door that was stencilled with the words 'Commissioner Harris', in bold letters. His legs had carried him across the street, through the doors of the Police HQ and up the three flights of stairs to the top cop's office.

It's amazing how you can get lost in your thoughts and are still able to function.

"Come in, James," Peter Harris's deep voice said.

Clara was already sitting in a dark green leather buttoned armchair, one of a pair that matched the office chair that Harris sat in. Peter sat with his hands clasped in front of him at his dark hardwood desk. All the furniture was placed on top of a maroon carpet. The room had no natural light. Clara held a glass of bourbon in her hand.

"Drink?" Harris said, and before James had time to answer, Peter had walked over to a panel in the dark wood wall and lightly pressed it. A door opened revealing a liquor cabinet. Harris poured James a double bourbon and handed it to him.

"Thank you, sir."

"You're welcome James," Harris said, sitting down in his office chair. The room was illuminated by red press lamps. One was glowing softly on Harris's desk, the others lit oil paintings of legendary commissioners on the dark wood panelled walls.

Harris sighed and reclasped his hands. "What happened at the slums?"

He already knew, but he wanted Clara and James to tell their side of the story.

"We apprehended a clockwork man," Clara blurted out.

James grunted. "Obliterated a clockwork man more like."

Harris held up his hand requesting them to be calm. "At ease, the pair of you. I don't care for these mechanical monsters anymore than you do, but I need to tell Theodore Spencer and Jedidiah Lewis something."

"Sir," Clara said, raising her hand like a child in class. "I think you need to point out that the automaton couldn't distinguish between police officers and supernatural beings."

"Are you saying the robot malfunctioned, Clara?"

"Yes, I am sir."

"James, what is your assessment of the situation?"

"I think the fucking thing needed to be stopped before it went rampaging through the city and killed everyone."

Harris sat back in his chair and sipped his drink.

"If I tell them that it nearly killed two of my officers and may have killed children fleeing the scene, I think it'll shut them up."

"There's something else we noticed sir."

"Go on James, what did you find?"

"We found charred remains of vampire children laying on the floor."

"Ah, for fuck sake. There won't be anything left now. I think the wind will have carried their ashes away. Were your goggles recording at the time?" Harris said, looking at both of them in turn.

"The cameras were rolling all of the time, sir," Clara said.

Harris smiled. "I will need you to hand your goggles into the forensics team for analysis. We need this footage kept under wraps. We don't want Antony Wright getting hold of this film. When the time is right, we'll release it to him."

"Antony Wright, or Weasel Wright as we like to call him," James said.

Harris half smiled. "I think his nickname is probably more well-known than his real one."

Harris steepled his fingers. "We have digressed. Correct me if I am wrong, are you saying this robot may have inadvertently awoken vampires from their sleep, forcing them to flee in direct sunlight?"

"Yes, sir. That is exactly what we are alluding to."

"Thank you, Clara, for clarifying that. I think I have a very strong case to present to Chancellor Spencer tonight."

Clara frowned.

"Clara, my dear, why do you spoil your pretty face with such an ugly gesture?"

Clara chewed her lip. "I am concerned, sir, that more and more of your meetings with the right honourable gentleman are occurring at night."

Harris waved his hand dismissively, "My darling girl, what are you trying to say?"

"Call me a hopeless paranoid fool, but didn't you say Zintius was present at the last meeting you attended?"

Harris huffed out a breath. "Get to the point, Detective Overton."

"Yes, sir. I have reason to believe that Zintius has turned Chancellor Spencer and his associates into vampires."

Harris grunted. "That's a bold statement, Clara. Do you have any proof?"

"No, it's pure speculation on my part. What time is the meeting?"

"Midnight tonight."

Clara and James exchanged glances.

"Look, you are jumping to conclusions," Harris said, laughing nervously.

"With all due respect, sir, if Clara suspects something, you should listen to her."

Harris looked at James and then at Clara.

"Okay, what do you propose I do?"

"I think you should visit the police armoury and pick up one of Horace's special guns. They have a UV setting. If a vamp tries to attack you, turn the weapon on it," James said.

"You are like family to me, Peter, You're all I have left," Clara said, her voice shaking, her eyes brimming with tears.

Harris rounded his desk and hugged her. "It's okay, my darling. I will take a gun with me tonight."

Clara looked up at him. "Thank you, You are the closest thing to a father I have. I would be utterly devastated if I lost you as well, Peter," she sobbed, her wet red eyes pleading with him.

James placed a reassuring hand on the Commissioner's shoulder. "And if you went to Spencer's place without a firearm and came back dead, I am too young to take your job," James said, smirking.

Harris broke his embrace with Clara and laughed heartily.

"You've got some bollocks on you, James."

"Yes, sir, they are made of Bronze."

Harris and Clara laughed.

"I'll take your advice, both of you. If I am not mistaken, you have about four hours until The Festival Of Life starts. Obviously, you'll be on duty when that begins. Go home, get some rest, and I'll see you in the morning. Dismissed."

"Yes, sir," they both said and left.

Peter smiled and shook his head. "Kids!" he said and laughed again.

Chapter Twenty: Pick a Side

"Oh my! We're finally a couple," Clara said, giggling and covering her mouth after she opened the door.

James furrowed his brow. "Um? Ah?" He examined his bottle green suit and his matching topper. He looked at Clara with a building smile. "You're wearing bottle green too. If I knew we were going to the archery range, I would have worn my leather armour set as well. I was under the impression I was taking you for a fine dining experience on a dirigible."

Clara's mouth fell open. "Are you saying I am under dressed?"

Before he could reply, a loud crack of thunder rumbled across the jet black sky.

"It looks like rain. Come on Clara the cab is on the meter," James said, pulling up the collar on his black frock coat.

Clara stood on tip-toes and whispered in James's ear. "I don't care if I look under dressed, I have concealed weapons, and I hope you paid the maitre d' to look the other way."

James shrugged, a sly grin on his face as he opened his frock coat revealing two pockets, each one held a rifle.

Clara returned the smile. "That's my boy," she whispered, making him shiver and pull at the white collar of his shirt."

Sensing his body tense, Clara pulled away and held him at arm's length. "What's wrong, James? You look flustered."

"Im… Im… fine. Just a bit hungry, that's all. Let's go and eat."

"Okay," Clara said, leaning forward and kissing him on the cheek.

James smiled weakly, but squeezed her hand in his. They boarded the cab and James slid over to the window, watching the lightning flash across the sky and the rain drum on the carriage windows.

Clara retrieved a throwing knife from inside her leather jacket, flicked a switch and a metal emery board popped out. "You were right about that storm," Clara said, blowing off the excess keratin from her fingernails.

James's right leather glove squeaked as he gripped his cane handle, then he turned to face her. "Hmmm? Oh yes. There's something I need to tell you."

Clara leaned closer. "You have my undivided attention, my love, go ahead."

"The Festival Of Life will be taking place on the dirigible, so we will be making a series of stops to pick up all the dignitaries. I hope you don't mind."

Clara blinked slowly, put down her knife, then picked it up again. "Golly! What a marvellous surprise." A nervous smile sat on her lips.

"There's a bit more to it than that. I didn't have to bribe the Maitre d' at all. We are the air marshals on this flight."

Clara tightened her lips, her cheeks colouring.

"This is utterly preposterous. I thought this would be our time to relax before everything kicked off, James."

"Clara, my sweet, please don't be angry with me. We have two hours to have a beautiful meal before the airship picks up the first batch of revellers and representatives from the Dragon Mountain treaty."

The cab stopped and James helped her disembark.

Clara stepped onto the grass of the airfield. Angled flood lights illuminated the dirigible, tethered to the ground with ropes fastened with stakes. It looked like a silver bullet, harmless on its own, but deadly in the wrong hands.

"I remember the Dragon Mountain treaty. That was the one where I agreed to be the tethered goat."

James walked away, ran his fingers through his hair, looked at the ground and nodded.

When he turned to face her again, his eyes were filled with tears and his lips quivered.

Clara walked over and hugged him. "Come on, you silly man. We have a flight to catch."

James choked back a laugh, and they got on board the huge vessel.

There's something else about James's behaviour. Something he's hiding from me. I'll see if I can get his tongue to loosen up. If I ply him with enough drinks, his tongue will be looser than the village gossip's tongue. If that doesn't work, well, I'll just turn on the providentia charm.

Buildings crumpled as the toker sprayed bullets over the slums all over again.

Albi Lurcock covered her mouth with her right hand and wiped a tear from her eye with her left hand.

"I think we have seen enough of this gratuitous violence, Commissioner Harris. You can shut off this ghastly film now," Patrick Spencer said.

Harris suppressed the smirk he wanted to display, walked over to the table and switched off the film protector. The reel slapped on the side of the machine as it powered down.

"Jedidiah," Spencer said, looking at the industrialist. "You need to try and convince your employees to go back to work. I am sorry your wife and child left you, but here's your opportunity to save a little dignity. These Tokers, as the tabloids call them, are an embarrassment and unpredictable."

Jedidiah stood there with his mouth open. "Chancellor, I must protest."

"There is nothing you can say to change my mind, Lewis. Now, go and call a press conference."

Jedidiah stayed rooted to the spot.

"Lewis, get out of my sight!" Spencer roared, his face red, veins bulging in his forehead.

Lewis fumbled his way out of the attache room, tripping on a chair leg before he made it to the door.

Spencer slumped in his chair and drank a dark, coppery smelling drink from a glass goblet.

Harris grimaced. I think Clara might be right. Zintius has turned the Chancellor.

Spencer turned to face Lurcock, flashing her his warmest smile.

"Albi, you need to put your house in order. You have two hours to get rid of those frightful contraptions."

"Okay, sir. I'll get right on it," Albi said and then left.

"Commissioner Harris, I want to show you something. Come with me. Pour yourself a glass of red and bring it with you."

Harris did as he was asked and followed the Chancellor up an ornate white marble staircase. The staircase was wide enough to fit a carriage. Eventually, Patrick Spencer flung open large, heavy oak doors and stepped onto a balcony. Harris gasped as he took in the splendour of Lario at night. Smoke curled from the chimneys of sleepy cottages, inns, taverns and theatres. A train blew its whistle as it crossed the viaduct that Clara had saved just a few short weeks ago.

Revellers laughed as they shared a joke in the courtyard of the Monk's Inn.

Horse drawn cabs whizzed past in the direction of the play house.

"Look at her. Isn't she beautiful?" Spencer said, gesturing to the sprawling metropolis below them.

"It's an impressive sight sir, I can't deny it."

I have seen some impressive views from Lario before, but not from this building.

"Make the most of the view, Commissioner. This landscape is about to change forever."

Harris reached inside his frock coat and flicked off the safety catch on his pistol.

"I am sorry, sir. I don't follow."

"Zintius and Albi Lurcock have ambitious dreams. They are true visionaries, unlike Lewis."

Yeah, I saw how you threw Jedidiah to the wolves earlier.

"Would you care to elaborate on the plans Zintius and Lurcock have, please Chancellor?"

"It is quite evident that Lario and the rest of Tarnuz is not ready for an automated workforce, but they are more than ready to embrace a supernatural one."

"Sir, I am afraid there are flaws in both of these plans. My officers have investigated these faults numerous times. I object to children being forced into labour and being turned into mutants. I also have evidence that suggests corpses are being repurposed and used inside the Tokers. All of these practices are barbaric and inhumane. I cannot allow them to be executed in my city."

Spencer grinned a sharp toothed smile. "An interesting word, execute. It can mean so many things, such as carrying out or putting into effect a plan, order, or course of action or it can mean carrying out a sentence of death on a legally condemned person: "he was convicted of treason and executed".

Harris gripped the handle of his pistol. "Are you threatening me?"

Spencer held up his hand in surrender. "I fully understand that the supernatural trials haven't gone smoothly, but productivity of the test subjects has been promising. Supernatural employees are up to sixty percent more productive than human ones."

Harris made a low, short guttural sound. "It's still child labour, only you have denied them the right to be children. Robbed them of their basic right to enjoy a magical part of their lives. Every kid should be able to look at the world innocently with wide eyed wonder."

Spencer carried on smiling. "I can't see how anyone is denying anyone anything. A vampire child is still a child and still needs nurturing and guidance."

Harris had walked to the end of the balcony and Spencer was at the other. They faced each other like two gunslingers at high noon.

"Yes, but unlike werewolves, vampires are immortal and they never age. Which proves my point about a kid being denied a childhood. I can't see any provision being made for education for these youngsters. There is no record of these people at the IFSF. If there had been, myself and the rest of the police force would have worked closely with Agreeable Solutions on a rehabilitation programme."

"But any animal has to fend for itself eventually."

Harris sighed. "We're going around in circles here. If that's all you have for me Chancellor, I'll say goodbye. I have a city to…," before Harris finished talking, Spencer flew across the balcony and squeezed his windpipe. Spencer's eyes glowed red and two sharp fangs dropped down from the roof of his mouth. The Chancellor's face was as pale as alabaster and his features were contorted. Stars floated before Harris's eyes as he balled up his large fist and punched the other in the cheek. A maniacal laugh escaped Spencer's lips as Harris tried not to black out. Finally, Harris's fingers curled around his pistol again and he fired in the vampire's face. Screaming, Spencer recoiled, grabbing at his sizzling face, which was more ash than flesh now.

"One thing I learnt whilst I was a beat cop was never meet a vampire without a UV gun."

Still screaming, Spencer stumbled backwards and fell over the balcony. As he fell, Harris fired his gun a second time turning the former Chancellor to soot. Harris peered over the balcony and looked at the black powdery substance on the cobbled street below.

"You broke the law arsehole and the sentence is death," Harris said, gasping for breath.

Before the Commissioner composed himself, he heard a woman scream and watched helplessly as a gargoyle swooped down and carried the writhing woman away. Aiming his gun he fired off a few rounds, but missed the beast as the screaming lady disappeared from view.

"Fuck," Harris said, slamming his hand on the balcony banister.

***

Agonised screams and the roar of burning flames filtered from taverns and pub gardens instead of the sounds of drunken laughter and singing. Thick smoke filled the sky along with the smell of burning timber. Jedidiah Lewis buttoned up his mourning coat.

A hatchet-faced man doffed his cap at Lewis as he approached the back door of the TWLF. Hatchet wore a dirty dark blazer, waistcoat, trousers, and black shoes. He held out his hand and Lewis slipped six gold sovereigns into his palm.

"Gawd bless ya, Guv. I can't guarantee ya safety when in there, but I'll do my best to protect ya on the way in."

"I appreciate it, my good man. You are probably the only friend I have left in the city."

Hatchet looked at him flatly with his brown eyes. "It cost ya, though dinnit, governor?"

Lewis's smile faded, he swallowed hard, then he cleared his throat. "Yes…well… let's not keep the workers waiting any longer, lead the way. There's a good chap."

Hatchet scowled and led Jedidiah down a dimly lit corridor. They turned right, facing steps that led to a stage with the curtains still drawn.

They could hear the sound of muffled voices coming from the meeting hall.

"This is where I leave ya, mate," Hatchet said and walked away.

Jedidiah licked his lips, bounced from one foot to the other. He threw punches like a boxer and rolled his head from side to side.

"I have been given word that the filthy scumbag Jedidiah Lewis is waiting in the wings," Ned Jenkins, the new head of TWLF said. Boos and jeers went up from the crowd.

"I couldn't give a fuck what that fucking wanker has to say," a man in the audience yelled, and was rewarded with roars of laughter, banging on chairs and a chorus of "Yeah".

"I think every dog has his day. Let Lewis have his, then we'll decide our next move. Please welcome to the stage Jedidiah Lewis."

Everyone booed as Lewis shook hands with Ned before taking the microphone to talk to the hostile crowd.

"Good evening, my fellow comrades," Lewis said, looking at the stony faced men before him. "I humbly stand before you this evening and admit to you today that I have made a terrible mistake."

"You're not fucking kidding. Defenceless children were driven from their homes yesterday and some even lost their lives," A chimney sweep said, followed by murmurs of agreement from the union. The sweep continued. "And I for one," he said, pointing at his chest. "Want to know what you're going to do about it."

Jedidiah trembled, his facing turning ashen. "I…I…I… we, err, the Chancellor and I will work very hard with you good folks to ensure better pay and working conditions for everyone."

"Ya too late for that, mate. The Chancellor was seen plummeting to his death this evening," another mob member shouted.

Jedidiah rocked backwards on his feet, grabbed his handkerchief from his breast pocket and dabbed at his forehead.

"I think you're running out of options, friend," someone jeered.

"How are you going to bring back Patrick Spencer from the fucking dead, huh? Are you some kind of fucking mage or something?"

Jedidiah stepped away from the mic, a burning rage coursing through his veins. He turned his back on the crowd and when he turned to face them, his face was pale and his eyes were red.

The men let out a collective gasp and the human swarm stepped back.

"I might have fucking known," Ned bellowed. "He was a fucking vampire all along. Let's crucify him on one of the crosses in the town square."

Moving as one, the mob edged forward, but before anyone could touch him, he disappeared faster than a blinking eye.

"Where the fuck did he go?" a union member said, looking to and fro.

"Look, up there!" a man said, pointing at a corner of the ceiling.

Everyone moved their eyes to the corner of the room.

Ned pulled out his gun and fired at Jedidiah, but he vanished before the bullet hit him.

"Everyone load your weapons with silver rounds, but don't kill him, I want him alive."

Men took out their firearms and the hall was filled with the sound of revolver barrels spinning and guns being loaded. For a moment, there was silence as the mob scanned the room with their eyes, then the peace was shattered as Jedidiah let out a cackling laugh. Instantly, everyone raised their guns and moved them around the hall, every man fizzling with energy like a high tension wire.

"You can't kill what you can't see, gentlemen," Jedidiah said.

"Show yourself and fight like a man," Ned said.

Jedidiah chuckled. It had an eerie echo to it, and the men shivered as ice began to form on the windows.

I am going to call his bluff, Ned thought.

"A neat trick with the windows, Lewis. But when was the last time you fed?" Ned said, wrinkling his nose.

"What's that fucking smell?"

A skinny boy with a sheepish look on his face, gingerly raised his hand. "Sorry, Ned. I always do that when I am scared."

Ned placed a reassuring hand on the lad's shoulder and whispered. "It's okay Timmy, I am scared too." Timmy smiled, straightened up and puffed out his chest. Ned patted him on the back. "Good lad." and returned to the centre of the room, where he was greeted with more mocking laughter from the invisible vampire.

"You lot are pathetic. I haven't even begun picking you off yet and some of you are already defecating yourselves."

Ned planted his feet and raised his gun higher, breathing heavily. Show yourself, motherfucker. You're more annoying as a vampire than you were as a wealthy industrialist.

"You sound thirsty to me, Lewis. You may have great power, but you still need to eat."

For a moment, there was silence, then a scream, and the sound of slurping. Ned whirled around and saw Lewis sucking from Timmy's neck. Lewis looked up and smiled, blood dripping from his fangs.

"Gotcha," Ned said, pulling his trigger. Lewis's body shimmered, but before he could disappear, the silver shot caught him right between the eyes. A blood curdling scream escaped his lips, shattering the frosted glass, forcing the men to dive for cover.

When the debris had cleared, Ned looked at the men lying prone on the floor.

"Listen, men, which one of you is a nurse? A man with a mop of curly brown hair stepped forward. "Fredrick, do your best to save Timmy, will you?"

"You have my word."

Ned laid both his hands on Fredrick's shoulders and stared determinedly into his eyes and said, "Good man, I am counting on you sending this boy back to his parents."

Then he turned to the others and said, "We don't have much time. Lewis is already beginning to heal. Somebody fetch me some rope to bind him and some nails and one of the town crosses. I want to make an example of this fucking bastard."

10 minutes later, the men came back with everything he had requested.

"Thanks, lads. Oh, and I see someone remembered the garlic, too. Very good work. Look, the bullet hole is disappearing. Smash up some of the garlic and smear it on his head wound. Promptly, the men responded to his orders. Jedidiah writhed, convulsed and screamed whilst the men hammered the nails into his wrists, severing his median nerve. After this, they hammered his feet to the upright part of the cross, bending the knees at 45 degrees.

Once Lewis had finished screaming, sweat pouring from his forehead and blood soaking the cross, he said, "It doesn't have to be this way. Why can't you just chop my head off? That's one way to kill a vampire, right?"

A brute of a man with ginger hair and beard leaned over and said, "You'd like that, wouldn't you? We're doing it to send a message. No one fucks with TWLF," he said before he hawked and spat in his face.

"That's it," Ned said, looking over his shoulder as Fredrick bandaged Timmy's neck. Frederick glanced at Ned and gave him a thumbs up.

"He's ready, chief," one of the union members said.

"Excellent. Grab as many weapons as you can."

The men retrieved weapons from the armoury beneath the building and when they returned, Ned said, "Let's hoist this son of a bitch up."

Ned stood at Lewis's left arm whilst one man took the right side and another stood at Lewis's feet.

"Three, two, one, lift."

They lifted Lewis onto their shoulders and carried him out like pallbearers. Five minutes later they arrived at the town square, stepping over debris and trying to block out the sounds of screaming, burning flames and people sobbing over dead relatives.

Carefully, they lowered greedy Jedidiah Lewis and his cross into a slot cut into the cobblestones. Once he was in place they hurled abuse at him.

"Enjoy the sunrise, bitch. It'll be your last," Ned said, causing the crowd to cheer as they walked away from Jedidiah Lewis.

After the TWLF had walked for a mile or so in silence, Timmy, who had recovered somewhat, largely due to the painkillers kicking in, said, "What has happened to Lario sir?"

But before Ned could answer, a rider on a black horse hurtled towards him with a determined look on his face, his robes flowing behind him. As he drew closer, Ned realised it wasn't a rider at all, but a centurion counsellor.

Eventually, the centaur stopped and introduced himself. "I am Midapius of the Centaur Council. Ned Jenkins and the rest of the TWLF, we need your help on the battlefront."

"Battlefront? What the hell are you talking about?" Ned said, scowling and furrowing his brow.

"The death of Chancellor Patrick Spencer has triggered a civil war."

"Fuck. I wondered why the city was in complete pandemonium. When you say civil war, what do you mean exactly?"

Lowering his head, Midapius spoke softly. "I am afraid the children of Tarnuz…

"You mean the vaccine kids?"

"Yes, they are indeed the children I am referring to. They have turned on everyone in the country."

"Okay, who sent you, Midapius?"

"Councillor Dimitri."

"The vampire?"

"The very same."

"Fuck."

***

"'Ish wine is rearwy good, Clara."

Clara had decided that the wine was taking too long to have the desired effect, so she used her providentia charm on it, heightening the potency of the drink.

"James, you're drunk."

Whilst a good conjurer never revealed their tricks, she would come clean tomorrow. All she had done was to wrap her bare hands around his wine glass and think about the truth. Once James had drunk from the glass, the drink acted as a truth serum.

"Shush," James said, holding a finger to his lips, glancing around the fine dining restaurant, to see if people were watching him. "They'll all want some...Hic!," he said, guffawing loudly and clapping. "I do want to tell you something, Claaara, my sweet." He touched her cheek and nearly fell off his chair in the process. "Last night..." he said before emitting an unearthly burp.

"James!" Clara exclaimed.

"I had a dream, no, no, no, a vision, no thatsss not it eeeither. Anyhoo, a nightmare. Yes, that's what it was." Then he whispered, "A nightmare, shush, shush," holding his finger to his lips again.

"Oh, good God. The pain of waiting is excruciating," Clara said, grabbing James' hand.

Within seconds, her eyes had rolled over and she was under the power of a trance. A blurry face swam into view and when her vision had cleared, she recognised Eme's face, smiling. Clara's chest felt tight and when she looked down, she saw a leather restraining strap. Her hands and ankles were bound with leather manacles. Twisting her neck, she saw James struggling against his restraints.

With a gasp, Clara let go of James's hand, grabbed his wine and concentrated on sober thoughts. Drunkenly, he swiped at his glass and drank the remainder of his wine. A golden glow flourished on his face and the colour returned to his skin.

"Waiter, could I please have some water," James said, gasping, waving his hand in front of his outstretched tongue.

"Certainly, sir, coming right up."

"Thank you."

The waiter left to fetch a water pitcher.

"I don't know what happened to me just then. I felt like I had an out of body experience."

Technically, you did.

"Well, you managed to tell me about that premonition you had last night. I was awfully afraid."

"Is that the one where we strapped to an examination couch and Eme was staring over us?"

Clara nodded.

Children of Tarnuz

James rubbed his hand over his face and through his hair. "It scared the shit out of me."

"Yes, that was my experience too."

"What do you think we should do? Confront Eme?"

"You know what Eme is like. She will just laugh at us and blow cigarette smoke in our faces. No, we'll sit tight. I am sure an opportunity to talk it over with her will present itself tonight."

A clap of thunder rumbled outside, followed by a bright flash of lightning.

After that, the waiter arrived accompanied by a waitress.

"Your water, sir," the waiter said, setting the pitcher on the table with two glasses.

James thanked him and he left.

"Le salmon en croute?" Clara raised her hand and the waitress laid her food in front of her.

"Chicken with green beans and new potatoes?" James also raised his hand, then the waitress served him also.

"Would you like more wine?"

"No!" Clara and James said, in unison.

"Very well, miss, sir, and if you need any fink else, just give us a holler," the waitress grabbed the corners of her black maid's dress and curtsied, then she left.

Clara and James enjoyed the rest of their meal and almost forgot where they were, what they were there for and what time it was.

"Good evening, ladies and gentlemen. We are currently descending. When we land, we will be welcoming everyone from The Festival Of Life. On behalf of myself and all the crew, we hope you all have a wonderful time."

James cocked one of his rifles.

Clara also loaded her weapon.

"And so it begins." James said.

With a soft bump the dirigible touched down. Clara and James walked over to the large windows and watched the ground crew secure the vehicle to its docking station. Once it was in place, supernaturals and humans chatted enthusiastically about the evening ahead. And then Clara thought she saw something she didn't expect to see. Waving her hand dismissively, she turned away from the window. Curiosity got the better of her, however, and her eyes bobbed over the boarding passengers again.

"I don't fucking believe it. That's Dr Alibi Lurcock with a fucking Toker," James said, verbalising her thoughts, his hands pressed up against the glass like a five year old at the zoo.

Clara rolled her eyes. *It's just as well that I love him. The breadth of his immaturity is utterly staggering sometimes.*

Clara nodded. "I think I need to extract some information from our Commissioner, don't you? Would you like to be the fly on the wall when I do?"

"Absolutely. Wait, have you heard from him? He could be hurt or he could even be…"

Clara held up her hand, signalling him to stop.

James felt his cheeks go red.

"Sorry, Clara."

"It's okay. I am sure he will communicate with us momentarily. Look, they have all boarded," she said, as the dirigible rose into the air again.

Hoofs and high heels clattered over the white wooden floor as people found their seats. Elves, shifters, dwarves and centaurs took their places behind magicians tables, loaded with props. Even Velorina had a table, but hers was filled with Moonlight Meals paraphernalia, the official sponsor of the event. Velorina met Clara's gaze and smiled. Clara raised her alcohol free martini and walked away.

Aarlon, the elf leader, stepped onto the bandstand, held out his hands with his fingers splayed and conjured a purple orb between his hands. Raising his hand, the shimmering globe floated above his head and stopped. Gasps and murmurs went up from the crowd.

"I could have used a microphone to speak to you, ladies and gentleman, but I thought a purple orb would be more fitting for the occasion."

People chuckled and Aarlon smiled in appreciation.

The elven elder continued. "I am not against modern methods of communication, but this is one way that us elves use for long distance phone calls, even today. If you would like to find out about ancient conversations between elves or anything elven, come and see me at my stand. Now without further ado, I would like to welcome you all to the Festival Of Life."

The diners clapped and cheered, and then the attendees began mingling around the room.

As Clara moved about, she stopped at the stall of Niq the shifter.

"This is a trick that a ten year old shifter can do. It is a skill that is unique to shifters and I am master at it, hence my name."

"But you can't have been born with that name, surely?" a male festival goer said.

Niq smiled. "I am a shifter, darling. Change is the name of my game," Niq said, holding her hands out, palms up, making her onlookers chuckle.

Still smiling, Niq put a bottle top on the table and Clara felt her heart go into her mouth. Helplessly, Clara watched as the bottle top transformed into a miniature frolicking foal. Sweat broke out on her forehead and she wiped her clammy hands on her green leather trousers.

Make it stop, please make it stop! Niq, I am begging you.

Eventually, the trick finished leaving a coppery taste in Clara's mouth. Clara touched her inside lip with her fingertip. Blood.

Not a smart move Overton. If there are rogue vampires on-board, they might smell the wound.

"Clara, you look like you have seen a ghost," Niq said, standing beside her. Clara was so worked up, she hadn't noticed that the shifter's display had ended and they were alone.

"I…erm…," Clara looked at the ceiling and shook her fists, bouncing up and down on the balls of her feet.

Niq frowned and spoke softly. "Clara, in here." taking her by the hand and leading her into a side room. Niq held out her hands and muttered a spell, camouflaging the door.

"No one will disturb us here. Everyone will think it's a dead-end and will look for somewhere else to fuck. Clara, take a seat."

Niq gestured to one of the red velvet armchairs with gold binding. The room was completely empty. Clara thanked her and sat down. Niq sat opposite, placing her champagne flute on the glass-topped table in between them. The room had a green carpet with a gold crown pattern. Behind Niq was a large rectangular mirror with a moulded gold frame. Scattered around the room were more matching table and chair sets. The room was lit by faux electric candles in sconces.

Taking deep breaths, Clara tried to calm her nerves. Closing her eyes, she concentrated on a woodland waterfall. A few minutes later, she woke from her trance and smiled weakly.

"And tough street cop Clara Overton is back in the room," Niq said, smiling out of the side of her mouth.

Clara giggled, then swallowed hard. "I have been privy to that type of magic before and when you said that only shifters could perform it, I realised someone I trusted wasn't… Niq held up her hand and Clara sat there with her mouth open.

"My goodness Clara, take a breath. If I am hearing you correctly, you have seen the bottle top horse trick before, and it wasn't performed by a shifter?"

"Correct." Clara nodded profusely.

Niq's glass clinked on the table when she set it down again. "Who performed the spell?"

"Emmeline Miller," Clara said, using her full name, as if she was trying to distance herself from her friend.

Niq leaned forward, her eyes wide, her mouth open. "She's a providentia like you isn't she?"

Clara nodded a pained expression on her face which Niq reciprocated.

"Look at me having empathy with an empath," she snivelled.

Clara tried to laugh through her tears.

Niq folded her hands in her lap and said. "I am of the mind-set that your friend

Emmeline Miller has been replaced by a shifter."

Clara blew her nose and said in a nasally voice, "I have churned it over in my mind, and I have arrived at the same conclusion as you, Niq."

The shifter stood, her black trousers rustling as she did so. Looking up, Clara noticed how stunning Niq was, making her body tingle with sexual energy. Clara coughed and tore her eyes away from the beautiful redhead.

Niq didn't seem to notice and flexed her fingers repeatedly as she walked over and looked at her reflection in the mirror, exposing her supple back and elegant neck, making Clara gulp and blink expeditiously.

She's wearing a backless ruffle shirt and no bra. Are changelings always this promiscuous? Clara put her hand over her mouth. What if Niq is the person who has replaced Eme, who knows?

Clara clicked the safety off on her gun, and pointed it at the shapeshifter, just as Niq turned around, revealing a choker around her neck. The diamond in the centre of the choker sparkled as the shapeshifter raised her hands. "I am sure you have many enemies being a police officer and everything, but I can assure I am not one of them. I don't know the circumstances surrounding Eme and the horse spell, but I do know I want to find the person who is pretending to be your friend."

I think she is telling the truth. She is so alluring, my mind is a blur. I am so distraught by the whole Eme situation, I don't know if I am coming or going. Is Eme safe? Is she even still alive? And more importantly, who is this fake masquerading as my best friend, for fuck's sake?

Clara slid the safety catch back into position. "I am sorry, it's the way we are wired, I am afraid."

Niq lowered her hands. "It's okay. You're a cop, I get it. Besides, shifters have this stigma attached to them."

Clara snorted. "Beggars, scoundrels, thieves…"

Niq made the surrendering gesture. "Okay, enough of the insults already!"

Both women laughed, breaking the tension.

Niq sat down and clasped Clara's hands in hers and said softly, "I am here to help you. I want what you want. I want what the Dragon Treaty wants. I am proud to call myself a Tarnuzian, and I will fight until my dying breath to bring a better future to the country I love."

Clara smiled. "Okay, that's truly marvellous, but you can let go of my hands now."

Niq blushed, laughed with embarrassment and let go. "Oh, Clara, I am so sorry. I barely know my own strength."

"That's okay. I needed total reassurance from you, and I think I have it now," Clara said, flexing her hands, trying to restore the circulation to them.

"I am glad we are on the same page," Niq said, a smile growing on her face. "Clara, I want you to try and think of someone that has a grudge against you. Someone who has history with you."

Clara stared over Niq's shoulder at the mirror. Who could it be? William, the barman at The Arch Tavern? No, he disliked me, but not enough to want me dead. Some members of the gang that I kissed with my deadly lipstick? That reminds me, I must put that on.

Clara took out her gun and opened the lipstick cavity on the weapon. She walked over to the mirror, puckered her lips and applied the protective lip balm, then the poisonous makeup, then she returned to her seat.

"I would have kissed you with or without the lipstick."

Clara felt her cheeks burn. "I am with James, remember."

"He's a very lucky man, but if you happen to split up, here's my number." Niq handed Clara a business card and Clara tucked it in her inside pocket.

Clara looked at her flatly. "Thanks for the card. I may need to contact you, anyway, if this case ends up in court. If you kissed me with this lipstick on, you would have minutes left to live."

Niq sat ramrod straight in her chair and folded her arms. "You may want to tell James you've put that stuff on, or I will see you in court, but for a different case."

Clara raised her right index finger. "Point taken. I'll tell him right away."

A look of realisation came over Clara's face.

"Abigail Price, that's who is impersonating Eme!"

"I know the name, but I can't put a name to the face. Are you sure, Clara?"

"No, not completely sure, but I saw her at the docks a few weeks ago when James and I were investigating the murdered sailors."

"This is interesting. Are you certain it was definitely Abigail Price you saw?"

"Well, if it wasn't her, it was somebody that looked bloody similar."

"What did she do when she saw you?"

"She smiled at me, put her hood up and then she disappeared."

"It certainly sounds like her, Clara. She wanted you to know she was around again. We need to find someone who can help us."

"I saw Albi Lurcock join the other passengers this evening. She works for the robotics department at Agreeable Solutions. Maybe she knows something."

Niq nodded determinedly. "Let's go and find her," Niq said, breaking the spell and opening the door.

***

Zintius stood on a mountain top overlooking The Field of Fallen Heroes. Driving rain pelted his face, and the fierce wind made his black cape flap. He watched as Dimitri led a rag tag mob of supernaturals and humans against a horde of genetically engineered mutants. And he smiled.

"That pitiful little band is no match for the sheer power of my monster army."

"I wouldn't underestimate my son or the humans if I were you, Zintius."

"Raqaknoff. I might have known. You can't help interfering. You spend too much time with elves. You're all harps and tree hugs."

"Just because I believe in harmony, doesn't make me weak. You are nothing more than a blunt instrument, a resounding gong, a clanging cymbal."

Zintius turned to face his adversary. "You've gotten so soft you have forgotten what it means to be an apex predator. To be a god among men. We were worshipped, adored and revered. People lived in fear. They respected us, they wanted to be us. All of that has gone. I am trying to restore dignity and pride in everything we represent. You, on the other hand, are content on running a silly little business supplying meat to the humans. Pathetic."

Raqaknoff rolled back his shoulders and raised himself to full height. "I've found a way to coexist with humans, instead of murdering them for their blood. Men can teach us so much and I'm prepared to learn from them."

Zintius shook his head. " I see now that it is fruitless to try and convince you to join me, and this is why you must die."

The two vampires drew their swords and circled each other. Zintius led with an overhead cut, but Raqaknoff jumped backwards and landed softly on a higher ledge. Zintius landed opposite him and Raqaknoff followed with a thrust and kicked him in the belly, winding him. Zintius clapped his hands.

"Bravo, bravo. You still know how to fight. It isn't too late to join me, you know."

"You don't have anything to offer me."

Zintius lunged, Raqaknoff dodged and cut the other's bicep. His arm sizzled as the wound gushed blood. Zintius grimaced and wrinkled his nose.

"That is a low blow even for a vampire. Why did you lace your sword with garlic?" Zintius gasped, the veins in his neck turning black. He pressed the ruby on his necklace and an airship floated down, producing what looked like a drainpipe. Raqaknoff thrust at Zintius' midriff, but he parried and drove his sword into Raqaknoff's eye socket. Raqaknoff fell backwards, and, just before he lost consciousness, Zintius turned into smoke and disappeared up the pipe, then the pipe retracted and the blimp flew away.

For a moment, Raqaknoff lay there waiting for death, then there was the sound of beating leathery wings and burning flames. Raqaknoff heard the sound of creaking metal followed by an explosion. A scaly foot lightly touched his chest giving it a golden glow. He let out a loud gasp of breath and raised his head. He opened his good eye and saw Targem, Vywrath and Kiada's son.

"It's good to see you, old friend. I heard you attack Zintius' airship. Is he dead?"

"Hard to say. As the dirigible disintegrated, it jettisoned an escape pod."

Raqaknoff coughed. "You may have to fight Zintius again one day, but I won't be around to help you."

"What are you talking about? I have used my magic to heal you."

Raqaknoff laid his head down and smiled weakly. "I appreciate it, but this is my last day on Remina. It has been prophesied. Does your mother and father need your help rounding up the dragon mutants?"

"No, they said they had it under control, and they told me to look after you." Targem paused, then he said, "They knew about the prophecy."

Raqaknoff laughed weakly, it was more a croak than a laugh. "Pull this fucking sword out of my eye, please."

Targem laughed and the sound reverberated around the canyon below. Daintily, Targem clamped his teeth around the hilt of the blade, pulled it free and spat it out. Placing his foot on the vampire's chest again, he closed his eyes and breathed deeply. Another golden glow appeared in the other's eye socket restoring his vision. Raqaknoff felt the back of his head. There weren't any signs of the wound at all.

"Thank you, Targem," Raqaknoff said standing up. "I now feel fully restored."

Targem scratched his neck with his back foot, his claws sounded like sandpaper rubbing against metal.

"I don't understand. If you are fully restored, how are you supposed to die?"

Raqaknoff smiled. "You are part of the prophecy too, my winged friend. Why do you think your mother and father sent you to me? I will fulfil my last wish, to watch the sun rise for the last time. I haven't seen the sun in 500 years. I am old and I grow tired of this life I have lived. My time has come."

Targem sat on his haunches. "Raqaknoff, sit on my back and we can watch the new day sun together. The rain has stopped now and the dawn is only a few hours away."

Raqaknoff patted the beast on his wing before climbing up the dragon's spine onto its back, wrapping his hands around the reptile's neck. With giant steps that shook the ledge, Targem walked to the edge of the cliff and stood there. Both of them waited for the sun to appear on the Eastern horizon.

"Just so that you know, I don't like prophecies. Not ones like this."

Raqaknoff snorted. "I have lived, if you can call what I have a life, a long time and most of it was spent shedding innocent blood. My kind can live as long as me or longer, but I come from an evil race. Most creatures don't get to choose how they die, but I have accepted my fate and embraced it. Now let's wait for the sun."

Targem turned his head and looked out the side of his eye, a single tear formed there and dropped to the ground. Suddenly the earth trembled and a crack appeared. A tree grew in the earth and the crevice disappeared.

"I have created the tree of life in your honour, Raqaknoff. Whoever comes here in search of healing or resurrection, will be healed. When people taste the golden apples, they will be reminded that everyone has a second chance if they turn from wickedness, even a vampire. If they seek healing for their own selfish gain, they will die instantly and will not be revived."

Raqaknoff nodded.

***

Clara and Niq stepped out of the conference room to the sound of voices and silverware clinking on china plates. A jazz band was playing ballads softly on the stage. When they turned the corner, they saw James going from table to table, presumably asking about Clara's whereabouts. Eventually, James looked up, saw Clara, waved and came over.

"Thank goodness I have found you. I was looking everywhere for you," James said, leaning in to give her a kiss. Clara stepped back before his lips touched hers.

James's jaw went slack; his hand flew to his chest. "Clara, what's wrong?"

Clara stood on tip toes and whispered in his ear.

When she had finished talking, he stepped back and nodded thoughtfully. "I understand."

"Don't come any closer or she gets it."

A male voice yelled from the back of the dining hall. James and Clara's hands flicked off the safety catches on their guns; they turned in the direction of the voice. Women screamed, men swore and the band stopped playing.

A skinny, sweaty man in a dark peak cap, grubby dark trousers and scruffy tan boots had his arm around Dr. Lurcock's throat. A pistol was pointed at her temple. Her eyes were wide with fear and she gasped for breath.

"Take it easy, mate. No-one needs to get hurt," James said, holding out his hand.

"I lost everything because of this bitch and her fucking tokers. I was a bricklayer, see,

Children of Tarnuz

and they lays me off, don't they? I was surplus to…"

Before the man could finish, Lurcock's Toker knocked him out with his mechanical arm. Women screamed again, and people scattered in all directions. Eventually, the crowd dispersed and locked themselves in their cabins. Niq and Velorina had disappeared too. Clara and James dived for cover behind an upturned table.

The dirigible began to descend.

The pilot has tripped the silent alarm. "We will be landing soon," he said, over the intercom.

"Quick in here," Lurcock said, to Clara and James, opening a metal door. Clara stepped through the door first. When James stepped over the door jab, Lurcock threw a knife into his back. He pitched forward, unconscious. Clara turned and pointed her gun, but Lurcock flicked her wrist again, launching a blade, catching Clara in the stomach. Clara's jaw slackened, a look of horror on her face as she slumped to the floor.

***

Ned Jenkins stood in line with the rest of the TWLF and the humans. His boots squelched in the muddy ground as he adjusted his stance. An icy wind blew through his chestnut hair and beard. He faced Dimitri and his supernatural horde, who waited at the top of the hill.

Tolerus, the caramel coloured centaur, trotted up to Ned and stood next to him.

Shit! Why didn't he stay at home with his family like I asked him to?

"Hello, Ned."

"Tolerus." Ned looked at his boots. "What are you doing here, centaur?"

Tolerus drooped his shoulders and furrowed his brow. "I have come to fight alongside you, my brother."

Children of Tarnuz

Ned gave his friend a flinty stare. "You're not my brother. Today, you fight with them." He pointed at the top of the hill.

Tolerus stumbled over his feet. "But we have known each other since we were kids. I agree with your cause, and I want to fight alongside you."

Ned picked up a rock and threw it at Tolerus's hindquarters. The centaur jumped forward and winced with pain.

Ned bared his teeth. "Go and fight with the other freaks."

Tolerus hesitated, his eyes searching Ned's face for empathy.

Ned set his jaw and said nothing.

"Suit yourself," Tolerus said, spitting on the ground and galloping up the hill.

Ned watched as his ex-friend joined Dimtri's army.

After Dimitri had welcomed Tolerus to the troupe, he addressed Ned's battalion.

"I am not your enemy, Mr. Jenkins. Nor is anyone at the top of this hill."

"You're a vampire. My men and I have crucified one of those already tonight." Ned's crowd cheered, banging swords against shields.

Dimitri waited until the commotion had settled down, then he said, "I am aware of Jedidiah's fate, and if I were in your shoes, I would have done exactly the same thing."

A burst of flame shot out from the mountaintop above them. A dirigible caught on fire, its metal frame creaking as it disintegrated and fell to the ground. Then, a flaming projectile escaped from the burning wreck and disappeared into the blossom forest.

Ned's army murmured amongst themselves, pointing at the sky.

After a pause, Fredrick said "I think he's bluffing Ned,".

Ned thought about this, but before he could verbalise his thoughts, Dimitri spoke again.

"Neither myself nor the vampire council are responsible for turning Lewis. He was converted by Zintius, he was more than just the face of Agreeable Solutions. He was a vampire overlord that needed to be stopped."

"Dimitri, you're referring to Zintius in the past tense. Why is that?"

"Ned, we have all just witnessed a dramatic fireworks display. This was the climax to a ferocious battle between my father and Zintius. Whilst I sense that my father still lives, I know that tonight will be his last night."

Ned's men muttered again. "Can't you blood suckers heal yourselves?"

"Yes, you are correct in your assumptions, but my father must die to fulfil a prophecy. I can assure you that Zintius is no longer a threat and the vampire council is a peaceful organisation."

"If you are serious about peace, lay down your weapons."

"As you wish," Dimitri said, laying down his sword, nodding at his troops to do the same.

"Yarrrrrr," Fredrick cried, waving his battle-axe in the air and charging into the middle of The Field of Fallen Heroes. For a moment, nothing happened, then a small red dragon flew down and grabbed Fredrick by the shoulders and carried him off. Swinging his axe desperately at the reptile's front legs, Frederick tried to free himself from the monster's steely grip. In the confusion, Dimitri's archers fired at the tiny dragon whilst Ned's bowmen fired at Dimitri's army and the dragon.

As the battle raged on, a sound of leathery wings filled the air.

***

Clara opened her eyes but her vision was blurry, and she heard the sound of machinery humming. She felt something fastened around her chest. She was laying on some kind of couch. She looked down and saw a leather strap. She tried to move her hands, but they were secured with leather bracelets that were chained to the side of the couch. Gasping, she tried not to panic, but her mouth went dry and she had stomach pain. Her hands were clammy and her sweaty hair stuck to the side of her face. As her vision started to clear, she saw Emmeline Miller smiling down at her. She realised with horror that she had seen this scenario before and she started screaming. As she did so, she heard someone writhing around next to her. With a turn of her head, she saw James, who was also strapped to an examination couch.

"Clara, it's okay. I am here."

"Ah, this is so sweet. True love really runs deep," Eme said.

"Let him go, Eme, or whomever the fuck you are."

"Oh this face is one of many," Eme said, shifting from Eme to Albi Lurcock.

"If you have hurt Eme, I will hunt you down and kill you."

The shifter threw her head back and barked an evil laugh. "I can assure you they are quite safe. An associate of mine, Dr. Marcus Thimble well, is taking very good care of Miss Miller and Dr. Lurcock."

"And whom am I communicating with right now, may I ask?"

"Polite to the last, even in the face of extreme circumstances and almost certain death. I mentioned many faces, and yet, you have only seen two. I suppose it's time to take the mask off," she said, shifting into Abigail Price.

"I knew it! You were loitering around the dock that day when James and I were investigating the Pelham case."

Abigail raised her hand like a girl scout. "Present, miss. That filthy little weasel took something from us. Come on, hand it over," she beckoned with her fingers, the sleeve of her dark blue bustle dress rustled as she did so.

On the side of her blond head, she wore a mini black topper. She would blend in with any crowd, hiding in plain sight, the art of a true shifter. Over the top of the dress, she wore a white surgeon's apron, with a pocket on the front filled with instruments of torture.

Clara smirked. "Do you mean a little gold box?"

"The very same."

"I don't have it. It is deep in the bowels of the police headquarters. It's probably being examined by forensics as we speak."

In truth, Clara had forgotten about that piece of evidence. She thought she heard a police squint say he was completely stumped and had passed it onto Horace and Adamar. If anyone could figure it out, they could.

Abigail shrugged her shoulders. "It's not a problem, after you're dead, Clara Overton. I'll pose as you and take it myself."

"Not if I have anything to do with it," James said, straining against his restraints.

"Er-her-hum," Abigail said, pretending to cough. "Girls are talking," Abigail said, pointing at Clara with a truncheon then at herself with it.

"Hey, that's mine," James protested.

Abigail made a small "O" with her mouth and lightly touched her lips.

"Oi, officer, stop thief. Would you like your precious truncheon back?" she said, moving her hand up and down the shaft and licking her lips.

"As a matter of fact, I would."

"No James, no," Clara protested.

Abigail tightened her lips together and clubbed James's wrist until she heard the bones break. With every single blow, he screamed in agony and Clara whimpered like a tortured dog.

Abigail looked at Clara and smiled bitterly, then she yanked James's broken hand towards her and made him clasp his fingers around the baton. He cried in pain and sucked air through his teeth.

Abigail brushed her black lace gloves together, as if she was wiping off imaginary dust. "There, that wasn't so bad, was it," she said, first looking at James's face, which was a sweaty mask of pain, and then at Clara's red eyes and tear stained face. Her make-up had run, but she was still stunningly beautiful.

"I think it's time for a commercial break, don't you? All of this fun has to be paid for somehow. Flint," she said, clicking her fingers.

"Yes, Miss Price?" replied a metallic voice.

"Would you be a dear and bring in the television set, please?"

"Certainly, Miss Price." he said, walking away like he was wading through treacle, his hydraulic springs hissing every time he planted his feet.

A steady hum could be heard in the silence, and Clara looked at the metal struts and bolts and realised they were on a dirigible.

"Are we on the same dirigible as the Festival of Life, or did you build this one solely for conducting your diabolical dastardly deeds?"

"Diabolical dastardly deeds? What a wonderful phrase? Bravo!" Abigail said, giving Clara small, mocking handclaps. "So, your private education didn't go to waste after all?"

"Apparently not. Are you going to answer the fucking question or not?" Clara said, listening to James's heavy breathing.

He must have passed out. The pain was obviously too much for him. Hold on tight, darling. I am going to get us out of this.

Abigail tutted and shook her head. "That type of language isn't very becoming of a lady, is it?

"I am afraid this isn't either," Clara said, flipping Abigail the bird.

Abigail narrowed her eyes and glared at Clara. Shortly after that, they heard the heavy copper feet of Flint clattering on the metal gangway and the sound of castors rolling along the floor.

Abigail smiled brightly like a housewife expecting her dinner guests. "Just wheel it into the centre there, would you?"

"Yes, Miss Price."

Flint moved into position and Abigail pointed a remote control at the screen turning the device on. If circumstances were different, Clara would have marvelled at this technology, but all she cared about now was James.

"In answer to your question, this is my dastardly dirigible," Abigail said as she waited for the picture to appear on the screen.

Clara heard the sound of a battle, but had to rest her chin on her chest to see the TV.

"Can you see that okay, Clara? Abigail said.

"No, not really."

"Just a sec." Abigail reached behind the TV stand and raised the height. "How's that?"

"Perfect."

"Jolly good. Now, let's see. Oh, how delightful. It looks like civil war has broken out in Tarnuz. Come here, Flint."

The robot stood in front of her and she took both of his metal hands in hers, and they jumped up and down making the steel floor shake every time they landed. Unfortunately, they didn't have the decency to stand in front of the screen, and Clara watched an elf get his hand chopped off plus a human lose an arm. Clara's lips quivered and her face contorted, then she heard the sound of large leathery wings and Peter Harris's commanding voice.

It's not over yet Abigail Price. This could be the final hurrah.

***

"Adamar now," Peter Harris yelled from Vywrath's back.

Horace and Adamar were riding on Kiada. Horace was sitting behind Adamar. The dark elf screwed his eyes shut tight, held out his hands with palms exposed and fired a blast of energy. A large transparent wall formed in front of the two warring factions. The force field pulsed with electrical power, but rippled like water.

Stunned and confused, the fighting foes stared at the barrier with slack jaws. Adamar moved his right hand away from his left and encased Fredrick and the baby dragon in a magical bubble, whilst maintaining the existing barricade on the battlefield.

From the back of Vywrath, Peter Harris addressed the crowd below. "Ladies and gentlemen of Tarnuz. Our country is in turmoil right now which has been brought about by independent actors whose only purpose in life was to bring death and destruction to Tarnuzian soil."

The crowd talked amongst themselves, some of them pointed at the dragons.

Harris continued. "Now, may I suggest you put down your motherfucking weapons and shake fucking hands because we have dragons, and we ain't afraid to use them."

Vywrath and Kiada roared and somewhere in the distance, Targem roared too. The dragons did it for dramatic effect, but it didn't matter because everyone laid down their weapons and hugged, kissed or laughed. Adamar let out a breath, and the force fields vanished. The tiny red dragon opened his right leg and let go of Fredrick. Dimitri saw the nurse tumbling to the floor and flew up and caught him. Then he lowered him to the ground gently. Cheers and whistles went up from the crowd. Dimitri smiled broadly as people applauded him.

***

Aiming the remote at the screen, Abigail turned the set off.

"I was bored of that anyway. Flint, put that fucking thing away."

"Yes, Abigail Price," the automaton said, wheeling the entertainment unit away.

"You call him Flint. Is he, by any chance, Lucius Silas Flint?"

Abigail smiled proudly. "The very same."

"You are remarkably talented, Abigail. You are an expert vaccine researcher and robotic scientist. Very impressive."

Abigail pulled out a fan from her dress pockets, wafted it and fluttered her eyelashes at Clara.

Massaging her ego seems to be working. Keep it up Clara.

"Why, thank you Clara, I am truly flattered."

Flint stood next to her and Abigail put her arm around him, her sword clinking against his copper body.

She has a sword? How did I not notice that before? Clara thought.

"Flint here is the prototype. Of course, his purpose is completely different now. He has no need for his wife Hannah or his son Elijah. A blunt instrument that lives only to serve my every whim."

Children of Tarnuz

I had a wife and a son? That's who those people were in my dreams? Flint thought. I must find a way to set these people free.

"Oh silly me, I forgot to torture you," Abigail said, touching her lips once more.

Oh fuck, oh fuck! Think Clara, think.

"I have accepted my fate, but could you grant a dying woman her last wish?"

"Why, of course. What is it sweetie?"

"I was very turned on by you stroking that truncheon and licking your lips. I feel silly."

Abigail stood over her with a sultry smile on her lips, her breasts rising and falling with excitement. "Go on, Clara."

"Your lips are so inviting I…"

Abigail kissed Clara fully on the mouth, breathing heavily, then she pulled away.

"I heard you were kinky. Let's dial it up a notch," she said, drawing her sword and staggering backwards. Her lips and face turned blue as she started to choke. Blood filled her eyes as she collapsed on the floor, her sword making a loud clang as it slipped from her fingers.

Flint had found some smelling salts and was waving them under James's nose. After sneezing, James opened his eyes. "Is she dead?"

"Yes I think she's dead," Clara said.

"Ooo, careful there, fella. Ah, fuck. My wrist hurts like hell," James cried, as Flint unlocked his manacles. Then he undid his chest strap.

Flint set Clara free and she embraced James, but a look of terror spread across his face and blood poured out his mouth. Clara screamed and backed away.

"JAMES!" she yelled looking in horror at the tip of Abigail's sword poking out of his chest.

Abigail smiled, from the floor. Flint took Abigail's sword and cut her head off, which rolled along the floor and rested against the wall of the airship, her eyes staring, her lips split with an evil grin. A crimson geyser spurted from her neck and her body went limp.

Clara rushed to James and touched his chest, closing her eyes. She concentrated very hard on healing and the sword fell away from his body. As she continued, the bleeding stopped.

As she tried desperately to revive him, there was a loud creak as the airship door was pulled back like a sardine can.

"Thank you for opening your mind to me, Clara." Velorina said, stepping through the gap she had made. Dimitri followed.

"Smear this on James's wound. It should heal him," Dimitri said, handing Clara a jar of paste.

"Thank you. What is it?" Clara asked, unscrewing the lid.

The paste smelt of apples and Clara almost dropped the jar in surprise. Dipping two fingers in, covering them with gloop, she applied it to James's injury and watched the

Children of Tarnuz

hole disappear, she saw James gasp and sit up.

A robot voice said over a speaker, "Self-destruct will take place in T-minus five minutes."

"That is the program that Miss Price set up. The dirigible is on a head-on collision with the communications tower that transmits to the goggles," Flint said, over a cacophony of alarms and flashing red lights. "You need to leave...now!"

"But what about you Flint?"

"There's nothing left for me now. Go! Go!"

Velorina took Clara's hand and James took Dimitri's, and they leapt from the airship into the early morning air. The sun was just an orange thumbnail on the horizon. Like pointed arrows, the vampire siblings sped towards The Institute for Supernatural friends.

When they reached their destination, the sun was rising and the vampire's skin started to singe. Doctor Stokes flung open the front doors.

"Quick, all of you to the underground infirmary."

They hobbled down the steps as Dr. Stokes barked further orders to her subordinates. " Get James Bronze a bed and the two vampires some blood and a pair of coffins, please."

***

"Albi? Albi? Are you awake?" Emmeline Miller said, as she shook her friend, making the dormitory bed creak.

"Huh, what? Emmeline, what do you want?"

"Abigail Price and Zintius are dead. That means they will come to rescue us! I read it in the newspaper earlier."

Albi turned on her side and stared at the ceiling. "Emmeline, I hate to break it to you, but they don't know where the fuck we are."

Emmeline slid down the side of Alibi's bed and put her head between her legs. "I hadn't thought of that."

"I had. Now go back to bed."

"I know someone who can find us. Clara Overton."

"Whatever."

THE END

Clara Overton will return in **Emmeline Miller Is Missing** - A steampunk crime adventure.

Thank you to my readers for buying this book. Please do leave me a review on amazon at xx or goodreads at xxx

Children of Tarnuz

Children of Tarnuz

Children of Tarnuz

Printed in Great Britain
by Amazon